First Publication November 2022
Indies United Publishing House, LLC

ISBN: 978-1-64456-437-0 [Hardcover]
ISBN: 978-1-64456-438-7 [paperback]
ISBN: 978-1-64456-439-4 [Mobi]
ISBN: 978-1-64456-440-0 [ePub]
ISBN: 978-1-64456-441-7 [Audiobook]

Library of Congress Control Number: 2022934185

INDIES UNITED PUBLISHING HOUSE, LLC
P.O. BOX 3071
QUINCY, IL 62305-3071
indiesunited.net

The silent bear no witness against themselves.
Aldous Huxley

To Lee, the sun in my universe.

To Eddie,
my dear friend,
hope you enjoy this!
Please stay
in touch,
Lisa

The Ridders

A Political Thriller

Lisa Towles

INDIES UNITED PUBLISHING HOUSE, LLC

Look closely. You can see them. Ants scuttling through brush and debris in their oscillating dance of obscurity and emergence, death and resurrection, intending not to deceive but to exploit the natural patterns of nature.

Look closer and they are not ants. And it's not so random what they're doing. They're not just foraging for the most obtainable food supply. They watch. Monitor. Calculate. Track. They can sense heat, and their antennae can smell smoke. They look for forest fires to lay eggs in burning trees, their three-hundred-million-year-old DNA designed to survive uninhabitable climes.

Now reach in and peel back another layer. The stench makes your eyes water, a heat that liquefies skin and bone and, before that, an insidious cold that prowls the shadows, numbly setting the stage for the inevitable next - *rebirth*.

PROLOGUE

I clean my gun the same way an art collector cares for an original Picasso—with white gloves, tweezers, soft brushes, syringes. An owner of an antique sword might use fine-grade steel wool to remove superficial rust, abrasive paste to clean the brass, and lemon juice to dislodge hardened residue. Distraction, for me, meant taking apart my precious Browning .9mm semi-automatic—a gift from our dead partner Archie Dax the night he died—scrubbing out the bore, wiping down the frame and barrel, regardless of whether it had been shot or not. Like people, guns age when they're ignored. But tonight I couldn't concentrate on anything but that envelope, and the clock was ticking to find out what was inside without actually opening it. Fifty-five hours, to be precise, within which I had to deliver something to a hotel lobby lest I got myself garroted, shot by a long-range sniper rifle, or otherwise permanently rubbed out of existence, such as it is.

Ray, my degenerate roommate, slipped past me in his swift, lopsided gait heading to the bathroom in the same dirty shorts he'd had on all week. He shook his head when he caught me polishing the polymer grips at the kitchen table.

"Keep it up, BJ," he warned. "You'll never hit your target."

"Is that so?" I said, feigning interest.

"It'll slip out of your goddamn hand."

1

"Ray, you're a landscaper. What do you know about guns?"

He poked his head around the corner. "Dude, everything in life is about grip."

Speaking of grip, I heard him peeing with the door open. I hate that. Two more months of this and his lease was up. Counting the days.

I got up and snagged the last beer from the fridge, knowing he was probably planning to do the same on the way back to his smelly lair at the end of the hall. I'd already found a company to do a "deep clean" the day after he moved out. If he leaves. Fuck Ray and his landscaping gig and stupid grips. I honestly had bigger problems than a slippery gun.

"I know you snagged the last beer," he bellowed.

I took a long, ceremonial sip. "Flush the damned toilet." Asshole.

CHAPTER 1

What would you do if someone offered you a million dollars to bring an envelope to the reception desk of a luxury hotel? That's it. Sure, a no-brainer. A relatively inconsequential risk, easy money, right? Trouble is, anything involving a million dollars might not be what it seems.

So many questions. Namely why me, BJ Janoff, should be offered this seemingly innocuous task. There were no answers available, no consultants waiting with details or clarifications. One million dollars in cash to perform this social experiment. Right now. Yes or no?

I know what my older brother Jonas would do. He'd say no because of the multitude of potential hazards his paranoid mind would concoct, keeping him tied to the past, still wearing the same ugly khakis from ten years ago, stuck in the protective bubble of his big house in Ladera Heights and his geriatric Mercedes. So, of course I didn't tell him. Yet.

Then there was Lacy Diaz, the girl-next-door-turned-lawyer, who drives a car flashy enough to get a speeding ticket if she goes over fifty on the freeway. "Hell, yeah, I'd take it," she said, with about a hundred caveats. What do you expect; she's a lawyer. "Wear rubber gloves," she said. "Ask to see the contents of the envelope first. If it's money, fan it out so you can see the bill denominations.

Take photos of the payor."

"Photos of the payor?" I laughed and closed my eyes, a response Lacy inspired by pretty much everything she did. "Excuse me sir, would you mind if—"

"I'm just trying to protect you from potential—"

"Potential. Now you sound like Jonas. His whole world is so much potential there's no room for now."

"He's your brother. You can't choose your family so get over it."

So be it.

A million dollars? Hell yeah, of course I said yes, I'm not stupid. Luckily, the task was intended for not only the most beautiful hotel in LA but the one I went to almost every morning. Sure, the cappuccinos were okay at the Peets counter, but the staff was even more noteworthy.

"Good morning," I said, loping up to the counter.

"Is it?"

"Pretty sure." I didn't let my eyes fall below Raquel's neck, given her choice of a low-cut blouse.

"Usual?"

"Yeah."

I watched the Westin Bonaventure Hotel staff moving wordlessly through their tasks today. A keen observer of human behavior, I knew something was going down when Mario the bellhop pushed an empty cart past me and lowered his eyes to the floor. No banter, humming, rapping, high fiving me. No smile.

"Hey?" I called after him. "What am I, invisible?"

Alena, who managed the daytime housekeeping staff, hurried after him toward the elevators. Her face looked like she'd been crying all morning. No makeup and she was buttoning her uniform top while she walked. Maybe I'm paranoid.

Raquel was moving slowly and clearly not interested in talking. So I took three steps to the left to get a view of the reception desk. The typical chorus line of coiffed, perky concierges today included a confused, twenty-year-old in a wrinkled t-shirt. Something, no doubt related to the FedEx envelope I'd tucked into the back of my pants, was afoot. Out of coffee sleeves, I burned my fingers on Raquel's cappuccino and hunkered low on a lobby sofa watching and sipping.

4

A cadre of men in identical black suits marched to the reception desk. Here we go.

I calculated my distance to be roughly fifty feet from the polished, walnut counter, maybe forty-five. Lucky for me, the acoustics in here rivaled the Guggenheim and I could hear everything. One suited man in front, nine underlings huddled behind awaiting instructions. I heard the word envelope posed as a question. The misplaced pothead behind the counter looked like he might start crying any moment. He gazed through the suits into the cavernous lobby space. Don't look at me, buddy, I don't exist right now. I took three more sips of coffee then back to my morning theater.

My phone buzzed with an incoming call. Jonas, who I suppose qualified as my business partner even though I wasn't paid an equal salary, and there was no legal agreement in place that formalized our working arrangement.

"Hey, bro," I whispered.

"Hey, bro?" Repeating was one of his annoying traits. He had so many.

"What?"

"Where the fuck are you?"

"On a job," I lied. "Where are you?" I laughed inside, knowing this would unglue him. He hated the idea of my taking side jobs because he felt I was unqualified to be a private investigator. When our partner Archie Dax was still around, we used to laugh about this. He and I were so similar. He understood me almost better than anyone. I'd only had my investigator's license for less than a year when he died, but he never thought that mattered. Said I had the right head for PI work. Aww, Arch. My world's not the same without you.

"Job? What job?"

Poor Jonas. I still hadn't told him.

"Okay look, we've got the Bergman family coming in at nine tomorrow morning and I need the…" He exhaled long and hard, specifically to relay his frustration and inspire guilt. That ploy never worked with me.

"What, Jonas—WiFi? Maybe you've heard of something called the internet. Yes, I know, and we're good."

"Router! Router. That's it."

Lord. "It's not the router, it's the modem speed and the unit will be upgraded within the hour. We're fine. Just let them in when they arrive."

No response.

"Are you crying?" I asked. "Pacing? Take your pill, Jonas."

"Fuck off. Say hi to Raquel for me."

I hung up and the phone rang again. "Dude, what?"

"And please don't wear your stupid backwards baseball hat. Please? I beg you. The Bergmans have money, a lot of it. We need that right now."

"Okay Jonas, no hat. Happy now?"

"We'll see."

* —◈ ◈═▶ ✦ ◀═◈ ◈— *

Okay, so about the Bergmans. Jonas had been talking with them, Sten and Estelle, for the past two days about their vanished eighteen-year-old daughter, Anastasia, heir to their multi-billion-dollar estate, and how her net worth made her an especially enticing ransom target to what they described as "the underworld". LA's not utopia but not sure I'd call it an underworld.

Just two more errands today. First, I put a five-dollar bill in Raquel's tip vase even though she didn't see me. She still deserved it for being open at 6 a.m. and for looking so goddamn beautiful first thing in the morning. Then I held a small, black plastic ball in my hands and set it on a side table with a perfect view of the hotel's reception area. The table was on the other side of the seating area so that meant roughly thirty feet from the front desk. The plastic ball, a nanny cam designed to look like an air filter, was partially concealed by the fat leaves on a fake rubber tree plant. Unless someone moved that plant, or the filter for that matter, I'd be able to see the front desk of the Bonaventure Hotel for the next twenty-four hours via an iPhone app, which I suspect would be time enough to see why someone would pay a stranger a million bucks to deliver a stupid envelope.

CHAPTER 2

I woke up restless at 6 a.m. and again an hour later, remembering the sad anniversary, and checked the nanny cam feed on my phone to make sure it was working. It just didn't make sense, other than the money guys wanting to avoid the ten suited men who kept showing up at the front desk. Three sips of weak coffee and a two-minute shower, I was out the door by 7:30. The traffic gods favored me because I hit the parking lot by 7:58. I entered in slo-mo, starting in the back of the southwest entrance, craning my neck to scan for Lacy's notorious yellow Lotus. Can you imagine? Not just a Lotus but Solar Yellow parked in a dirt lot in this neighborhood of Venice. And it's never been broken into, so she said. Maybe thugs felt like the obvious alarm system wasn't worth the aggravation.

Born one month apart, Lacy and I were two years younger than Jonas, and growing up next door, we were all essentially siblings. When Jonas turned his MBA plus preoccupation with crime into an entrepreneurial venture, of course I was tapped for IT and networking support, given my degree in computer science. Lacy, being a lawyer, didn't specifically work for Jonas but offered early morning consultations on some of our cases before she went to her real job at her daddy's law firm. My implacable get-there-first rivalry with her was a leftover vestige from elementary school, racing down the street to see who touched the front door of the school first. So immature. But when it came to women in my life, she was the yardstick to which everyone else was compared. The Lotus wasn't there yet, and I was delighted to pull into the space she designated as hers. Life's a bitch, deal with it.

Only because Jonas begged me, I left my collector's item Dodgers baseball cap on the passenger seat and instead brought my briefcase, a useful prop for billionaire meetings. Little did they know there was nothing but a paperback book in it. On second thought, I pulled out the book and tucked it under my arm. And it wasn't till I was standing in the dirt lot gazing at the morning sky that I again remembered what day it was—the anniversary of our mother's death.

"Good morning, Mister Jonas," one of the cleaning crew shouted from the second floor and waved.

"I'm his brother, BJ." I waved back, never quite sure what they did up there though Jonas seemed to think it was storage for an eBay business. Must be a very successful eBay business.

I opened the office door slowly, glad that Jonas startled easily and hoping to scare him.

"Hey," he said, eyeing my attire and immediately clicking into the briefcase and book. He didn't smile but I felt his soul relax a tiny bit. Shit. The Bergmans were already here. Where was their car?

"Excuse me, Mr. and Mrs. Bergman, I'm Jonas' brother, BJ. Sorry I'm late." I switched the briefcase to my left hand and offered my right to Mr. Bergman. A single, hard shake, watery blue eyes, ruddy face. What kind of a name was Sten anyway? At least twenty years older than I expected, same for the Mrs, who remained seated with her arms crossed and eyes squinted. I could tell she was a pistol. How could a couple in their seventies have an eighteen-year-old daughter? Adopted, maybe a granddaughter instead of a daughter? Or maybe they were just full of shit.

"Ma'am," I said, and sat to their left. Jonas returned to the chair directly across from them.

"See, Estelle, a reader," Mr. Bergman commented, pointing at my book. I knew that would be a good idea. "You always say young people don't read. I told you they were good boys."

Estelle Bergman's hairstyle was something to behold. A teased, multicolored mass that resembled a sort of modern art storage container. She could seriously hide a ham sandwich in there and no one would ever see it. I averted my eyes and tried not to laugh. It wasn't working. Jonas shot me a death glance. I got up to get a glass of water and used my palm to muzzle my hysteria. I knew I was punchy from not enough sleep and obsessing over that freaking envelope. Come on BJ, hold it together. Okay. Breathing. I'll be fine.

"What are you reading?" the woman asked in a taunting whine.

I came back from the kitchen sipping the water and tried not to look at her. That was probably the most respectful thing to do given the expectations of their generation.

"Arturo Perez-Reverte," I said. "It's called *The Club Dumas*, about the Three Musketeers. Amazing story."

Jonas stared, unblinking.

"I know, Jonas, you have the master's degree but I'm the bibliophile. Deal with it." I winked at Mr. Bergman and smiled at the Mrs. "Brothers, you know…"

"Anyway, Mr. Bergman," Jonas cut in. "You were about to tell me of a new development about Anastasia. Please continue."

"She hasn't come home, if you were wondering," Mrs. Bergman said with a humph.

"Have you filed a missing person's report with the police?" I asked. Jonas expressly told me not to talk during the interview.

"Brock, can you—"

I hated that name. Jonas knew that.

"Three days ago," Mr. Bergman answered. "Nothing happened. We don't even think they're looking for her."

"Have you considered offering a reward for any information leading to her return and any media support?"

Jonas looked like he was about to explode. "Brock, please," he whispered. "You know nothing about this case."

"What does he mean by media support?" the woman asked her husband, who looked at Jonas, who looked at me with his palms out. "Not going on TV, I hope? All those TV execs are a bunch of rapists."

"No, nothing like that." Still trying not to laugh. "I just meant a strategically placed news article in a reputable newspaper for print and online coverage, with a picture of your daughter and some compelling details about her life that might make readers sympathize with her disappearance and want to help."

"That's not a terrible idea," Jonas managed.

"High praise," I joked.

"Good. When can you have it done?"

"Me? I'm just the IT guy. Besides, I've got another case."

"Here - the last two boyfriends Anastasia spent time with. Addresses and phone numbers. I don't have their emails." Mr. Bergman placed a handwritten index card on the obscenely luxurious white, marble coffee table, Jonas' unapologetic MBA gift to himself. Admittedly it was the only piece of furniture in here that I liked. It would look great in my living room. Then again, better to wait until Ray left.

"That's helpful, Mr. Bergman. I'll move on this right away. Meanwhile, Brock and I will work on the article and we'll be in touch in the next day or so."

Mrs. Bergman spent five minutes getting up from the couch. Jonas saw them out.

"Stop calling me Brock," I told him. "That's Dad's name. Not mine." Our father's name was George because he chose to take his middle name.

"How old do you think she is?" Jonas asked, presumably of Mrs. Bergman.

"Somewhere under a hundred? How should I know? That hair, dude. I almost had to go back out to my car."

"I know." Jonas took the same chair and I sat across from him on the mushy sofa. Now I felt bad for laughing at Mrs. Bergman.

"You know the daughter's probably just bored," I said, "bedding down some ghetto crackhead for fun."

The office phone rang. Jonas went to the desk and answered it on speaker. "Janoff Investigations."

"It's Sten Bergman. Tell your brother I have a book for him since he likes to read so much. I'll drop it off for him tomorrow."

"Will do, thank you sir."

Jonas came back to the couch and sat, sizing me up the same way Mrs. Bergman had. We both loved the *Supernatural* TV series growing up. Even now. I was only ten when it first aired, and my mother forbade Jonas from letting me watch it with him thinking it was too scary for me. The one and maybe only advantage to her long illness was that she went to bed early, usually before eight, and since our father was always traveling that meant no one was around to stop me. Jonas was too cool for school at that age, but I knew he liked our weekly ritual of watching it together, enjoying the recurring banter about who was who. Even though I was younger, I was clearly Dean Winchester, the dysfunctional risk-taker, tactical loose cannon with a bad car, while Jonas was the more stable, strategic, level-headed Sam, both of us unwittingly united in our search for our father. For us anyway, we knew where he was, or we thought we did. We just didn't know why.

"What's up, *Sam*?" I joked, knowing there was never a wrong time for *Supernatural* references.

"Dean," he replied staying in character. "Bergman's dropping off a book for you tomorrow."

"Great."

Jonas was grinning.

"What, pray tell?"

"You're wearing a jacket. Like a suit jacket. And you walked in early, with no baseball cap, carrying a briefcase no less."

"Uh-huh…"

"Who are you and what have you done with my little brother?"

"I work here, what's the big deal? And maybe I've been known to *adult* from time to time. Look, I need to tell you about something."

"Okay, but I don't have time right now. I've got some research to do on another case and I want to try to track down one of the boyfriends on Bergman's list. Call me while I'm driving?"

"No, I'll go with you."

CHAPTER 3

I gave Jonas the basics and waited for his inevitable barrage of questions.

"What's in the envelope?" he asked, taking forever to pull away from the curb. He literally turned his head left and right five times.

"Dude, what are you waiting for?"

"I'm a cautious driver. What's in the envelope?"

"I don't know."

"What do you mean you don't know?"

"If I open it before it gets delivered, they'll kill me."

"Come on. Seriously?"

I took off my grown-up jacket and sighed. "It's paper. It's fucking paper. I don't know what it is. I can't open the goddamn thing." Except that it wasn't paper. It was small, amorphous in shape and form. I'd felt it but I honestly had no idea what it was.

"You mean you won't get paid if you do."

"I already got paid," I mumbled sort of under my breath.

Jonas took a hard right and veered clumsily to the sidewalk, where he let the motor idle in park. For a moment he stayed quiet, staring at the odometer.

"You got paid a million dollars? Are you fucking kidding me?"

"Not kidding."

"Where's the money?"

A call came in on Jonas' car Bluetooth. Lacy. He sank forward and reluctantly pressed the green button. "Hey," he said.

"I need BJ. Is he with you?"

"Present," I chimed.

"Dude, focus here," Jonas said. "Where's the money?"

"You told him?" Lacy asked. "I thought you weren't going to."

"Oh, well, that's even better. Why am I always the last to know everything? Where's the money, Brock?"

"Stashed."

Jonas sighed and turned now, the car still idling. "Okay. Okay. Gimme the rest."

"I have to deliver the envelope, or they'll kill me."

"What a preposterous story. Seriously, it's preposterous. Who the hell does that? Okay, back up and start from the beginning. Where were you?"

"Third Street, coming out of Union Bank on the corner, and you know how you can feel when someone's following you?"

"Yeah."

"It was this dinged up old Pontiac, like something out of *The French Connection*. I kept walking and didn't change my pace because I knew if they were following me, running would be the worst thing I could do."

"What'd you do?" he asked.

"I kept walking but farther away from the curb. The street was packed, so my strategy was to blend in with the crowd and sort of disappear without having to run."

"Good plan. And?"

"Some guy with a beanie and a European accent yelled 'hey' out the window enough times that I couldn't ignore him. I didn't walk over to him but I slowed my pace, and the car pulled over with the window down. The guy said he had something of mine. I was kinda cagey, but he'd piqued my interest."

"Did you tell him what he said?" Lacy asked. "That he called you by name?"

"Lacy, shut it," Jonas barked.

"Sor-ry."

"He asked me if I wanted to earn a million dollars for delivering an envelope."

"BJ come on. You seriously can't be that stupid."

I looked at my brother. "Sure about that?"

"Where?" he asked.

"What?"

"Deliver it where?"

"The reception desk at the Bonaventure."

"Unreal." He shook his head. "And you were right around the corner at that point, right?"

"Right. Of course I noted to the guy that if I delivered it, they could easily just take off and get away with not paying me."

"What did he say to that?"

"Nothing."

"What'd he look like?"

"Short hair, almost a crew cut under a black beanie, milky complexion, dark glasses, kind of a round face, and tall."

"He was in a car," Jonas noted. "How do you know he was tall?"

"The top of his head was touching the roof of the Pontiac, that's how. So the guy says to me, 'Proper relationships are based on trust. So we give you money first.'"

Jonas smirked at my impression. "What kind of accent? You said European. Like Germany, France?"

"Russia, Chechnya, maybe Ukraine."

Jonas tapped his fingers on the steering wheel. "Lacy, what do you make of this?"

"Oh, I'm allowed to speak now?"

"Sorry."

"What part, specifically?" she asked.

"A guy says BJ deliver this and I'll give you a million bucks and he's like, yeah, okay."

"That's not what I said."

"But-you-took-the-envelope, Brock, so that means you've accepted their offer."

I shrugged. "Okay, but I haven't delivered it yet."

"How long do you have?"

"Three days."

"And how many of those days are left?" Lacy asked, always the clever one in the bunch.

"Two."

"Did you tell him what happens if you don't deliver it?" Lacy asked me.

"Um…"

Jonas flicked both brows up. "Bye, Lace," and he disconnected Lacy's call.

I sulked in the passenger seat like a scolded teenager, trying to tolerate Jonas driving thirty miles an hour in the right lane on the freeway.

"Dude, seriously?"

"Jonas, please. I was walking down the street and a man cut me off in his beat-up car and handed me a briefcase filled with money. I didn't know what the fuck I was doing, but he forced me to take it and drove away. What else could I do?"

"A lot of things."

"Where are we going?" I asked. "You're just gonna knock on the door and ask for Anastasia Bergman?"

"I want to see what these addresses are so I can plan a strategy for approaching them. That's what private investigators do."

"Oh, this again. Nice dig."

"Don't you think it's useful to see if the addresses are to an office, an apartment, a storage facility, or a hunting shack in the woods?"

"Yes, Highness, but given the fact that I only have two days left to deliver an envelope, shouldn't we be using that time to determine what the fuck is in it?"

"Haven't you been doing that already? What have you been doing for the past day?"

"Surveillance."

Jonas tipped his head sideways the way he did when he knew I was right. "Okay, look, we'll be thirty minutes, tops." He turned to check me out.

"What?" I asked.

"You look sad."

I was deciding whether or not to mention it. But when it came to not only business partners but brothers, guilt can be a powerful leverage commodity. "I guess I'm a little sad that you don't seem to remember what day it is."

Another head tip. "Of course I remember. She died in my house while I was taking, or supposed to be, taking care of her."

"Don't go there, bro," I said. "Least you were there with her." The implication was that I'd been out surfing the day she died and not there helping Jonas, hearing her last words on earth, reminding her how much I loved her. My chest felt tight with grief. Three years. Still now.

"You and Lacy were right, Brock. We should have brought her to hospice, to a facility that specialized in that. Maybe they could have helped her hold on longer."

"Maybe, but I'm not sure it's what she wanted at that point."

That was three years ago, and it still felt like yesterday. We drove in silence to the first address on the list—a business park with no obvious front entrance, which had its advantages. The second address, designated as the home of Anastasia Bergman's second serious boyfriend, was a large, residential home in Silver Lake. And the third address referred to a street that neither of us nor Waze had ever heard of. Was that even possible?

My phone rang. I reached around to pull it out of the right pocket of my jacket where I'd put it. But it wasn't in my right pocket. It was in my left pocket.

And it wasn't my phone. OMG.

I shot Jonas a panicked look and held out the phone like it was toxic waste.

"What?"

"Not my phone, dude."

"What do you mean it's not your phone?"

"It's not my phone!"

"Whose phone is it?"

I stared wide-eyed, unsure what to do, searching my brother's eyes for an answer. It kept ringing.

"Shit," Jonas said. "How'd you…how'd they—"

"Fuck if I know. What should I do? Quick!" The ringing was driving me crazy, like a gong going off right next to your ear.

"If you don't answer it…"

"I know, I know. You're right." I pressed the green button.

"He-hello?" I stammered.

"Mr. Janoff." It was the same voice as the man in the car. "How you doing today?"

"I'm fine, thank you for asking." I had no idea what etiquette to use for gangsters, other than what I'd seen in Quentin Tarantino movies. "Who is this?" I asked, even though I knew.

"Your new friend, remember? You deliver envelope for us, like you agree. You not forget, no?"

"No. Scout's honor, your envelope will be delivered on time."

"Scout, what is scout? I do not know this term Scout but will look up. I have many dictionary in house for many language. Do not forget, Mr. Janoff. Tick tick. We will be watching."

"Um...thank you?"

"And my regards to your dead mother."

CHAPTER 4

Fuck, fuck. Fuck fuck fuck. Now we had irrefutable confirmation that we were being surveilled with some kind of wiretap. Was it in the glove box of Jonas' car, or in the same pocket where they'd somehow placed their gangster burner phone? Jonas hadn't said a peep since I hung up, and no wonder, right? His face looked like marble. I took a deep breath, and my phone rang again. Jonas and I stared at each other in a panic, then I smiled realizing it was my own phone. But I didn't recognize the number. Good God. Not again.

"Hello?"

"Hey BJ, it's Langley."

My chest relaxed allowing me to take an actual breath. "Hey, Langley. Got my message?"

"Yeah, and I've got some time later this morning if you want to bring the envelope you told me about."

"Can you do it soon, like now by any chance?" I blurted, dispensing with any hello how are yous. "I'm kind of on a schedule."

"Kind of?" Jonas mumbled.

"Uh…sure, I can do it now if you can get over here in the next thirty minutes or so, and you'd be coming to my house, not the office. You said you wanted to keep this under the radar, right?"

Understatement of the day. "Right."

Jonas was heading back to our office so I could pick up my car.

We didn't say a word, and when we got there I found a pen and legal pad on his desk and wrote, *Going to have the envelope x-rayed, back by lunchtime. Don't call my phone anymore, they probably cloned it. Call Jay Langley if I'm not back by one o'clock: 310-259-7598.*

Jonas read the note and stood close to me, then gave a sober nod of agreement.

◦ ◦◈◕◌═ ✦ ═◌◕◈◦ ◦

Before I left, I snatched a Sharpie and the legal pad off the desk, then sat in my car handwriting a note to Jay, assuming there was also a listening device in my car. Motherfuckers.

Even though we'd met in college, Jay Langley was who I hoped to be like when I grew up. Me with my aimless computer science degree, and he, the smart futurepreneur, with his business/engineering double major. Aside from his current paycheck, I envied his expert planning skills and career focus. He was probably making over a hundred thou. Jonas and Lacy would attest to the fact that I was still essentially fourteen, just slightly taller. They were right.

I swear a dark blue Honda Civic had been two cars behind me for the past fifteen minutes. Could be a coincidence, though I was starting to believe there was no such thing. I'd been here, to his parents' house in Torrance, twice during parties our senior year, and remembered now that one of the front steps caved in when I stepped down on it and nearly fractured my ankle.

I used the edges of the stairs to approach the front door and resisted the urge to look behind me every two seconds. I chose a knock instead of the doorbell. When Jay opened the door, I displayed the legal pad sheet and held it over my chest. His hair was shorter now, no facial hair, and wrinkles had formed on his forehead. I didn't even want to think about how I looked right now. Jay leaned his head down to read the notebook and motioned me in with his hands. I closed the door tight and followed him.

It smelled wonderfully fresh in here, like lemons, which suggested he'd been smoking weed and wanted to impress a woman with his clean house instead of smelling like an opium den. I kept my eyes peeled for women's underwear swept behind a door. Jay was never short on dates, but his slightly pudgy physique failed to

19

explain his sexual success. He turned on a stereo and raised the volume, then motioned me toward the back door where we stepped outside. He stood close to get a good look at me and held out his hand. Did he want money? No, of course not. He was asking for the envelope. I spent about a second too long deliberating. By the time I reached back under my shirt, he was already down the back stairs heading to the garage. I followed him, feeling bad like I'd disappointed him. Was Jay on the list of people I no longer trusted? What's the matter with you, BJ?

Instead of cars on blocks or camping equipment, Jay Langley had a bona fide, 21st-century tech lab hidden out here in his small, dreary garage. Geez. Now I felt even further behind him.

"Whoa," I said.

"Home away from home, I guess. Come on in."

I took the liberty of looking around. 3D printer, an 8-screen surveillance system and on the opposite wall was something that looked like the metal, conveyor belt machines at airport security. He held out his hand once more. I could tell he wasn't in the mood for delays. I pulled out the 9x12 FedEx envelope. He placed it gently on the belt and pressed a button to advance it directly under the view sensors. I moved closer to the screen, knowing full well that I'd lied to Jonas about there being papers inside but not prepared for what I saw now. I stood on my toes to lift my view a few inches and squinted.

"Cocaine?" I whispered.

He shook his head.

What was I looking at? I moved closer to the screen and saw the outline of a small Ziploc bag, about two inches by four inches, with some kind of material inside.

"This machine's equipped with a contraband sensor, so I don't think so. Also, the particles look too big. They almost look like pebbles, but they look neither polished, tumbled, or uniform. Whatever they are, the fragments look to be all different sizes. Unique."

We went back and forth whispering in each other's ears, like talking in a movie theater. For me, I had the excuse of their listening devices. But what would account for his discretion?

"Nothing else in here? No papers?"

"Looks like one piece of paper." He pointed. "But it's folded, and I can't see what's on it."

"No way to read it?"

"Nope," he said, then shrugged. "Not unless we can find a way to access UCSD's x-ray fluorescent spectrometer."

"What is that?"

"It's mostly used on archival documents to add light and visibility when old, dirty, discolored, or smudged paper was used. The art department has one for their historic art collection."

"Unfortunately I don't have the luxury of time right now. I can't explain how I got this, but I have to give it back soon."

Jay blinked back. "How long do you have?"

"A little over a day."

"Until what?" he asked.

"Don't ask."

"Let me make some calls." He acted put out, but I knew he loved shit like this, puzzles, especially unsolvable ones. "Meet me back here after work," he said. "I should be home around seven tonight."

"Thanks, man, I appre—"

"And leave this with—"

"No way. Are you kidding? And if you share any of what we've been doing here with anyone, not only my life will be in danger."

"Seriously?"

"Yeah man, seriously." Staring contest now.

Jay bit the inside of his lip, deciding, blaming me for putting him in this position.

"Look, I'm sorry. I wish I could tell you more. And if you can get back to me any sooner than seven—"

"Well, I assume I can't call you, right?"

"Right."

"I gotta go."

CHAPTER 5

The whole ride back from Jay's house to our office, I lamented the fact that I'd gotten him involved in what should only have been my problem. Jonas of course and, in a small way, Lacy who had heard part of our conversation in the car. What if I'd put all of them in danger by soliciting their help? But what choice did I have? I was targeted by a Russian mobster to complete a task he either wouldn't or couldn't do himself. And I still kept coming back to the *why me* question.

For some reason, I parked around the corner and peered in the back door before opening it, checking for anything that looked suspicious. Jonas was the neurotic one who second-guessed every decision he ever made. Now look at me. I knocked three times on the back door. I heard Jonas' footsteps from the kitchen, where he was probably making more coffee and pacing, wondering why I was late. 1:25. Poor Jonas.

He opened the door. I held out the notebook and Sharpie with outstretched arms.

We sat on the sofa side by side, handwriting messages back and forth like seven-year-olds playing spy. Ridiculous.

How'd you do? he wrote.

The envelope contains a small Ziploc bag of something white, I wrote. *Large particles, but not hard like pebbles. More spongey like*

Styrofoam or something, but in random shapes and sizes. One piece of folded paper, which I might be able to get a look at when I meet Jay back at his house tonight. He knows someone at UCSD who has different equipment.

He grabbed the legal pad and nodded, reading what I'd written. My hand was already getting tired. He flung the notebook on the coffee table, sat back and crossed his arms. My sentiments exactly.

"I know," I said out loud.

He grabbed the Sharpie and wrote, *Where's the fucking money*?? in large letters. It reminded me of *The Big Lebowski* but failed to crack me up today. Jonas formed his eyes into his don't-fuck-with-me look. I had a couple of choices here, and either would have a notable influence on my immediate future. I could, of course, refuse to tell him, thereby protecting him from whatever thugs were watching and monitoring me right now.

They might be monitoring me already.

My shoulders felt tighter than the morning after one of my Planet Fitness workouts. The pounding that started in my head yesterday had moved from my forehead to my temples and, honestly, I couldn't fit any more lies in there right now. Even of omission.

I returned Jonas' stare and gestured toward the front door with my finger. He pointed to the door and looked back with a question in his eyes.

Yep, I nodded.

The front door of the office had a tiny, square foyer, some hooks on the wall where I kept an extra baseball cap and where Jonas kept this hideous, old-man cardigan hanging by the label. I added a threadbare gym towel to the rack for effect. On the floor below them sat my extra pair of running shoes, and a rumpled, black duffel bag, typically filled with dirty gym clothes that I hadn't gotten around to washing. Jonas kept his gaze fixed on the door, then looked back at me with eyes widened as if to say, *That?*

I nodded again and smiled. Yep. That. The heavy-as-shit briefcase the thug had handed over was in my apartment, specifically hidden in the back of Ray's smelly closet. He always wore the same clothes, never did laundry, so it was as good a place as any to hide something. I was proud of myself for that little trick, but I felt certain I'd do something stupid here very shortly to underscore that singular, clever moment.

My phone rang. Lacy. I couldn't answer it. I clicked to disconnect it and immediately texted that I'd meet her in the parking lot of the office out back.

Jonas, in a moment of sudden courtesy, or maybe fear of my impending doom, brought me a cup of coffee in a real mug, made to my exact specifications of one sugar and no milk. He made one for himself and we sat together on the top step of the back staircase, waiting for Lacy, sipping in silence.

"What am I supposed to do here?" he asked, in his normal speaking volume.

"What do you mean?" I whispered, unsure if their listening devices were installed in the office and if we could be heard out here.

"When you leave. You're gonna leave me here—"

I put my hand over his mouth in case they'd installed a listening device somewhere in my clothing. I knew he was about to say *with that,* and I didn't want Scary Russian Guy to think that money had any connection with this office.

"Dude, we're outside. We're fine."

The yellow Lotus pulled into the back lot.

"There's only one Lacy," I said.

No business suit, today she wore long, loose, wide-leg black pants, a white flowy shirt, and black sandals. An otherwise casual outfit that, on her, still looked elegant despite her constant attempts to remain a tomboy.

"Don't you boys look cute. Lemme take your picture."

"Shut up."

She pinched her lips and pulled a folded piece of paper from her pants pocket and handed it to me.

"What's this?" Jonas grabbed it out of my hands. "Who is Oleg Kokov?" he asked, reading from the page.

"Shut the fuck up, dummy," I hissed, then complimented Lacy on her sleuthing. "Well done, Watson."

"Later." She waved and headed back to the most ostentatious car I'd ever seen.

"I got the plate number off the Pontiac that approached me," I explained after Lacy drove off.

"And you think that name is the guy who handed over a million dollars and an envelope to a stranger?"

For some reason, yeah, I did.

"Oleg Kokov. Okay," he said. "Well, I did some research on our client's daughter, Anastasia Bergman, while you were gone. She was a model and started breaking into acting, with 1.7 million Instagram followers, a Tiktok account, and she was six months—"

"Pregnant?" I asked.

"No, six months from her college graduation. Kind of a promising young woman, on the surface anyway."

For some reason, when he brought up Anastasia, my mind went to the envelope. "Keep looking," I said. "I've got some research to do. Jay Langley at seven tonight and hopefully he can help me find out more about what's in that envelope. After that, well, we'll see."

⁕ ⬦⬅═+═⮕⬦ ⁕

I didn't tell Jonas I was preparing to deliver the FedEx envelope tonight, nor did I tell him how I had a day's worth of footage to review from the nanny cam I'd placed in the Bonaventure lobby. I know what he'd say anyway. He'd ask me what was preventing me from just delivering the envelope, and why I tolerated being left totally in the dark. The answer, of course, was the scary Russian mobster who was undoubtedly following me at this moment. The main floor restroom of the Bonaventure had the best chance of adequate lighting and enough privacy so I could stay there for an hour. I entered it by way of the underground parking garage and took the stairs to the main lobby where the men's room was fortuitously right around the corner.

I didn't go near the actual lobby, though it killed me to not check on the camera I'd left there yesterday. I chose the second farthest stall on the left side, locked the door, opened the app on my phone, and logged in. The great thing about this app is it had five different playback speeds. I started the playback at normal speed first. The position of the camera was perfect.

At one point, a man was standing directly in front of it, blocking the view of the front desk, but that only lasted about thirty seconds.

I increased the speed to 1.5 and watched a steady stream of businessmen, women in high heels dragging overnight suitcases, two families of four, and one woman in a long evening gown with what

25

looked like a bodyguard behind her, then no activity for four, five, six minutes.

I sped up the playback to 1.75 speed and watched more of the same: singles, a few couples, nothing, and then one man in a watch cap. I widened my eyes. Could this be Scary Russian Guy, Oleg Kokov? And why would he have a car registered to him in his own name? Gangsters didn't do stupid things like that. I watched the man, who wore black pants and a black leather jacket, hoping he'd turn toward not away from the camera when he walked away. When he got up to reception, he leaned into the desk lowering his head slightly, forearms on the counter, waiting for the concierge to ask his co-workers or manager if someone had dropped off the FedEx envelope that I still had tucked in the back of my pants. I could see the concierge shaking his head: young, dark hair, dark skin, glasses. Come on, Oleg, turn this way, turn this way…he turned, and the pit of my stomach clenched when I saw the familiar face with its slightly crooked nose. I sped up the camera this time to 2.0. Oleg came back twice, once again alone and another time with a taller, thinner associate, no doubt asking if the envelope had been delivered yet. So this exercise begged the question of who would be receiving the envelope, and how could I provide proof of delivery?

CHAPTER 6

Well, my little camera was still recording so I thought I might surprise Jay at work at the LA County Medical Examiner's Office, hoping he'd made some arrangements with his high-tech friends for the next step in my investigation—the folded paper in the envelope. I fucking loved this place, morbid as it was. For someone learning about crime scene investigation and, as Jonas loved to remind me, his protégé, a forensic crime lab was like a candy store. Like most crime labs now, the front office consisted of a glass wall with a numbered keypad module on the right. No code, no access. I knocked quietly on the glass.

A stern-faced security guard angled his head to see my face. "Yes, sir. Can I help you?" Formal, but not completely unfriendly.

"I'm here to see Jay Langley."

"Is he expecting you?"

"Yes, sir," I lied. I'd already pissed Jay off earlier today. Maybe he'd give me what I needed to just get rid of me. I hoped.

I saw the top of Jay's pointy head towering over the security guard. His shoulders sank when he saw me. I was all too familiar with disappointing people, so I was used to it. Wasn't that what this whole mission was intended to fix? A million dollars to right all the prior wrongs of my life? Start fresh. How many people had those same aspirations? Then again, how many of those people died before they got a chance to spend it? Was I destined to be part of that elite group of losers?

Langley came through the security door and motioned me to the elevators around the corner.

"Sorry for coming unannounced. I thought you might potentially have some information for me sooner."

"Yeah, yeah I know, desperate times, BJ. Isn't that always the case?"

Damn, throwing shade. Okay, noted.

"I'm not gonna be done here by seven and I know you're on the clock. What's your email address?" he asked.

"Bjjanoff91@gmail.com." I watched him type that into his phone. "Okay cool. I'll email you the digital files that I took from my machine this morning. Let me do that right now, actually, so in case I don't get finished in time tonight you can contact my friend at Grace Imaging yourself."

"Grace Imaging?" I asked. "I thought you said UCSD."

"Same thing. Ask for Kayla. I told her you might call tonight."

"I can email her the digital images and she'll be able to open and scan them?"

"Yes. She has a better lab and more expensive equipment than I do, so she's likely to be able to see more. Your files are DICOM, dcm format, which is an industry-standard so they should work fine."

I wanted to ask him how I could open the image, but I stayed quiet and listened to his plan. Kayla, Grace Imaging, dcm format. It all sounded plausible. So why was my head pounding and my palms sweaty? And why was there a knot in my stomach when I thought about Jay Langley? For one thing, I hadn't had anything to eat or drink all day. Not good.

"Still plan on meeting me at my place at seven tonight," he said. "I'll text you if I can't make it." He reached out and grabbed my hand with one single shake. The heavy security door clinked hard when it closed, like something in my life was about to change forever.

❖ ❖❖ ✦ ❖❖ ❖

The next symptom to add to my headache and anxiety was dizziness. I death-gripped the railing walking out of the Medical

Examiner's office and sat in my car for a good twenty minutes to drink stale BPA-poisoned water and steady myself. I looked at my watch. 5:45 p.m. Shit. Rush hour in midtown. Wherever I drove right now would be a parking lot anyway, so I might as well stay here. The question was whether to deliver the envelope now, how to arrange for proof of that action, wait to see if Jay would be available at 7 p.m. as scheduled, or if I should head to Grace Imaging now where a woman named Kayla was supposedly going to help me answer the *Why me?* question.

I couldn't call Jonas for consultation, nor could I call Lacy because of my suspicion that my phone had been cloned. Did I have any proof of this other than watching gangster films? Not specifically, no. Had I been away from my phone for any period of time, when Oleg and his thugs could have taken it? No, but they also found a way to implant a burner phone in the pocket of my jacket. When had they—ahhh. Now I remembered the dewy-skinned starlet who'd turned my head walking out of Peets at the Bonaventure. I was holding the door for an old woman coming out and a starlet crashed into my left side, apologized, and that was the pocket the burner had been in. I paused to remember her face. She no doubt worked for Oleg. Wow. These men were not amateurs.

I made a sort of grid in my head. Oleg at the top left, his tall associate from the lobby video in square number two, and now starlet in the middle left. Her luminous complexion startled me, dark eyes set far apart, and...wait.

"I sorry, I so sorry," she'd said when she crashed into me, rather than *I'm* sorry. Was the Starlet also from Russia and working for Oleg? I'd call her Natasha for the moment. I pretended I was playing an iPhone game because frankly it was less terrifying than reality. By accepting a million dollars, I think I'd unwittingly sealed the certainty of my early demise.

Turned out that Grace Imaging, if I had the right one, was on Grand in LA and not actually in San Diego on the UCSD campus. I knew how to get there on surface streets to avoid rush hour traffic on Highway 10. Taco Bell on the left and a Gold's Gym on the right, Grace Imaging was a white, two-story building with large glass windows on the west side. I got two tacos and a large Coke from the drive-through. I was too stressed to eat. Even so, I forced myself to take three bites of the chicken taco, hoping the protein might balance me. I parked and entered the Grace Imaging building and headed up a long staircase. At the top was a suite with the door open. The dark gray carpet smelled old and smokey, not at all what I expected. I was ready to introduce myself as my adult name, Brock, not BJ. But no one was here.

"Hello?"

A man in a lab coat entered the reception area and looked behind me into the hallway.

"Yes?" Thirtyish, clean-shaven, medium height, sweaty-faced, and nervous.

I explained I was there to see someone named Kayla and I was sent by Jay Langley.

"Who?"

"Jay Langley, from the Medical Examiner's office."

"Look, whoever you are, Kayla is…I don't know where she is actually. I'll let her know you were here, okay?" The man rushed off down an interior hallway and I heard a door close. Odd.

Back in the safety of my car, the tacos smelled delicious suddenly and I downed two of them with about half of the Coke. What I needed was water. That would be next.

I checked my phone, hoping, hoping, yes it was here: the email from Jay with the file attached of the interior of the envelope. I knew there were software programs that translated file types for Windows and Mac. Looked like there was something called DICOM Viewer for Mac for viewing image files like MRIs that might work. And that was only a contingency plan anyway. I had Jay and Kayla helping me with this. Didn't I?

I checked my phone again: 6:30, just enough time to get to Jay's house by seven and hope and pray he was there to tell me what was so important about a little Ziploc bag that was worth a million dollars. I felt a wave of fear and isolation, suddenly, afraid to talk to anyone and, for obvious reasons, feeling afraid to go home. Had I fucked up by putting the briefcase in Ray's closet? Now I was second guessing everything. Wasn't that Jonas's department? Certainly not me.

Jay's car was parked out front. Whew. I took a moment to breathe. I might be able to drop off the envelope after knowing more conclusively what was inside. What was on the folded paper? A handwritten note, a receipt, a description of the contents?

I knocked on Jay's door and waited. Maybe he had just gotten home. Maybe he was doing bong hits in the back bedroom and couldn't hear the knocking. So I rang the bell. Once, twice, and waited. Ten, twenty, thirty seconds. I rang the bell again. More waiting. I counted back from 100. At sixty, I headed down his driveway to access the tech lab in his garage. Thinking of the keypad at the ME's office, I wondered why he didn't have something like that here, given the sophistication and cost of his equipment. I knocked on it.

"Jay? Jay, it's BJ. You in here?"

I waited, listened for any noises inside, expecting him to come out the back door of the house and invite me inside.

Cars, motorcycles, and some voices on the next street over were all I heard. I knocked again on the garage door, then turned the knob. The door was unlocked. He'd flicked a light switch on the wall earlier today. Now the light switch didn't work. Interesting.

I pulled my phone out of my pocket and used the flashlight feature to light up the room. I moved my arm right to left. All the equipment looked intact, nothing out of the ordin— Oh! Oh my God. Jay! Oh no. Please no.

I suppressed the urge to jump to the floor to try to revive Jay, who was lying half on his back and half on his side. I didn't move, knowing the risks. I stood there in the entry, the door still open behind me, completely frozen in my movements but feeling a spinning sensation under my feet. I gripped the edge of the door, knowing I shouldn't touch anything but feeling like I might fall over if I didn't. I cried a little out of shock, more like a sneeze with a momentary outflow of tears and guttural sobs, which instantly disappeared. Jay didn't respond to my shouting his name. And when I ran the flashlight beam over his face and neck, I could see red ligature marks on his neck. God no. His face was blue.

CHAPTER 7

Out of some kind of survivalist trait I never knew I had, I managed to delay my reaction long enough to wipe my fingerprints off the garage door handle, close the door, and make my way back out to my car and in the middle of rush hour traffic. Had I stepped in any blood? No, he wasn't bleeding, or not that I could tell without moving him. Hiding in a sea of jampacked cars seemed a prudent place to be right now, somehow using claustrophobia to buffer out the scarier emotions. Then again, why did I wipe my prints off the door handle? I'd been there earlier today and probably touched every single piece of equipment in there. Great.

I had to call my brother.

"Hey."

"Why are you calling me from your phone?' Jonas asked. He'd just gotten home, I could tell by his terrier, Sasha, barking in the background.

"Because it occurred to me that they probably hadn't had time to orchestrate dropping off the burner phone in my pocket and also clone my phone because I wasn't without it long enough."

"Jesus, Brock. Where are you?"

"In rush hour traffic. I only have a minute so listen up. The person Jay told me to go see is missing, and Jay is dead."

"What?"

"I just found him strangled in his garage."

"Holy shit, BJ, what have you gotten yourself into?" He paused, thrusting all the air out of his lungs. "Deliver the fucking envelope. I mean it. Do it now!"

"I'm not giving back the envelope," I said, almost surprised by the words.

"Are you high? They'll…they'll…you know. They'll kill you."

"Think about it, Jonas. Why me? Oleg, the gangster's been going to the reception desk at the hotel to see if I dropped it off yet. What's the point of this exercise? I mean, if he was doing that, why couldn't he drop it off there himself, and why did it need to be dropped off at all?"

I threaded my car through the lines of cars. I changed lanes and, naturally, that one slowed to a complete stop.

"I-I don't know. Did you tell me about these men in black suits? Maybe he was trying to avoid them getting it? What are you thinking?"

"It's a game, Jonas."

"Dude, you just finished telling me that Jay Langley's dead. How is that a game?" His voice cracked.

"I don't know but I'm gonna find out what this is all about. You won't see me for a while but I'll stay safe, I promise."

I hung up quickly before he could change my mind. It was an evil thing to do to someone as neurotic as he is, but it couldn't be helped. Jay Langley, my college friend, was lying dead alone on the cold floor of his garage. That meant everything's changed.

I got off at the next exit, swirling back around to head to my apartment. Thank goodness Ray wasn't there, so I was able to get in and out with the metal briefcase from his disgusting closet in less than two minutes. The last thing I saw before locking the door was my White Butterfly plant on the kitchen windowsill, which had been begging for water since last weekend. No time.

I headed back south to Venice. I drove 65 miles per hour in the middle lane, didn't turn my head left or right, and was completely calm and steady. I no longer had any of the physical symptoms I'd had earlier. It was like another version of me had woken up when I saw poor Jay Langley's dead body crumpled on the floor. Dead, Jay. It was still too shocking to fathom. And it was all because of me.

I parked in the back lot of our office and grabbed the empty briefcase. I turned off the alarm first, then calmly transferred the cash from the rumpled gym bag in the foyer to the briefcase, arranged exactly as I found it two days ago. I closed and locked it, could barely lift it with one hand but managed to get it back out to my car, on the floor of the backseat. I returned to the office, found a roll of shipping tape in a drawer in the kitchen area, pulled a canvas painting off the wall. I fixed two long pieces of tape to my sleeve while I turned the painting over to show the recessed backside. I taped the FedEx envelope directly onto the back of the canvas. Luckily it was thick enough to not show it when I placed it back on the wall. It was taped so that it stuck to the canvas and, if it fell, it would still be concealed within the wooden frame. Good enough for the moment.

I used my own phone to try to reach Kayla at Grace Imaging. The same harried guy answered the phone. I recognized his voice, and he said Kayla hadn't come back and he had no idea what happened to her. He said happened - interesting choice of words. That implied that he thinks something did happen to her. Didn't it? Oleg and his team of goons were probably following me, but I didn't care. I drove quickly to the Bonaventure and stood in line at Peets, hoping and praying that Raquel was working late.

A woman with short, blonde hair walked into view. "Can I help you?"

Survivalist Brock clicked on, putting fear and uncertainty to sleep for a while. Who was this new person?

"Hey, I'd like a large, iced mocha and I have a little favor to ask you." I winked when I said it. Had I detected a slight drawl in her voice? "It's this silly family thing, but I need to prove to my brother that I'm bringing his briefcase back to him today. It's this sort of contest we play."

"Sure, let me make your coffee first," she said, only slightly amused. "But it's slow right now. What do you need me to do?"

"Just take my picture when I bring this briefcase to the reception desk."

"That's it?"

"That's it," I said.

"Sure, no problem."

While she made the coffee I had no intention of drinking, I put two pieces of masking tape on the briefcase and used my Sharpie to write Oleg Kokov on it in large lettering. I handed the girl my phone, instructed her to stand in the middle of the lobby, and take one picture of me placing the briefcase on the reception desk, and another of the concierge taking it.

I sipped the coffee. "Best coffee in town," I said, and it was most of the time. "You ready?"

"Sure," she said. "What happens if you win the contest?"

"I'll find out soon."

I handed her the phone and stood behind one woman. Someone else appeared behind the desk. "I can help you, sir. Are you checking in?"

"No, I was instructed to drop this off for someone named Oleg Kokov. He's expecting it. May I leave this with you?"

The woman blinked back, then said, "Certainly sir." She struggled to lift it with both hands, then clunked it on the floor at her feet and pushed it under the desk. "Is there anything else I can help you with?"

"That's it, thank you so much. He should be here shortly."

"Alright, sir, have a good evening."

I turned. The blonde woman and my phone were nowhere in sight.

CHAPTER 8

A busload of seniors filtered in through the revolving doors and crowded the lobby. I moved through them back to the coffee stand and found the girl, thank God, frothing milk behind the counter.

"Sorry," she said. "I had to get back to the counter."

I nodded but watched her eyes. Was she too part of Oleg's crime ring? Was everybody?

She reached in the pocket of her apron and handed me my phone. "Hope those came out okay and good luck with the contest." She flashed a momentary smile that somehow didn't match the look behind her eyes. Did she know something? Was she in on it?

I nodded, thanked her again, checked the photos. Big sigh. There were two that were exactly what I asked for. Zooming in showed me holding the briefcase, and the woman taking it from me. Perfect. For security, I texted them to Lacy with a *will explain later*.

Back in my car, I pulled Oleg's burner phone from my glove compartment and dialed the number that my earlier call had come from. I knew Oleg wouldn't answer it himself. Why? Because I was starting to understand my new adversary. Oleg Kokov needed something from me. Not just from someone but from me specifically, or why else would he orchestrate this whole deal the way he did? And Oleg cared about appearances. That's why he brought his underling with him to the reception counter. He had his team of goons, probably two at least, and answering his own phone calls would make him sound too eager when, of course, he didn't have a care in the world. Right? Right.

"Who is this?" a man's voice answered, accentuating the *is*.

"You know who it is. Oleg Kokov please." I counted to five. The man snorted, placed his hand over the phone and mumbled something.

"Meester Janoff. Learned some things I see. How you doing today?"

"Mr. Kokov, I am well, thank you for asking," I mocked.

"What can I do for you?" he asked mechanically, struggling to remember what little English he'd learned, knowing whatever he got wrong would subvert the strength of his public image. I loved that.

"I've made my delivery. Good day."

I hung up, texted the two photos the blonde barista took to Oleg's phone as proof of my delivery, removed the SIM card from the burner phone, smashed it with the heel of my shoe, and added the phone number to my list of contacts of my own cell phone in case I needed to call him again. I strategically left my car in the hotel underground lot, unlocked, and took off on foot to board the Flower Street and 4th southbound city bus near Figueroa.

If Oleg had been tailing me, they knew I'd returned the money instead of the envelope and were probably planning to take my car apart piece by piece. My poor car. I was now living out my personal version of a Quentin Tarantino movie. I could never touch that car again. Thank God I'd paid it off last year.

CHAPTER 9

Welcome to Brock Janoff 2.0. I'd spent the night wrestling with myself on a hard park bench on the grounds of Griffith Park Observatory. I knew it was a popular homeless gathering spot open all night and, since City administrators hadn't yet formulated an action plan for homeless housing, it ticked all of my boxes: secluded, unsupervised, dark, and crowded. Even if Oleg and his goons followed my bus and then Uber ride here, it was completely obscured under a cloudy sky. How would they find me? I was just another skinny dude in a dirty baseball cap and oversized hoodie, and other than my blond hair there was nothing noticeable about me.

Before trying to sleep, after telling him I was jumped and robbed and had my phone and wallet stolen, a nice old man let me use his phone to text Jonas a quick *I'm ok* message. The poor guy felt bad for me and offered me some of his dinner. BJ Janoff 1.0 would have carried around guilt from that moment like a lead treasure weighing him down for the next decade. Today I was someone different. Indomitable and determined to survive.

Jonas was right, too. I was named after my dad, George Brock Janoff, whom I never wanted to be like. There was nothing wrong with him. He lived the American dream the best way he knew how: by working the only eighty-hour-a-week government job that ever existed and cheating on my mother with not one but two of his office assistants. Fucker. It was the kind of US State Department job that no one talked about: accountant. I couldn't even imagine the risk factors he encountered every day managing all the dirty deals of shady politicians, black ops projects, congressional tribunals. I would have had an easier time understanding heavy drinking, even drug use than philandering. It just didn't seem like him and, in my bones, never felt completely true. Maybe I was just afraid to consider scarier alternatives, like his entire existence was a lie. My mother joked while we were young that they'd only had sex twice, accounting for Jonas and me. So when we found out about his 'two cookies' as my mother referred to them, it just seemed like a bad cover story. I sort of checked out after that and neither of us has talked to him since Mom died three years ago. Yesterday, come to think of it.

I dreamt of my father, and it was always the same dream. But I never woke with any urgency to call him. I no longer kept track of his whereabouts. He told Jonas and me lots of stories growing up explaining the reasons behind his frequent international travel, and why he wasn't allowed to bring our mother with him. Mostly Europe, the trips were once a year for some kind of conference that he could never talk about. Netherlands one year, Germany the next, then Austria. "I make sure there's enough money to support our interests," he used to tell me and, he'd say with a wink in his eye, "I make sure everyone's spending it properly." It never occurred to me till later to ask who he meant by 'our'. And when you're seven, words like properly in the context of financial contributions don't register as corruption. Then the once-a-year international conferences later turned into many trips in preparation for the conference, checking the books, visiting banks, meeting with lawyers, and none of it was tangible enough to discuss at the dinner table. "Daddy has a very important job," my mother would say and then quickly shift to homework.

In the dream, I was looking at a picture of my father and four other men and, because the laws of dreams defied the laws of space-time, I was able to reach into the picture, touch my father and pull something he was holding out of his hand. But I never got far enough to see what it was. A book, a pen, a vase. Something very old and very valuable was all I ever came away with. Where was that picture now, and had it ever actually existed?

I woke with indentations in my right cheek from the slats on the wooden bench. But there were advantages that offset my bad night's sleep. 1) I was still alive. 2) I'd returned Oleg's money so no one could accuse me of being a thief. 3) The envelope was safe at the moment, temporarily anyway. 4) And this one was the most important: I had the DCM image file Jay sent me of the contents of Oleg's magic envelope.

The image Jay died for. I could still hardly believe it.

The way I understood it, having read about airport security x-rays, the machine was designed to reconstruct an image of the contents of bags based on low and high-energy x-rays. By comparing the output signals of both x-rays using detectors, the machine outputs an image of different colored objects depending on their density.

The disadvantages of my present situation of course included being homeless, carless, no cell phone, my murdered friend, who very likely died because of my project, and the only person who could help me with the next step in my research, Kayla, was missing. Naturally the option to just open the envelope had crossed my mind, given my dire circumstances and the current chain of events. But something about those mysterious contents was, to Oleg Kokov, worth a million dollars. Probably more. So whatever it was had danger attached to it. Out of homage to Jay, I was determined to find out what the hell was in that Ziploc bag.

First, coffee. Luckily I'd taken a hundred bucks cash out of an ATM two days ago and I still had that in my wallet. Wait. I pulled out my wallet and checked. It was all there. I sat up slowly, pretending to stretch while taking in the scene and scanning for Russian gangsters. The nice man who had offered me half his dinner approached me again and asked if he could sit down.

"Please," I said, and motioned. I still felt bad for lying to him about being robbed. "Where can someone get a cup of coffee around here?"

"The café in the observatory is open now," the man said. "They have very good coffee. And breakfast."

"I had some money stashed in my pocket, which the robbers didn't take," I explained. "Let me buy you breakfast. I'm BJ," I said, realizing a second too late that I should have used a fake name. Or another fake name.

"James," he said, and shook my hand. He had the face of either the kindest person you'd ever met or a practiced con man. I couldn't decide which yet, time would tell. Round head, light skin, medium-length brown hair, large features. Either way, this was perfect. Fuel up and fill the belly of a homeless old-timer. Turns out James was a Brit and a former Postmaster General in London. I bought us both omelets and toast, coffee, and orange juice. I gave him a ten-spot and asked if I could stay in touch with him and call him sometime. He wrote down his phone number on one of his old postmaster business cards in slanted script, with a pencil no less. Who knows when I might need a man like James.

"What's the most secret way out of this park?" I asked him, realizing he probably lived here every day, off the grid.

"You mean without being seen?"

"Exactly."

"I'd take the trolley down to the Red Line Metro Station."

⁕ ⁕⧼ ✛ ⧽⁕ ⁕

I rode the trolley and kept my eyes peeled for mysterious onlookers, evidence of surveillance, or anything out of the ordinary. Once I got on the red line, I pulled out my phone, lowered the volume, and watched the lobby footage from my nanny cam, intermittently keeping an eye on the crowd around me. Ten people in my car including me, five men and five women, all looking at their phones. No one looked up to meet my gaze. I took a deep breath, my chest still tight from anxiety.

Okay. I was headed back to North Hollywood where Jay Langley lived, which was the wrong direction. I kept my eyes on my phone and so far nothing. What the fuck?

I sped the playback up to 1.75 and made sure to not look away. No Oleg, no silver briefcase. I kept watching, but there was nothing. And that introduced a hundred new questions.

Was the money actually in the briefcase that he gave me? Yes, because I'd packed it in there myself. So if he hadn't picked it up, maybe Oleg didn't care about the money and it was never about that, and always about the envelope, which was luckily still in my possession. Even so, I kept watching. Now it was close to midnight on the video. Two women approached the desk with luggage; a bellhop met them, no Oleg. Fuck.

I searched my memory trying to remember who had taken the briefcase from me and remembered the pictures that the coffee barista took. I stopped the video, closed the app, and found them in my photo folder. By describing her, I could easily find out her name, call the front desk, and ask her about the disposition of Oleg's briefcase. An incoming call interrupted me, again from a number I didn't recognize. It could be my new mafia friends, but my gut told me no. I picked it up.

"Hello?"

"Mr. Janoff?"

I paused to assess the unfamiliar voice. A young-sounding woman with a strange, faintly European accent. "Yes."

"This is High Society Custom Tailor calling to tell you that your suit is ready."

"Oh, excellent." I didn't own a suit and I'd never been to a tailor in my life.

"If you can come in today for a fitting, we're open till five o'clock."

"Sure," I said. Why? Because everything in my life already felt completely unreal. What harm could come from one more thing? "What times do you have available?'

"Eleven, or else 2 p.m. today."

"I'll see you at eleven, thank you. Can you remind me of your exact address?"

"3000 Wilshire Boulevard, Suite 110."

"See you soon."

CHAPTER 10

I smiled as I got off the Metro at the North Hollywood station because this stunt had Lacy written all over it. And she was known for doing terrible accents. I found an Uber right there and managed to snag it despite a line of other travelers. Honestly, after sleeping on a park bench all night I deserved to be carted around town by other people. I stayed in the Uber for a minute looking out at the place, staring into the glass doors, waiting. I knew I was a sight and probably smelled bad. Hell, I could actually use a new suit for whatever future was awaiting me.

I tipped my Uber driver on the app. "Thank you," I said, and stepped onto the curb, feeling vulnerable in the fifteen steps to the entry.

I opened the heavy, glass doors. The carpet was thickly padded, the space was library-quiet, and it smelled like…something. Not bad, just noticeable. I moved slowly to approach a man at the helm of this operation. "I'm Brock Janoff and I believe I have a fitting scheduled for eleven."

An older man, understatement, looked down at a notebook using his finger to follow a string of names. "I don't have any fittings scheduled for that name, sir. Could it be another place?" he asked, probably hoping it was.

"I thought it was here, and I received a call from—"

"BJ."

Lacy. I knew it was her. "Hey there, I'm just buying a suit," I told her. "Be right with you."

"No problem. You need a new one anyway."

I looked at the man. "My sister, she knows best, right?"

"Of course, sir. Let's get you measured. Did you have a color in mind?"

Ah, changed his tune, did he? Now that he knew I had money to actually buy something. Problem is, I didn't.

"Tan. I've always wanted a tan suit."

"Very good sir."

"And I need something off the rack if possible. I have an event I want to wear it to today."

"I'm not sure that will be possible, but let's see."

I let the man measure my arms, shoulders, legs, waist, then he disappeared into a back room.

"Lace!" I hissed.

She emerged from a display of Italian wools. I hugged her and something in my chest loosened when I felt her arms around me. Other than my mother, she was the only woman I'd ever loved, even though she was like a sister. I wiped my eyes on her shoulder.

"You okay?"

"Fuck no, I'm not okay. Thanks for the rescue."

"Always here for you, bro." She touched my cheek. "Are you hurt?"

"Not that bad. But I suspect I don't smell very nice right now."

"I'm used to it," she smiled. "Go get your suit, I gotta call my dad back."

Lacy's father, Jerome Diaz, started out working at a shipping company, as in intercontinental shipping, then he inherited the company from his father, sold it, and now he's a millionaire venture capital guru who opened a law firm, bought his daughter a Lotus, and sent her to law school. When Daddy calls, you better answer. What I loved about Lacy is that she still lived in the same dingy studio apartment she had ten years ago and never allowed her family's money to change her, with the exception of the car.

"Mr. Janoff," the man said as a statement. I was surprised he remembered my name.

"How'd you do back there?" I asked.

He held out a tan and blue suit. "One option that will need to be hemmed, and I can't do that till this afternoon, and one other option that should fit you like a glove," he said of the blue suit.

"Blue."

"Yes sir. Summer weight Italian wool. It should look divine. Would you like to give it a try?"

I'd try it just for his use of the word divine. Lacy came around the corner again. "I'll cover this," she said, directly to the tailor.

"Very good, Miss."

Lacy, my sugar Mama.

"Will that be all for today, sir?"

"You need a shirt," Lacy said. "A turtleneck," she said to the man, "and same shade for a monochromatic look."

"Right away, Miss."

⁕ ⚬⚬⚬ ✛ ⚬⚬⚬ ⚬ ⁕

I belonged in a Benetton ad or a Saturday Night Live skit. This was good because I didn't look or even feel like me in this fifteen-hundred-dollar getup. Lacy put a camera around my neck and rolled up the sleeves on the jacket and shirt. Then she stood back for a better look.

"Perfect," she said and giggled. "Come on, I've got a car out here."

"Your car? A little conspicuous, don't you think?"

"Not the Solar, another one." She pointed when we got outside to an old, dirty, dark blue Rav. "Get in, driver's side," she said, and handed me a set of keys.

"Um, okay. Where are we headed?"

"Santa Monica Pier."

"Sure. Are you off today?"

"Sort of." She grinned.

"Did you tell your manager you'd be out? Or are you playing the Daddy Owns This Law Firm card again?"

She giggled and stared. "You look good in a suit. I barely recognize you."

"Come on, I look like a talk show host."

Lacy nodded with a smirk, reminding me once again that she

45

was always two steps ahead of us. She was right. I didn't look at all like BJ Janoff right now, which was probably good.

"Let's just say Jonas and I have been frantically looking for you. He's sort of, how shall I say this…"

"Undone?"

"Good word. Now," she said when we'd both closed our doors. "Tell me what's going on."

I pulled onto Wilshire and headed for the freeway. I started with Jay.

"Oh my God. And you found him?"

"Yeah."

"I am so sorry. And you were there with him earlier leaving all your forensic evidence all over his lab?"

"Yep."

"Who the fuck are these people?"

"Russian gangsters, I suspect. As to what they really want, I haven't figured that out yet. But what I've pretty much confirmed is that they care much more about the envelope than about the million dollars."

"Why do you say that?"

"I returned the money."

"And kept the envelope??"

"What's even more interesting is that I don't think they've even picked up the money yet, which brings to mind a host of new questions."

"Jesus, BJ. Was that wise?"

"What, return money I never earned and wasn't mine to begin with, and was probably stolen from someone else? Sure. Was it risky? Look, my friend is dead and it's because of me." My voice gurgled when I said it. "And now I'm under surveillance, Jonas might be as well, and I know I'm being targeted. Why me? Why was I chosen for this nightmare? There's some connection with me and my family. I need to know what that connection is."

"Okay, okay. I get you. Watch the road. Turn off here." She pointed.

"Where are we going?"

"My father's crash pad that he uses when he's working late and doesn't want to wake my mom. She's a bad sleeper."

I held my tongue, remembering my father and what resulted from his late-night meetings.

"You can stay here through the weekend, maybe part of next week, I'll let you know."

"You're a lifesaver, you and your dad. Where are we, 4th and Pico or something?"

"Yeah, park down here, on this side street, there, Bay Street. You can have this car for a few days but only go out after dark."

I turned to look at her. "You're giving me an apartment *and* a car? What did I do to deserve this kindness?"

"You've got a hitman after you. Besides, it's only for a few days. I recommend not going out at all and just ordering food in. If there's anything you need from your place, let me know, and either me or Jonas will drop it off outside your door."

I tried to take it all in. Tried and failed. "Okay. What's the address?"

"2002 Fourth Street, gray building with businesses on the first floor. You're on the third floor, 316."

Good number. "Got it. Are you coming up?"

"No. There's a spare cell phone on the kitchen counter that you can commandeer for the time being, my number's already in it under Greta."

"Were you, like, a spy in another life?" I asked, seriously wondering.

"The key's on the ring," she said and pointed to the ignition.

"Greta. Is that your Starbucks name?"

"Sometimes." Finally she smiled. We sat there in silence for a few beats, both tuned into the gravity of my precipitous life change on the run from Russian gangsters. I let out a long sigh and she echoed that, nodding. We stayed there like that in the parked car, while I sorted through the chaotic mass of details lighting up my head.

"I'm not asking you about the envelope right now," she said.

"Good. Don't. It's fine for the moment."

"Does Jonas know where it is?" she asked.

"Hell, no. The less he knows about any of this, the better. Just tell him I'm safe."

"I will."

"WiFi password?"

She pointed upstairs as if to say, "you're good". She'd thought of literally everything. I couldn't help but laugh at this magical little fairy who was saving my life right now. How many times had she done that today? "Thank you," I managed as a sad understatement and kissed her cheek. "Nice having friends in high places."

"You look like a badass in that suit."

Or a drug dealer.

CHAPTER 11

As fate would have it, the crash pad was upstairs from a) a dry cleaner and b) a secondhand clothing store, with the added bonus of a little corner market in the same block. And the best part: I could access all of them through the back or the private courtyard entrance for upstairs tenants. First, I showered and tried to fit into some of the clothes in the bedroom dresser. The shirts were fine, but all the pants were about two inches too short. So I put on my new Italian wool slacks, a clean t-shirt, and went looking for a computer. There was a state-of-the-art 40" TV, an expensive but pared-down stereo, so logic told me a VC guy had to have a spare laptop somewhere. If I asked Lacy, she'd need to ask permission first before letting me use it. So in the spirit of keeping a low profile, I rummaged through closets, luggage, briefcases and, sure enough, a backpack in the hall closet that had a laptop that weighed as much as a coffee table. I guessed it was a decade old, probably with no software updates. Great. I really needed my computer right now. The question was how to get it without going outside.

I got some water to start replenishing what I hadn't drunk in the past two days and stretched out on one of those posh sofas that had a chaise on one side. Omg, heaven. This guy must be loaded. I went back to my own cell phone and opened the app again for the hotel nanny cam. So far I'd only gotten through half of what it had recorded. I could even see how much charge was left in the unit I'd placed on the side table: 35%. Pretty good energy efficiency. The problem was there was no way for me to safely pick it up to charge it. It seemed strange that none of the hotel staff had seen it yet. Surely they cleaned the lobby every night. Did it look so common to a hotel lobby that no one noticed that it was the only one in the whole place? I added that to my growing list of anomalies. I fast-forwarded through an hour's worth of video, then sent Lacy a text from the new phone she'd left me.

Dear Greta, Need laptop. Am desperate. It's at home. Ray can let you in.

Ray? Ewww. That porn star mustache? Must I talk to him?

He said you're a hottie.

So gross. Let me see what I can do.

Thank you, angel. I knew from her Instagram how she was a sucker for emojis, so I added two pink hearts.

Another thirty minutes of hotel lobby and nothing by way of the metal briefcase, or even the woman who'd taken it from me. Did she even work there? I had the pictures that proved I gave the money back. Was I to believe that it was a million dollars that nobody needed in the world?

I hadn't given up on that video, but I felt way more need to determine the contents of the FedEx envelope. I pulled out Lacy's father's laptop, not that old actually and it booted right up. A Windows machine, HP Pavilion. I started by updating all the Windows security updates, updating the antivirus, which had expired two years ago. Her father obviously used this as a spare and never needed it. After all that, I tried to connect to WiFi, no go. I'd need a Bluetooth dongle or a network interface card. I had both of those in my laptop bag. Hopefully Lacy wouldn't mind seeing Ray long enough to pick it up. Lacy, geez. The suit she'd bought me today alone—I owed her big time right now. I needed to make this right.

An hour later, everything was updated on the old relic and it was connected to WiFi, but internet surfing was painfully slow. I logged into Google and was able to access my email from here. I opened the email that Jay sent of the image files from the envelope, and I tried to download one of the applications that can read a DNC file. One download down, I opened that new application and from there tried to open the file from Jay. It didn't recognize the file type and threw back an error. Shit. Come on, Brock, think.

I had one more available option with DNC conversion tools. This one required a subscription with a monthly fee. I subscribed, fully intending to cancel it as soon as I no longer needed it, like tomorrow. Voilà, it opened the file. For some reason, I felt like closing the street-facing curtains. One of the biggest advantages of this place was the large sign out front that blocked part of the street view, probably designed that way. It allowed me a line of sight to the street without being seen.

The program was able to read the file, but it was taking a while to scan and then reproduce the images from the super outdated graphics card on this laptop. I heard a noise in the bedroom. It was Oleg's burner phone. I didn't answer but a lightning-panic bolted through my body as I wondered if it had a tracker on it.

Fuck.

Okay Brock, deep breath and don't go off the deep end. Do I have a gun? Yes. Is it with me here? No. And I don't want to have to ask Lacy for that. It was bad enough I'd need to inflict my disgusting roommate on her to pick up my laptop. So, no gun, no protection. That was my present situation and I'd make the best of it.

I glanced out the front window at the street view and saw no one suspicious. The program was still opening Jay's file, so I returned to the hotel lobby video. Did I see what I think I just saw? I sat properly on one of the kitchen stools, where the light was bright enough, and rewound about thirty seconds. It showed a man in a black, leather jacket with his arm wrapped around the neck of a young man, no visible gun so far. The man pushed the young man to the ground and walked out with the metal briefcase through the left-side lobby entrance. I played it again. The man was in full view when he exited the reception area. This was not Oleg Kokov, nor was it the taller associate I'd seen with him on the earlier part of the tape.

So then, who just took Oleg's money?

The man moved through the lobby, getting closer to the nanny cam. Too close. Had he seen it? He took a hard right and moved out of view but I kept my eyes glued because I just had a feeling. I saw a group of people sitting in the lobby, talking, buying coffee, two young students with laptops, and here he was again, the money man carrying a cup of coffee now and holding something in his other hand, moving not only toward the cam but getting lower and lower. When he got a few inches away, he held up something that had writing on it. "Dead Man Dead Man Mr. Janov Dead Man."

CHAPTER 12

My hunger instantly vanished. In its place, a white fear in the pit of my belly unfolded. The fact that Oleg's soldier had misspelled my name somehow made the whole thing worse. They'd found my nanny cam. That was fine because I had their briefcase pickup and threatening note saved in the app and preserved for either posterity or trial. The facts: Oleg had his money back, so maybe they'd let me just keep the envelope and its enigmatic contents. Highly unlikely. Even so, I still needed to figure out what was in it and why I'd been chosen for this hapless mission.

I texted Lacy on the burner phone to call me. In the meantime, I checked the laptop for the completion of the image file download. Ninety percent. Any minute now. I opened then closed the fridge and all of the pantry cabinets. Nothing looked appetizing, because I kept replaying Oleg's Dead Man elegy in my head. What I needed was a drink, and one of the living room remotes opened a wooden cabinet with a full bar. A beloved genie granting me my first wish. I poured myself a vodka tonic in a heavy crystal glass, enjoying the first moment of this day. Okay, week.

Sunk low in the mushy sofa, legs outstretched with the ancient computer on my lap, the first of the DICOM images finally displayed on the screen. It looked exactly as it had in Jay's garage laboratory, very similar to how toiletries looked to airport security under their x-ray machines: a full-sized, folded sheet of paper containing some writing on it wrapped around a small, Ziploc bag that contained what looked like white balls or fragments of something. They were all different-sized shapes and almost looked like fabric, or snowflakes. It was a natural part of human cognitive function to make associations. Something is like this, or looks like that, or reminds you of something you saw before. Well, the contents of the Ziploc bag looked like nothing I'd ever seen before. Of course, considering what I knew of Oleg, the possibility of it being a biohazard or some kind of biological weapon crossed my mind. The material formulation was completely unfamiliar, though I knew almost nothing about chemical warfare. What I really needed was to see the material up close. Since I was already a dead man according to Oleg, I had nothing to lose.

I called Lacy on her father's phone. "Hey-ey," I said, with a vodka-infused lilt.

"Someone found the bar, I see."

"Yep. Hey, I know you're already bringing my laptop over, but I have another request.

"I think you might be out of favors today, dude. Seriously? I bought you a suit, gave you a car and an apartment. Now what?"

"And made me a prisoner in your father's flat. I know I know, and I'm sorry to ask. But Lace, I-can't-go-there myself."

I heard the wheels turning in her complex brain. "You need the envelope, don't you?"

"Yes." I waited. Counted to five, ten.

"Where is it?" she asked.

I had to think of a riddle, in case my pursuers found a way to track this phone, too.

"In the...Okhtorkram."

I put Lacy on speaker and poured drink number two while she worked it out. Three, two—

"What do you mean by in?"

Damn, she was fast. We agreed to meet at the Griffith Observatory café at 9 a.m. tomorrow morning. That would hopefully give her enough time to go to the office and pull down the Mark Rothko painting. And time enough for me to drink too much and dream of death by strangulation.

THE RIDDERS

I woke at 3 a.m. after dreaming about Jay Langley and the last time we'd hung out after college graduation. My half-drunk, malnourished brain superimposed my dream-body in Jay's parent's house in Torrance one minute, and Jay's house in North Hollywood the next, reminding me of everything I'd touched in his house, every surface, chair, counter, which would no doubt come back to haunt me. At 3:15, I realized I was starving. I gnawed on crackers right out of the box, drank water, and realized I'd had enough sleep. Please God, let there be coffee in this house.

Oleg's burner phone rang a little before four. I checked the street out front and saw nothing but a stray dog roaming around. Even so, the call meant that they were on to me and looking for me. If not right now, then soon. I had to take off. Without answering it, I packed a duffel bag from the closet with a few spare t-shirts, clean underwear, and one pair of baggy sweatpants that were miraculously long enough to not look stupid. I grabbed all three phones and disabled location tracking. Then I grabbed chargers, two bottles of water, the laptop relic, and headed down to Bay Street, where Lacy had me park the old Rav. So Jerome Diaz had a spare apartment, a spare car, did he have a spare wife too? It was none of my business. I put the laptop in the trunk and the duffel on the floor of the backseat. Maybe I'd see my friend British James again in Griffith Park. It was 5 a.m. Four hours till prime time.

CHAPTER 13

Luckily, the parking lot opened at 5 a.m. Even better, the bench where I slept the night before was unoccupied. I already had a plan for James if I saw him. I had nothing on me but my wallet, keys, and Lacy's burner phone. I left Oleg's phone in the duffel bag. I think I fell asleep the minute my head rested on the crook of my shoulder and woke to a woman tapping my arm.

"Morning." My voice hadn't woken up yet.

"You smell nice," the woman said.

I felt the drag of her hair on the top of my head. I didn't move.

"Hope you don't mind I was smelling you."

"Glad to be of service." I sat upright and checked her out. Old hippie. Harmless.

"I've got this bench at six," she said.

"No problem." I rubbed my eyes, getting used to panic-wakes and scanning my surroundings. "Do you know an old English fellow named James?"

"He was my friend first," the woman countered. "What do you want from him?"

Blinking through the cold morning air, I saw two fiery green eyes and a once-beautiful face framed by tangled, stringy dark hair. She weighed eighty pounds at most. I might stop to buy her breakfast, too. Who knew I had a humanitarian in me? She reminded me that the café didn't open till noon today, which meant I'd need to let Lacy know so we didn't transact our business out in the open. And if I didn't reach her, I'd be needing James more than ever.

"Ten dollars if you can bring James to me."

The woman examined my sweatpants, probably wondering if I had any money at all. So in the spirit of Oleg's business practices, I pulled out my wallet and paid her upfront. "If you run and don't bring me James, we'll never do business again." I squared off with her and she seemed to understand the economic potential of a mutually beneficial arrangement.

"I know where he is," she said. "Stay here."

While she started on her errand, I pulled the hood of my sweatshirt over my head and researched Google Maps for the nearest place to buy food. Franklin's Café and Market was a seven-minute walk from here and a useful opportunity to explain to James what his next mission would be. I zoomed in to see the path, zoomed out to see three public restrooms along the way, and when I zoomed out further, I saw a business just north of us up the hill. Maybe it was lack of sleep and food, or too much vodka last night. Or maybe seeing Jay Langley's dead body on the floor of his lab. But something pinged the back of my brain when I saw the words Abilene Cremation Services.

◦ ◈ ⬦ ✦ ⬦ ◈ ◦

By six, I'd explained the mission to James, he accepted the job, and I now had a legitimate spotter, meaning someone who looked like he belonged in a homeless hangout. Three hours till Lacy arrived with the payload. T minus three. I'd texted her twice already to request an earlier meetup time. For her, ignoring a text meant no. Her social media notifications were set to let her know about every single interaction and she got them from her phone and smartwatch. So James and I sat on a curb outside Franklin's eating breakfast burritos and sipping coffee, leisurely taking in the morning like a couple of aged millionaires gently greeting the day.

"My friend died today." James whispered the words gazing up at a closet of dark clouds hanging low over us. Did he even realize he'd said it out loud? And when today? The sun was barely even up.

"I'm sorry to hear that," I said. "How did he die?"

"I don't know." He sounded mystified.

"So how did you find out?" I asked.

"You know. They tell us. Happens a lot."

I had no idea what he was talking about. But the odd exchange made me wonder about James' age. Was he old enough for dementia, or could dementia develop from other mental illnesses or chronic malnutrition? God knows how long he'd been living on the street. I stopped chewing and turned to watch him. He barely looked fifty, which would be twice my age.

"What did they say about your friend? You must have heard from them early, it's only past six."

It was so quiet suddenly, no foot traffic on the street, no cars, not even any sounds from the café inside. The sky had an eerie orange cast to it. I imagined a bunch of eyes opening up and watching us. Was James hallucinating and hearing voices? Is that what he meant? I watched him chewing. He'd ceremoniously take a bite, chew, and pause to look at the sky, almost like he was listening to it. Was that where he heard about his dead friend? I felt so alone, suddenly, on this empty curb at the top of the hill. I wondered about Jonas, our office, our clients, friends I hadn't seen in months, the Planet Fitness I used to work out at with a view of the ocean.

Somehow everything in my life had folded into my new profession as a private investigator, learning from Jonas, who was not only an experienced PI but a smart businessman to boot. Had I ever told him that, given him a single piece of positive feedback like ever in my life? No. At least not yet. If I didn't hurry, I might end up like Jay Langley. I shuddered, snuggling back into the weird huddle with Postmaster James.

"We hear about the deaths on the network," he said, finally.

"TV?" I asked.

He turned and met my eyes. "Phone," he said.

"You have a phone network, okay, and that's how you heard about your friend?"

"That's right."

"What was your friend's name?" I asked, fishing for something, though I wasn't sure what.

"Oh, I can't tell you. I'd be violating the NDA."

"A nondisclosure agreement? And that's for your phone

network?"

He didn't answer and shifted uncomfortably on the curb.

"That's okay James, I don't want you to say anything that will get you in trouble. I was just wondering your friend's name, his first name I mean, because I thought I might light a candle for him in church." Exactly when did I become such an eloquent bullshit artist? Seriously, church? Where the fuck did that come from?

"You go to church?" he asked.

I smiled without specifically answering. "There's one around the corner from my brother's house," I said. Something told me to just keep talking because James was deciding something right now.

"You said they tell you about the deaths. Who's they?"

"It's a bit hard to explain."

"Do a lot of people die here, like up in this neighborhood? Seems like a lovely area."

"Oh, yes, it certainly is," he said. "It's a lovely place to die."

I repeated that phrase in my head a few times before responding. A lovely place to die. That's right, Abilene Cremation Services. Something about that name on the map worried me.

"Is there a funeral home around here, James?"

"It's right up the road."

I was careful with my words now, extra careful, because this conversation could have everything to do with not only the FedEx envelope but my future.

CHAPTER 14

"Hold on, my friend who's meeting us here is texting me." She wasn't, but I desperately needed an excuse to type some notes into my phone before I forgot them.

British James: Phone network, the deaths, NDA, a lovely place to die.

And Lacy did text me while James and I were talking.

"Is she still coming?" James asked.

"Sooner than expected," I said. "Looks like she'll be here shortly."

"Fifty dollars?" he asked. It was what I'd offered him. His face was wide and expectant.

"Fifty dollars." I nodded.

"Cash only."

"You got it. Do you make a lot of money through the phone network, James? You get jobs from them, yeah?" I tried to sound casual.

"Oh yes, sometimes more than I need."

"More money than you need?" I clarified.

"No, no, I mean sometimes they give me more jobs than I need. I'm old, you know," he explained. I couldn't help but love this guy. "Older than I look maybe. And I'm not in the best of health, I admit."

"So you need to turn down some jobs so you can rest. That

sounds reasonable to me."

"Thank you, BJ. I think we understand each other. And in this crazy world, that's something."

James started to get up and I felt an invisible door closing. Now or never.

"James?"

"Yes?"

"I'm not sure if you're allowed to share or not, but do you think your phone network might have some jobs for me? I could use work right now. I'm sort of in-between things."

"Well, all of us up here are between things. Sometimes I even feel like I'm between the between."

I nodded, waiting.

"Can you stay up late?" he asked.

I wasn't sure I'd heard him correctly. My face must have shown it.

"If you can stay up late and if you're good at keeping secrets, you'll be fine."

He bit his lip and studied me, deliberating, deciding whether he could trust me and if I was worth the risk.

I stayed quiet and waited.

"I can share some things with you, but not the names of any of the deaths. That's the part we're not allowed to speak of."

"No problem." I showed my palms. "After my friend meets us, could you maybe take me up there? To the beautiful place to die place?"

"Oh no." His brows scrunched low over his eyes. "We don't go up there during the day. Only at night."

Great. "Okay, you're the boss. You just tell me where and when."

Now that I had Lacy's dad's spare phone, not to mention his laptop and half his wardrobe, James and I traded numbers. While I was at it, I added *Abilene Cremation Services* to my list of British James terms. James took off somewhere but assured me that when my friend showed up, he wouldn't be more than five minutes away.

The plan was for Lacy to enter the largest stall in the ladies restroom down the hill from my bench here and wait for me. Then

I'd enter the same stall while James kept watch outside. She would remove the envelope from her backpack, and I'd tuck it into the back of my pants as I'd done before.

New problem: I was wearing baggy sweatpants today and the envelope might slide down, and I also wasn't wearing a jacket to conceal the shape of it under my shirt. Shit.

Mitigation plan: She'd need to leave the backpack with me. I texted her and told her as much in way too many words.

Fine, she wrote back.

I crawled under some low branches of a ponderosa pine behind my sleeping bench, empty now, which gave me concealment with a view of the whole Observatory Park. Jonas hadn't answered any of the texts I'd been leaving him since last night. He always kept the volume down on his phone and never heard incoming calls, ongoing problem. Was he as worried about me as I was right now? When I angled my head back, I could see what looked like the top of a tall building behind the observatory. Could that be Abilene Cremation Services? And was that where British James and his secret phone network were running some kind of sub-economy? If he kept his word, soon enough I would find out.

I'm here, Lacy texted.

Wait 5 minutes, I wrote back, then texted James, all the while scanning every face and human form for any trace of the Olegs. Right now it was a few homeless people still camped out from last night, some tourists with cameras, and students with notebooks.

Another text came in. *I'm right behind you*, James typed. Wow, what a pro. Surprisingly, he seemed to grasp the finer points of discretion. Of course I didn't turn around.

To Lacy, I wrote, *Head to the ladies room now. Do you know where it is?*

Bottom of the hill, right?

Right.

Go now, I wrote to James and saw him emerge from behind me. I liked the way he sauntered casually down the hill. I started counting, still scanning the crowds. Was I feeling paranoid? Hell yes. Fuck Oleg, though. I returned his fucking money so now he had no legitimate hold over me. So why was I so nervous? The question that still nagged me was why he orchestrated the whole mission in the first place. What looked like a high school couple flooded past me, the guy grabbing the girl's arm and her pulling it away.

"Ash," he shouted. "Ashley, wait. Come on. It's not like that. Ash!"

That name…*ash*. Jesus, what was wrong with my brain? Of course.

I'm in position, Lacy texted.

I could see British James leaning against the restroom exterior wall holding out a donation cup. It was a great prop, and I suspected it was just theater because he was likely getting paid plenty from whatever scam they were running up the hill.

Heading down, I texted. James didn't make eye contact with me when I approached. I entered through the ladies room door and said, "Greta."

She coughed and I opened the door to a large stall at the end of the row. God, she was a welcome sight. She wrapped her arms around my neck and held me close for a moment, then whispered in my ear to slide the backpack off of her shoulders and put it on myself.

"Is it in there?" I whispered.

She nodded.

"Where's Jonas?"

"There's no sign of him and he wasn't in the office at all yesterday."

Shit. "Thank you for this."

"There's a gift in there for you," she said and left first.

Still good out there? I texted James.

Affirmative.

I hung the backpack on the large hook on the back of the stall door and unzipped it just enough to see the top of the FedEx envelope. I reached my hands down into the pack to make sure it felt the same as before, a thin package with one sheet of paper and a small Ziploc bag. It was all there. Plus my laptop. Thank you, Lacy.

CHAPTER 15

James led me down the hill, me trailing a safe thirty-foot distance behind him. We split off at the entrance to the Observatory parking lot where I picked up the Rav, dropping the backpack on the floor of the front passenger side. I so wanted to drive past Jay Langley's house, almost as if I wasn't completely certain he was dead. Was he passed out, diabetic coma, asthma attack? Come on Brock, you saw ligature marks on his throat. Someone entered his lab, found what he was working on (my project!), and strangled him. Was one of Oleg's goons watching me right now? I scanned left and right. No one was in view, which didn't mean I wasn't being watched.

Forcing a mental redirect, I tried Jonas' mobile again, then his landline. Hard to believe anyone still had such a thing. From Griffith Park, I headed south on 101 to 110 and then west on Highway 10 toward Ladera Heights which, this time of day, only took fifteen minutes. I loved how unlike our tastes were for things like cars and homes. Jonas' condo was an eighty-year-old Mediterranean style and gutted and renovated ten years ago. He loved the nexus of old and new world. I preferred Bohemian flophouses, hence my untidy lair. His car wasn't there and I knew it wouldn't be. So why was I here? To use my spare key to snoop around and because our umbilical connection told me he was out investigating something other than the Bergman's daughter. So why was he ghosting me?

THE RIDDERS

I got James to agree to take me up to Abilene Cremation Services tonight after dark. We would meet at the Café at 11 p.m. Something told me not to bring the envelope with me. I needed a new place to stash it. And I had the perfect idea.

⋄ ⋄⊰⊱⊹⊰⊱⋄ ⋄

I left Jonas' place and texted Lacy.
Did you open it yet? Lacy texted.
No. Need more information first, I wrote back.
Can I be there when you do?
No objections but—
BJ, where are you?
Headed to the flat.
I'm around the corner. I'll come up.
KK.

I certainly needed the company right now, and it could be useful to have a lookout as I scoped out a new location for the envelope. But how did we know Oleg hadn't installed listening devices in this car and in the apartment for that matter?

I slipped into my temporary apartment through the courtyard entrance and took the stairs. While stowing the backpack in the bedroom closet, I saw the gift Lacy brought me: three pairs of jeans. Thank God. I put on the dark gray pair and took the stairs down to check out the ceiling tiles in the 2nd-floor laundry room. I'd seen the laundry sign from the courtyard and that gave me the idea.

The staircase was unlit, and the unfinished concrete steps felt taller than usual. Seemed like both of those things would have been building code violations. I kept going. The second-floor door was propped open and on the wall was a sign that read Laundry with an arrow pointing left. Cool. The door was closed, unlocked. The long rectangular room was empty with no machines going. I checked the handle and you could lock it from the inside. Bonus.

I turned the lock and discovered a pattern of small, square foam ceiling tiles. There was a single chair positioned at the end of each row of washers and dryers. With what looked like seven-foot ceilings, I was able to stand on the chair and reach to tap on one tile. I pushed it up a few inches and then stood on one of the dryers to see up there. Dust and rafters. Perfect. I pulled the envelope from where it was tucked into the back of my jeans and slid it above the foam tile, then positioned it back in place. I counted one, two, three tiles from the back corner. I unlocked the door and, before I left, took note of the cost of each machine so I could do laundry here and have a valid excuse to be in this room next time. $6.00 per machine. What a rip-off.

Lacy was standing at the door when I got back upstairs. "Up to no good?" she asked.

"You betcha."

"Where were you?"

I unlocked the door and held it while she entered, a moment of chivalry. "Doing laundry." I winked.

"You mean doing laundry without actually washing any clothes? I know what you were doing."

"Yeah, well," my voice trailed. "Desperate times, desperate measures."

"Why don't you just open it?" It was a legit question.

"Because I need to know that the people around me won't get hurt if I do. If it was nothing significant, then the Olegs wouldn't be doing their dirty deals to broker it. He's still calling me, you know. It's either a small sample of some very dangerous material, or else no intrinsic danger but, if found, would expose something at great risk to others.

She blinked back with her thoughtful eyes and long lashes. "Let's eat." She took burgers and fries out of two crumpled bags and opened two cans of soda from the fridge. "When was your last actual meal?"

"Breakfast, and before that, I can't say." I joined her in the kitchen and stared out the windows.

"What?"

"Where the fuck's my brother?"

I watched her wash her hands, put the burgers and fries on two China plates and fold two napkins. She leaned against the sink facing me. "I know something, but you're not gonna like it."

"Okay…"

"He sent me a text this morning, that—"

"Why didn't you tell me?"

"I'm telling you now."

"Please I beg you don't tell me he's gone after Oleg."

She paused. "He's been tailing him for the past two days."

"Fuck. How did he find him?"

"I don't know. I asked him. He said he 'knows people'. He was very cagey about it. He said something about Anastasia Bergman."

I took two bites of the overdone hamburger and forced it down, then two swallows of soda. "Thanks for dinner."

"I'm not even sure this qualifies as food."

"Bergman's missing eighteen-year-old daughter. She's like one of the Delevingne sisters, wealthy, beautiful, bored. What would she have to do with this?"

"You know her?" Lacy asked, and it might be my imagination but I saw a twinge of jealousy in her eyes. OMG, too funny. I took a mental snapshot of that look and stored it away in the back of my brain. Delicious.

"I don't like *know her* know her," I said soaking it up. "I'm guessing. But I have a sense about people."

"Oh really?" She giggled behind her hamburger bun. "What sense did you have about me?"

"Like…the first time I met you? In our side yard? When we were five? That you were always gonna get us in trouble."

"Oh, right!"

I loved the freedom and the intimacy of this random human moment, eating hamburgers with my childhood BFF. I was honestly starting to think I might not make it to twenty-six. Lacy was my salvation, right now anyway.

"Okay, well, childhood maybe, but I spent my entire adolescence getting you out of trouble. Admit it."

"No way," I said, but of course she was right.

"Okay, so we're saying that my paranoid, hypochondriac brother who never leaves home without his pill pack of vitamins has gone off on walkabout chasing Russian vigilantes? I'm not feelin' it, sorry."

"He said he had some help and wasn't doing it all himself. He had someone staking out the Bonaventure."

"Who?"

"Who did he call the last time he put someone under surveillance?"

"Oh, God no, please not him. Ray? My fucking degenerate roommate?"

"Why not?" she argued.

"All Ray cares about getting high. And grips."

"What?"

"Never mind."

"For someone like Jonas, Ray's the best game in town."

"Where are they right now?" I asked her.

"I don't know but they've got him, they're tailing them right now."

"Them?"

"Oleg and two others."

It was early, nine o'clock and we were both tired. Lacy spent the night in the full bed in the spare bedroom and I took her father's palatial suite down the hall with a king poster bed. I hadn't told her about my late-night appointment with James. I was lucky to have this place to hide out, but I missed my apartment, all the insignificant objects with which we define our life, the convenience of everything you need within an arm's reach or a ten-minute drive. Such was life living in a big place like LA. You could find anything here, have every need met. Almost. I missed my brother. I missed our Sunday afternoon chess ritual and I missed having his brain-on-overdrive helping me puzzle through all this. I hadn't told Lacy about my epiphany at the top of Griffith Park, when those two teenagers ran past me and the guy called her Ashley, and then her nickname of Ash. *Ash.* I hadn't told Lacy because I hadn't yet puzzled it out. Was that what was inside the Ziploc bag in the envelope? No – ash disintegrates in your hand and has virtually no mass. It couldn't be that. So then what was my exhausted brain hanging onto?

CHAPTER 16

I dreamed of waking to the smell of breakfast and finding Oleg in the kitchen scrambling eggs with his menacing, gap-toothed grin. I found Princess Lacy snoring in the guest bedroom, too funny. Sometimes, when we would all camp out in a tent in our backyard, Jonas and I would record her. I sat on the edge of the bed and gave her wiry frame a gentle shake.

"Huh. What?"

"I'm going out for a bit. Should I take the keys?"

"Go ahead, I have my own set," she mumbled.

"Don't you want to know where I'm going?"

"To do a dirty deal."

I hated how easily she said that, considering she was barely awake. "I don't know if that's true."

"Just don't die tonight, okay?"

* ❖ ✦ ❖ *

I loved Lacy for saying that. British James said to show up at our designated spot at exactly eleven and not before. So of course I was aiming for ten to see what I could find out. I was dressed in all black, hiding my light hair with a hood. I found a parking spot not directly under but near enough to a streetlamp that I could see. I pulled out the pen and notepad I brought from the condo and pretended it was my bullet journal.

Agenda:
1. Don't die
2. Investigate Abilene Cremation Services
3. Find Kayla
4. Men in black suits
5. Synthetic bioweapons

British James and I would be investigating number 2 here shortly. I still had a little time to kill so I could look into Kayla from my phone. I did a Google search for 'Grace Imaging Kayla' and filtered for News first and then an image search. Nothing at all came up, which was noteworthy.

Plan B: I tried LinkedIn and typed Grace Imaging and found the account, saw a link for "See all 10 employees on LinkedIn". She was the last name on the list: Kayla Babbin, San Diego metro area, dark hair, red lipstick, smart looking, labeled as Lead Imaging Technologist.

Next, whitepages.com. I tried San Diego proper first and a Kayla Babbin, age 42, came up in Ramona, which was about 40 miles north of San Diego. Then a general Google search for Kayla Babbin in Ramona, CA and there it was: her home address or at least one of her most recent: 42 Fernbrook Drive. That was the Irvings Crest area of a lot of empty space, new homes built in the late seventies, and horses as I recalled. New plan: drive down to Ramona tomorrow. I drew a box and put a checkmark next to number 3 on my list and wrote in her address.

Number four might take more digging. I think I'd watched all of the nanny cam video from the Bonaventure and only had footage of one visit to reception, at the very beginning, of the flurry of men in black suits. At the time I thought they were looking for the money and now I suspect it was the contents of the Ziploc bag.

I'd already been researching number five ever since seeing the contents in Jay's lab, but most of what I'd found were articles about engineered pathogens, which not only didn't feel right but seemed way too sophisticated for a grunt like Oleg.

10:30 p.m. Time for recon. From the edge of the Observatory lot, I drove north on East Observatory Drive, then right on North

Vermont Canyon Road, which wound up and around and then down to the Griffith Park trailheads, further past the Greek Theater, and Roosevelt Golf Course at the bottom where it intersected with Commonwealth Canyon Drive. There was a parking lot at the Vermont Canyon Tennis Courts and what looked like a ¾ mile driveway to the entrance. At home, meaning the meager apartment I shared with Ray the landscaper, I had night goggles, binoculars, and other surveillance gear I bought before I got my private investigator's license. A lot of good it did me now. But it was a straight drive in and I could see the looming building ahead. Odd that a crematorium would be three floors and lit up inside this time of night. I suspected something was going on in there that had nothing to do with funerals.

10:49 p.m. I was a few minutes early meeting British James in the Mount Hollywood Tunnel. I can't say I was excited about it, given the fact that my gun was still at my apartment and I had nothing on me with which to defend myself. I'd read an article about Griffith Park being cursed with a century of misfortune and a ghost that haunted that tunnel. Here I was walking up Mount Hollowood Trail in pitch darkness to meet a homeless man in a haunted tunnel. Great.

Normally the clearing just above the public restrooms would be filled with tents and other encampments. Tonight, nothing. Why?

Is that you, BJ? A text from James' phone.

Yes hello, I typed back, unsure why he wouldn't just catch up and speak to me. And odd that I couldn't hear him behind me.

Go through the tunnel and wait for me on the other side.

I was about twenty steps from the tunnel. No people, no cars, bikes, movement of any kind. I sorted my long list of questions in my head and kept walking. Not even a stick in sight, I kept my hands at my sides ready for anything. I heard footsteps behind me but didn't dare turn my head.

Are you behind me? I texted James.

No answer came, so I moved faster now entering the tunnel. My footsteps echoed. I started counting them. Twenty, forty, sixty, eight-five steps through the tunnel. I waited on the other side on the right, sitting on a berm under a heavy overhang of dense brush. I breathed the pungent night air deep in my lungs, barely able to remember my last experience in nature. I could hear crickets, frogs, night birds, owls, and a string of motorcycles somewhere below us. The footsteps were closer now. Someone was exiting the tunnel.

"BJ?" James called out to me in his regular voice.

"Here," I said, though I couldn't see him.

"Climb to the top."

"All the way?"

"Just to the top side of the tunnel," he said. "There's a path we'll follow into the facility."

I would have been happier if I could see him, but I recognized his voice and that was good enough for now. Just hoping the Griffith Park ghost didn't kill me first. Thank God I'd taken the time to install the flashlight app on this phone. Unfortunately, I hadn't checked the phone setting permissions and flashlight apps were notorious for location tracking and other privacy breaches when in use. For now, I needed it to climb up this craggy hill and make it in one piece. I found the top and could easily locate the path James mentioned would be here.

"Hey."

The sound rocked me and I spun around so fast I almost fell. James. He sounded out of breath. "Hey there."

"Are you alright?" he asked.

"Yeah, of course, fine. Just have, you know, quite a few questions. Like where we're going, what do I need to know, what types of jobs will I need to do."

James had this old-world butler way of staying silent with his mouth closed until you were finished talking. Refreshing, to say the least. "We all do the same job here. All of us are part of this sort of network that I mentioned." James started walking ahead of me on the path.

"What type of work is it?" I asked, trailing behind him a few steps. We were the only ones there, but I sort of felt someone's eyes on me.

"Sort of like the job I did for you and your friend earlier."

"Lacy?"

"Is that her name? Fetching."

"Yes, she is. Okay, so recon sort of work, security detail, that type of thing?"

"No weapons and not security. Just being a lookout is all. But it's very important to the enterprise."

Enterprise. I would add that word to my British James list. "What enterprise is that?" I asked, knowing full well he wouldn't, or couldn't, answer.

"You may get to meet the head scientist tonight. I've only met him once," he explained. "He likes to vet all the new guards."

I thought he'd just said it wasn't a security guard position. I went in a different direction with my questions. "What type of scientist?" I asked.

"His name's Dr. Anders Ek. He's some kind of biologist, I believe."

"What type of biology work does he do up here in a crematorium so late at night?"

"Saves people's souls."

CHAPTER 17

My pupils were dilating finally. Almost midnight, I was somewhere on the grounds of Abilene Cremation Services, just above the Hollywood Tunnel and northeast of the Griffith Observatory…in complete darkness. There was a name for the color you saw in this state, the absence of light, *eigengrau*, a dark gray everywhere I looked. It was cold. There were others here, but no one was talking. I could see them: men, women, hugging their arms around their bodies, shifting their weight, occasionally stretching their arms. James remained directly behind me, not in any sort of organized line but in the huddle. I never turned to verify his presence, but I felt him somehow. I had the unique sensation that an alien ship might appear above our heads shocking the lot of us with a sudden colossal spotlight. Too much Syfy Channel.

"Won't be long now," James whispered in my ear from behind.

I nodded.

"When the light comes on," he said, "they'll say how many guards they need for the next two nights. You'll come with me. They know me, so you've got a better chance than if you found the place yourself."

"Do people do that sometimes?" How could anyone randomly stumble upon this place?

"A few, yes. But they're dead now," he said.

Like…WTF? Okay. Seriously what the fuck was I doing up here? Pulling an invisible thread, I reminded myself. Everything that had happened since Oleg first thrust his envelope and metal briefcase at me had in some way led me to this place, to James, to this moment of truth.

Sure enough, a light flipped on, an exterior light coming from the back of the tall building a few hundred feet ahead. James tugged my sleeve and pulled me to the left of the crowd. He ran. I followed him but had no idea what we were doing.

"You need another name for tonight," he said, looking back. "And when they ask for ID say you got mugged and got your wallet stolen."

"Sure." Hadn't I used that excuse recently? It scared me how well practiced I was now at lying. James stopped and waved to someone, a man wearing a black suit.

Ten black-suited men. From the Bonaventure nanny cam.

The man stood on a concrete stoop looking out at what had to be thirty or more people.

"Hello James," the black suit said to James.

"Hello. I've brought a friend with me tonight."

"Is he reliable?" the man asked him.

"Oh, yes."

"Fine, come on up. I need two men and one woman tonight."

James pushed me ahead of him toward the man. The suited man looked down on us the way you gaze at ants crawling all over the ground at your feet.

"Name?" he asked, looking at me.

"Donald Upton," I said like I'd been saying the name my whole life.

"Fine English name. Do you have identification?"

"Oh, I'm sorry, no. I was mugged and they took my wallet."

"Very well." The man looked closely at James. "You'll vouch for him, James?"

"Yes, sir."

"You two can go in," he said to James, then said, "I need one woman," to the crowd behind us.

◦ ◦ ◦ ⬩ ◦ ◦ ◦

I'd never worked undercover before and felt suddenly nine years old again, playing international spy on hot summer nights with Jonas, Lacy, and two other kids from our neighborhood. I followed British James down two dark, empty hallways, the last of which had a set of double doors at the end. We waited. He didn't knock.

"Don't worry," James said. "They don't do fight games anymore."

"That's a relief." I tried not to laugh. Or cry. Another detail to add to my James list. "You mean they'd jump you and assess your fight skills?"

"That's right. They don't do that anymore."

"And they don't arm you with weapons when you're working?" I asked.

"Oh no. Too many people were getting killed."

I couldn't help but laugh now. "Well, they were in the right place. This is a funeral home, right?"

"There's a difference, you see," James said, lowering his head and his voice to answer. "A funeral home hosts a memorial service, deals with family members and all aspects. Abilene is a crematorium only. That means all they do is prepare the bodies."

"Prepare them? For what?"

"To be cremated."

"And then what happens?"

"Well, I don't see any other part of the business but I assume the cremains, that's what they're called, you know, are collected and packaged and distributed to the family."

"For a fee of course. Right?"

"I believe so, though I've never paid for that service."

"How long have you been working here?"

"Oh, I don't remember exactly. A few months now."

"Is the pay generous?" I asked, my brain spinning with three follow-up questions to his every answer.

"We keep watch when they're bringing the bodies in.

Bodies? What bodies? Who would be watching? It's a mortuary, so of course when someone died the family would arrange for the body to be brought here, right? If cremation was desired. And interesting that James answered a different question than the one I asked.

"Sometimes just innocent onlookers, and in which case we gently tell them that they need to move on and no harm will come to them."

Harm. Okay. I didn't think this night could get any more interesting.

"Once there was a TV crew here because the person who died, I heard, was a celebrity."

I nodded. "This is LA so that's understandable. But if most of the," I searched for the right word, "clients who arrive here are not celebrities, it seems like a lot of economic infrastructure to employ security guards for something that happens infrequently."

James blinked his watery blue eyes at me. No answer came.

"Do you know how many guards work every night?" I asked.

"Three of four, I believe. The place isn't that big."

Another round of motorcycle engines could be heard in town and, immediately after they passed out of audible range, I witnessed two things of interest: a police siren and the distinct sound of a pop-pop close by. It sounded like it came from inside the building. I felt the vibration of the shots under my feet. Hearing the police siren, James' head went down, and he eyed the area around the building. That was the job. *They were paying people, homeless people, expendables who wouldn't be missed, to look out for the police.* Who would be called, then, about the two gunshots that were just fired inside the building? My mouth went dry.

"Um, James…"

"I know, I heard it," he said.

"What happens if the police come up here?"

"Then we call Dmitriy. He takes care of the police."

Dmitriy. Another Russian name. I no longer believed in coincidences.

CHAPTER 18

There were two knocks on the double doors in front of us that came from the inside. James wide-eyed me, opened one door and vanished behind it with no explanation.

I took the fortuitous moment of solitude as a sign to text Jonas. *Where are you?* I hoped he'd both see the text and feel like it was safe enough to respond. Shouldn't he be out here in a freaking crematorium in the middle of the night instead of me? He had, after all, or so he constantly reminded me, a wealth of field experience. Wait, I was texting from a different phone. Maybe he didn't know it was me.

Working, he replied right away. Cagey bastard. This meant he knew it was me and didn't want me to know that he was out tracking Oleg Kokov's movements. *You?* he asked.

Don't ask.

I won't. Mr. Bergman dropped off that book for you.

Feel free to read it, I wrote.

Thanks, it's about wasps.

Excellent.

Is Betty with you?

In bed sleeping.

Funny. Betty was our childhood spy game code for gun. What I would do to have Betty with me right now. Donald Upton, Donald

Upton, I repeated silently, praying I didn't forget my real name when the time came to use it again.

Something smelled odd in here. I couldn't put my finger on it. Not food, not fire exactly, not a natural smell like the woods, but not a synthetic smell like paint either. Something in between and altogether unpleasant.

Without any knocks this time, James opened the door a crack, looked behind me, and motioned me in. I joined him in an all-white, empty room. I noticed how quietly he closed the door behind me. Why? The floors were white tile and polished to a slippery shine. Walls and ceiling, same. Like a level 5 decontamination facility.

"What are we doing here?" I asked.

"He's coming."

"Dmitriy?"

"No," he said, with a fiendish grin. "Dmitriy doesn't come up here."

Must mean the other guy, the scientist who ran this place. A door on the opposite wall slid open, a side-to-side automatic pocket door like you see in Star Trek.

"Hello, gentlemen," a man said. Scruffy longish hair, scruffy beard and mustache, white lab coat with a film of what looked like sawdust on it. Oh my God. Sawdust. Ash from burning bodies? I must be dreaming and have found my way into a World War II film.

"Hello, Doctor," I managed.

"James, nice to see you." The man took two steps forward, arms crossed. "And who have you brought us tonight?" The smile on his face was like looking at a T-Bone before it hit the grill. I recalled number one on my bullet journal list. Don't die. I'm trying.

* ◦ ◦⊰═⊱ ✛ ⊰═⊱ ◦ ◦ *

There was no facility tour or well-dressed women carrying trays of snacks. From the white room, we entered a dark vestibule, where two more of the seemingly identical, black-suited men patted me down—only me, one on each side. Thank God Betty was home sleeping after all. I was told to follow the man called Doctor, to whom I'd yet to be properly introduced, with British James behind me into a sort of lounge area, outfitted with actual armchairs, three of them, and a coffee table that was the wrong size for the room and the chairs. I pictured the beginning of *The Matrix* in my head, a suited man with a sales pitch, lofty ideals, a quintessential question and two colored pills. Red pill of alarming truth, blue pill of ignorance. My heart yearned for the blue pill, but if that was true, what was I doing in this place? Gotcha.

Then there was James, a loyal or well-paid soldier of this fortress. I could only assume, given the transactional potential of this place, that there was some kind of finder's fee or referral bonus available to him for bringing in fresh blood like Donald Upton.

We each took a chair.

"What brings you here, Mr.—" The man looked at James.

"Upton," I said. "Well, my friend James here said there may be employment opportunities and I'm between jobs."

"Are you now?" He barely moved his lips when talking, and James was a statue.

I didn't answer his rhetorical question and I wanted no part in the power play going on here. These people wanted something from me, so there was no balance of power. I was holding the cards. They needed to make their pitch.

"So, I'm interested in hearing what you have to offer," I said.

The room became a vacuum. I felt James' vibe change to outright panic, glancing from me back to the doctor, checking his face.

"I have the impression Abilene isn't your average funeral home. Am I right?"

"I'm not familiar with terms like average, Mr. Upton. A funeral home is a community resource intended for families. A mortuary deals strictly with the dead. And a crematorium specializes in a very specific processing service."

"I see." I nodded to simulate interest, when I was actually trying to place his accent. It was a mishmash, but not like the type Lacy simulated. His was real.

"And you have some supply chain gaps, I assume?"

"Please, elaborate, Mr. Upton," the doctor said.

"That's why you're hiring deadbeats like me in the middle of the night. You have a service that needs to be executed, and you're looking for reliable help."

"Exactly so. Are you the reliable sort?"

I nodded, still maintaining a look of disinterest, like I'd just as soon be home playing Xbox. I was sure I lacked the typical air of desperation among the doctor's other worker bees. This could either be to my advantage or disadvantage. He was intrigued with my strength of character, that was obvious. Poor James looked mortified.

"I'm still not completely clear on what you do here," I went on.

"What we do here, or me in particular?"

"Both."

The doctor rose. "I'm Dr. Anders Ek. I run this facility. And the service we provide here is cremation."

I tipped my head, which looked like I was trying to understand him. What it was meant to convey was a challenge, as if to say you're full of shit. "Seems like a very large facility for such a narrow scope of business, I have to admit. Much bigger than—"

"All the other crematoriums you've visited?"

"Okay, you got me there. Maybe not, then."

"The third floor is storage, the second floor is R&D, and the first floor is processing.

"Can I ask what you're developing that requires research?"

He didn't miss a beat. "More efficient ways to cremate human remains, of course."

I stayed quiet, enjoying the feeling that Dr. Anders Ek was selling me an idea. I knew already that I was the farthest thing from his typical soldiers. But I knew I'd piqued his interest. He might tap me for something else, which would be an opportunity to learn more about whatever was going on here.

"James?" the doctor asked. "Why don't you get started with your shift. I'd like to take Mr. Upton on a little tour of the place, show him around, ease his mind a bit before committing to a forward path. Are you alright with that?"

"Of course, sir. Goodnight, Donald."

I noted how compliant James was around Dr. Ek. More than that, the ease with which he spoke my fake name to say goodnight spoke of someone with practiced clandestine services skills. Honed skills. Skills that were developed specifically for a type of job or delivery. I was starting to feel like British James was the farthest thing from a homeless person, and that our chance meeting was the farthest thing from chance. Question is: what did that mean for me?

CHAPTER 19

One hallway, two hallways, an elevator, and a third hallway. All glossy, white-on-white everywhere I looked. Not a speck of dirt or a single scuff mark on the floor.

"Are you renovating a part of this building?" I asked.

Given the dimensions of the corridor, no carpet, and the ceiling height, there should have been an echo. But my voice disappeared as quickly as I spoke the words. Acoustic tiles could deaden a room, but why a corridor? The doctor maintained a two-pace lead, promulgating the lie of a facility tour when, naturally, he was planning on killing me.

I should have been scared. Normally I would have been. But something deep in my core felt this knowing that it was me who scared him. I was a sudden uncertainty that he hadn't planned on, and I suspected the good doctor didn't much like things he couldn't easily control. So, my advantage here was to just continue unraveling his composure by being my suspicious, disenchanted self. He hadn't answered my question. I knew he heard me. His pace slowed, then he turned back.

"Sorry, lost in my thoughts." What a liar. "Renovating did you say?"

"Yes."

"Why do you ask?"

"Because of the film of sawdust on your lab coat."

He smiled. "Not sawdust. Particles of some of the materials we use in the processing department. Occupational hazard, I'm afraid."

"Sure," I said.

"You're a keen observer, Mr. Upton. It's a great quality. We need more of that around here."

"Oh?" I let my question hang in the air to signal that I was still waiting for his answer to my previous question. What were the gaps in his supply chain that necessitated him hiring homeless people outside on the grounds at midnight?

The real question was whether British James knew that Dr. Ek was going to kill me. If not, it was up to me to reach Jonas and Lacy, or I was on my own. I wasn't seeing many opportunities for diversionary tactics in the endless hallways and, by now, I was deep in the belly of the building. The odd smell was stronger here, probably because I was on the second floor. Processing. What did that mean? I saw the flaw in my plan, suddenly, showing up here without explicitly letting Lacy know where I was going (in case I didn't return). Even more, my lack of due diligence to learn about the cremation process. If Dr. Death left me alone for a few minutes I might have time to read about it. I was sure they didn't just take bodies from a hospital morgue and burn them toe-tag and all. There had to be a number of steps in the process, to preserve and prepare the body for a funeral or memorial service, to comply with local, state, and federal regulations and standards and, thereafter, prepare it for its final phase.

We reached the end of another hallway. I was sure I'd lost about five pounds from the cardio workout to get here. Dr. Ek touched a module on the wall and a tiny, shoulder-height door slid open from the wall showing a tiny keyhole. The doctor pulled a ring off his belt and stuck a small key in, revealing something interesting dangling from the keychain by his wrist.

A four-inch miniature sword.

The full-sized door slid open before us, just as his phone buzzed in the pocket of his lab coat.

"Excuse me," he said. I heard a man's voice on the other end saying the word Sir. Yes, sir. No sir. I also heard the word disturbance. "Right." He hung up.

"Seems there's some kind of commotion going on outside on the grounds that I need to attend to. I'm afraid we'll need to continue our tour another time, Mr. Upton. I do apologize. Follow me and we'll go out together."

"Of course," I said, hardly believing my good fortune, knowing all the while he could easily lock me in a closet and I'd never be heard from again.

"Follow me," he said, again.

We were both running. I wouldn't need Planet Fitness for at least two or three days. He opened a door to a staircase, which I hadn't noticed the first time around. We jogged down one flight, then took another corridor to another flight of stairs that led back out to the loading dock where I'd started. I paid attention to his gait, speed, and body language to tell me how urgent he thought the disturbance was. What did you do, James? Set fire to the trees? I smiled inside, in a way that reassured my heart that I wasn't likely to die tonight after all. And now, I'd seen the inside of the fortress.

The closer we got to the opening, the more I could smell smoke.

"Thank God it's only outside," the doctor said, turning back to make sure I was directly behind him.

"I imagine your sprinkler systems going off could have disastrous effects on your work."

"Indeed," he said and turned. "There certainly is a job for you here, Mr. Upton, but not as an outdoor guardsman. No. With your clear head, observation skills, and obvious physical fitness, you could help my work in much more substantive ways. If you're curious, I pay generously, and I only work at night. It's up to you to decide." He shook my hand. "Now, I must attend to Dmitriy before he has a coronary."

⊙ ⋙ ✛ ⋘ ⊙

Dr. Ek turned right and I went left, careful not to run or even walk too fast through the woods. I don't know how, because I was too hyped up on adrenaline getting here, but I knew exactly how to get back to the tunnel, climbing down from the top. I did run once I got there and continued all the way down to the parking lot. I could see the Rav parked a few spaces down from the streetlight, which was still illuminated but dimmer. Funny the tricks the imagination plays on you. The night sky had darkened even more, or maybe it was just my mood. The air felt cool on my skin, and I smelled pine walking under a canopy of trees, now no trace of the smoke smell. I took in the sensations, hoping it would calm the storm of questions in my head. I squinted my tired eyes as I moved further down the path toward the parking lot, wondering suddenly who was sitting in the front seat of my car.

CHAPTER 20

Amazing how adaptable Brock 2.0 was becoming, because the minute I saw the outline of someone's head in the front seat, I immediately shifted my forward walk to backward without missing a beat. I think I missed my calling as a spy. Ten steps back now and out of view, I slowed to a stop to assess the situation. Was the head round like Oleg's? No, I saw hair, dark hair, a lot of it. And—ah, Jonas. Thank God. My brother to the rescue.

Though the eight-year-old version of me wanted to tear down the hill and run to my older brother and tell him everything I'd learned, I remained still and texted him instead.

Hi, I wrote, just to make sure it was him and to watch the figure in the car to see if he responded. My text showed "sent" next to it but not yet "read". Jonas, turn on your goddamn text notifications FFS! Should I send it again? No. Ten seconds, twenty. I sent it again, this time also calling him but disconnecting right away. The head in the front seat (of *my car*) hadn't moved a muscle and was staring out the front windshield. WTF?

Jonas, if it was him, hadn't yet spotted me walking down the hill. Using that to my advantage, I continued in stealth mode five…ten more steps to get a better look at him. It was him alright, inexplicably sitting in my borrowed Rav at 12:15 a.m. Okay…think, Brock. That meant he had to have met with Lacy to even know about the car in the first place. But Lacy didn't know where I was headed tonight. I hadn't told anyone. Only James knew.

Slow down, Brock. Let's not go turning on James already. I clicked my brain into analysis-mode before my imagination ran wild. I was still hidden enough from Jonas' view to avoid detection. *By him anyway.* Who else could be here right now as well? Of course, think Brock. Jonas has been tailing Oleg for the past two days. I backed up ten more steps very slowly without moving my head but using my peripheral vision to scan for movement, or reflections. Nothing so far. If Jonas learned what I was driving from Lacy, the only way he could have found the car was if he was tailing Oleg and Oleg had been tailing me. Jonas sitting in the driver's seat of my car was either a symbol to me that Oleg was nearby, or else he was using himself as a decoy to draw Oleg out. That's why he wasn't acknowledging my texts. He was pretending to be me. Jesus Jonas. Stop being a martyr and answer your phone. Besides, your hair's too dark.

I pulled open the rear passenger door and climbed in. "Fancy meeting you here," I said.

"Do you have any idea what danger you're in right now?" It only barely sounded like him.

"You're in my car. What did you expect me to do?"

"Read my telepathic message and stay away from here."

"Yeah, okay, I understand you sitting in the driver's seat of my car was code. Where am I gonna go, dude? I'm a lot more exposed if I'm on foot."

Finally, he turned his head.

"Oh my God, Jonas. What did he do to you?"

◆ ⋅◦❖◦⋅ ✦ ⋅◦❖◦⋅ ◆

I exited the car and climbed in the front seat so I could get a good look at my brother's mangled face. My heart shattered as I gazed at the swelling in the side of his mouth, a dark red splotch under his left eye, which would be black in a few days, and his left eye was nearly swollen shut. I reach out my hand to open his jacket and check for other injuries. But he flinched and pushed my hand away.

"Back off," he said, in a gravelly voice.

My hands were shaking. Part of me wanted to cry seeing him this way. "Okay, okay, no worries. Did he break any ribs do you think?"

He shook his head. "I was kicked a few times but—no I don't think so."

"Alright. How did you get here, and where's your car?"

"Uber."

I nodded, thinking. "Scooch over and I'll drive you home."

He raised his palm. "Don't-you-understand?"

I froze.

"They will kill you regardless of the envelope." Jonas looked directly at me now, showing both sides of his misshapen face. "They know you have it. They also know you're investigating what's in it."

"Jay?" My voice trembled. "They murdered Jay Langley, my friend from college. I fucking found him."

Jonas nodded.

"Okay, I hear you and I understand the danger. And now he's harmed my family, so the stakes are ratcheted up a few notches. Will you move over and let me drive?" When he didn't answer, I got out and walked around the front of the car, no longer caring who saw us. My family, my flesh and blood. Jonas had been harmed because he went after the criminals chasing me. I might never think of him the same way again.

❖ ❖ ❖ ✛ ❖ ❖ ❖

I wasn't sure if Oleg and his henchmen were following us, but I had more important things to worry about now. I needed to get Jonas to safety and assess his condition. As much as I longed for the secret wet bar at my crash pad, I drove us to Ladera Heights so Jonas could have all his creature comforts available, and to keep Oleg as far away from that envelope as possible. Even if they'd been following all of my exterior movements, there was no way they could have known where I'd stashed it because it was inside the building. I loved the feeling of being a few steps ahead of Oleg. Too bad the likelihood of that being true was so low.

I took 101S to 2W and then south on 405 to Ladera Heights. No talking on the way back. Not one word.

Man, it took almost two minutes and every drop of my patience for Jonas to struggle himself out of the Rav and step flat onto the curb. I stood back because I knew him. I knew he'd flail out at me if I tried to help him, and probably end up flat on the concrete. He inherited that trait from my father, who'd always hated my mother's caring ministrations and her "fussing", as he called it. Said it made him feel like an infant. Was that why he disrespected her by cheating on her with twenty-year-old women?

"Oh my God, bro, please let me help you."

"Shut up. I'm just sore as all. I'm getting there."

"You need to go to a hospital," I said.

"Just help me up the stairs and I'll be fine."

"We'll see how you are when we get there."

"Honestly, Brock, you have much bigger issues than my well-being right now."

That's where he was wrong, and maybe that's where one of those invisible lines lay between kid and adult. Seeing Jonas's swollen face under the streetlight clicked something into place deep inside me. Oleg could go to hell and I'd get around to dealing with him later. For now, I was taking care of my family.

"Let me tell you what happened," Jonas said.

"Let's get you out of this jacket—"

"I can—"

"Please, I beg you cut the crap! You have no idea what I've been doing tonight and my nerves are shot. You fucking belong in a hospital and if you refuse to go then I'll be examining you myself. Got it?"

Wow. I even surprised myself with that. Jonas closed his eyes.

"One or the other. You want to go get checked out at the ER? We'll probably be home in—"

"Fine. Doctor."

I carefully removed his leather jacket, feeling with my fingertips for bullet holes. He flinched every time I touched him. He was wearing a white dress shirt with no visible blood. But I could see where he'd been either side-punched or kicked by two dark smudges near his kidneys. He could have broken ribs or internal bleeding.

"Take your shirt off."

"I'm really o—"

"Oh, you'd prefer the ER? No problem. Lemme just call and let them know we're coming."

He started unbuttoning the shirt. I unbuttoned his cuffs and pulled the sleeves one at a time. There was a large, dark bruise on his upper abdomen and two that corresponded to the dark smudges in the back of his shirt. I pressed two fingers on each of his ribs, waiting for him to yell out in agony. First the left, then the right.

"Are you done?"

"Fine, no broken ribs, no ER." I collapsed on an ottoman in his living room. "Can I bring you anything?"

"I think we both need a drink."

CHAPTER 21

Jonas' liquor cabinet was a sad, too small, forgotten shelf next to the stove. Always seemed like an odd choice, especially because it should be stored away from potential combustibles and in a cool place. But I wasn't up for any reorganizing. This was emergency medicine. I looked at the three-quarters full bottle of Bell's fifteen-year-old scotch, which had been my mother's favorite. So far we'd shared a shot of it on her birthday every year since she died. I decided not to open up the painful topic and opted for the Johnnie Walker. After we downed two shots of it each, I brought him a clean t-shirt, sleep pants, a glass of water and two Motrin.

He said thanks with his eyes but said nothing, staring me down with a mix of fear, awe, and admonition.

"Where's Oleg?" I asked him.

"He and one of his men were driving up and down Observatory Road tonight, I think looking for your car. Meaning your actual car."

"They don't know about the Rav?"

"Not yet. I don't think so. Lacy gave me the car and condo details this afternoon."

I watched him swallow the Motrin with the last sip of scotch. Probably a bad idea under normal circumstances.

"How'd you know I was up there?" I asked.

"I didn't. I was just following Oleg. So are you gonna tell me where it is?"

"Hell, no. It's been moved a few times, though."

"I assume you haven't given it up because you want to find out what it is."

"That's part of it."

"Find out why your friend Jay died?"

I blinked back. Jay. Jesus.

"Okay, well, could you please explain to me your reasoning? Because I can't figure it out. I honestly don't recognize you at all, BJ."

That hurt. He never called me BJ. "Aren't you even a little curious why they chose me?"

"Of course. But—"

"No, you're wrong. You were about to say that there are more important considerations, right?"

"Obviously."

"There aren't," I said.

"What am I missing?"

"Why me, like, why me specifically? Not a rhetorical question, either. Let's think about it."

"Okay," he said, changing positions in the chair. "You're young, you seem smart and, logistically speaking, you're in love with someone who works at the hotel in question."

I scrunched up my face. Did he mean Raquel? "No I'm not."

"Are too."

"Am not."

"Are too."

We both smirked. "I've seen Raquel," he said, knowing he had me.

"She's pretty. So what. I'm not in love with her."

"Would you even know if you were?"

"Damn, that was cold. Besides, I barely know her."

"Since when is that relevant?"

"Okay okay, I go to the Bonaventure Hotel to get coffee a lot."

"Like every day."

"Fine, I'm a regular there. So it's likely if Oleg was looking to deliver something there, like the contents of the FedEx envelope, I'd be a logical patsy, that's what you're saying?"

He nodded. "Sure. But you're thinking it has to be more than that?"

"I know it does. Oleg's not just chasing that little Ziploc bag. He's chasing me. It's personal."

"How do you know that?"

"I just know, Jonas. And I need to know why."

Jonas got up and brought the clean clothes with him into the bathroom and changed. "Keep going, I can hear you," he said, through the closed door.

"Do you need help?"

"No. Tell me what happened last night."

I moved to the hallway and leaned against the wall so I could hear him if he keeled over. I told him about British James, the new terms I'd documented on my phone, and my visit to Abilene Cremation Services.

He opened the bathroom door, shaking his head. "Ever hear of something called backup? You shouldn't have gone there alone last night."

"I know. I thought I'd just be talking to a crew foreman or something, getting some sort of security guard job. Not talking to the guy in charge. His name is Anders Ek and he's running something out of that building that has nothing to do with mortuary services. It's like three or four floors and some significant capital invested in his R&D services."

He stood over me, vibing me with the older brother thing again. "Are you going back there?"

"Hell, yeah, I'm going back."

"You need backup then. I insist."

"Do you now?"

Negotiation-mode. Arms crossed. "You're an employee of Janoff Investigations, are you not? As your employer, I'm designating this undercover job as high risk and it's part of my Corporate Social Responsibility program to ensure the safety of my employees."

"What, Ray? You're suggesting my roommate Ray-the-landscaper as backup? He smokes weed eight hours a day. He did one job for us last year and botched it."

"Don't knock him," he countered. "I've had him working surveillance with me for the past three days now and he's been great."

"In what way? He's not technical so he wasn't running ops. What was he doing? Delivering coffee and sandwiches? Newspaper with holes in it?"

"He's a good shot, for one thing."

"How in the world would you know that?"

Jonas sank forward and sighed. He disappeared into the living room and came back holding up paper silhouette targets from a shooting range.

"What, all bullseyes? How do you know he didn't steal them from somebody else or buy them at an Army Surplus store?"

"Geez, paranoid much? He's your freaking roommate."

"Not for long, thank God. I didn't think he even had a gun."

We locked eyes.

"Betty?? Fu-uck," I moaned. "So you and Ray have been tailing Oleg all this time and, meanwhile, Ray's been carrying around *my* gun? What if he shoots someone, for fuck's sake? That gun's registered to me."

"Sorry about that, bro. That was my oversight. I didn't realize it was yours."

"Where's Ray and Betty right now?" I asked.

"I told him to take off last night when I was sure Oleg made me. One of his men, not Oleg himself, opened the driver's side door while I was parked, pulled me out and beat the crap out of me on the sidewalk, and told me continuing to follow them would result in not only my death but yours."

Hearing him say that and seeing his bruised face, my eyes welled up. "I'm—" I couldn't even get the words out. And the snide comment that was about to spill out about Ray got displaced with a well of guilt. Again. And Jay Langley? It was just too much. I went to the kitchen and pulled an ice pack out of the freezer and wrapped it in a dishtowel.

"I need to go pick my car up, by the way." He held the towel to his swollen eye.

"I can do that for you."

"No way, you're not doing it. Maybe a perfect job for Ray."

I raised a brow. "I mean, not that he's expendable or anything, but you're right he's not who Oleg's looking for."

"Why, who else were you thinking?" he asked.
I paused a second before I said her name. "Miki Fine."
"Is she even talking to us anymore?"

CHAPTER 22

I didn't want to tell Jonas that I'd been thinking a lot about Miki
lately. My current life circumstances required a wily, fearless sort,
and my situation seemed more desperate every day. I know. PIs and
informants have this sort of tenuous, transactional relationship. You
see them every day for a week and then not again for three years.
You pay them enough for their intel that they answer your call next
time, but there's usually nothing in between and that's just the nature
of it. People who live on the street have eyes and ears that others
don't. Miki wasn't just our partner, Archie Dax's informant. She was
Archie's best friend, backup, sidekick, who lived out of her car and
liked it that way. We always paid in cash, always paid well, she
refused all of our offers to add her to the payroll for legitimate
employment. "Legitimacy is vain," she explained more than once. "I
do lots of different types of work for different people and I like the
variety. If I wanted a penthouse, I could find a way to get it."

So when Archie got shot by one of our former clients, Miki
blamed herself and we hadn't heard from her since. Archie Dax died
the same month as our mother, three years ago. Maybe that was
enough time for Miki.

Jonas slept on and off for the next few hours, exhausted from the
chaos. He'd brought that book Mr. Bergman left for me. *The Wasp*

Factory by Iain Banks—the debut novel of a Scottish author that won all kinds of awards—is about a psychopathic teenager who kills his whole family. Great. Why did he want me to read this book? I flipped through it to check for a bookmark or yellowed store receipt tucked between the pages. There was a small, torn piece of paper stuck in the crook of the spine near the end of the book with writing on it. "Crossword: Cold Beetle". I had no idea and didn't care much for the musings of an old millionaire. I stuck the book in my backpack because it never hurt to have a contingency plan when your phone was out of battery.

I found a perfect spot to chill on the floor just under Jonas' street-facing living room window. Just listening. Sometimes to my own thoughts, birds, crickets, cars, motorcycles. Normally moving too fast to hear the world, these strange, new events were somehow attuning me to a deeper level of human perception. Hearing, seeing, smelling. Maybe it was the reality of Jay's body on the floor that somehow changed the weights of things in my life. Some things felt more important now, some things less. I heard Jonas moving around his bedroom. I had no idea what time it was but when wasn't it the right time for coffee? I made it the old-fashioned way because Jonas had a French press and bought whole bean coffee. I poured a cup and returned to my quiet spot on the polished, wood floors. Somehow it felt comforting.

"I smell coffee."

His voice startled me out of a half-sleep. "Fresh pot," I said and sipped. "Probably too strong for you."

"Isn't everything lately? You always did call me an old lady. I think you were right."

Another dagger in my heart. I ignored it. "Seems like you slept a bit. Your injuries will start talking to you when the Motrin wears off."

"I'll be alright." He stirred too much sugar and too much milk into his coffee, then joined me on the living room floor.

"You gonna tell me what you think is really going on here?" he asked.

"With what?" I knew what he meant.

"What's in the envelope?"

"You think I opened it? Holy fuck, Jonas. It could be a

bioweapon for all we know. An engineered pathogen."

"That's not what you think it is," he said, quietly. "I know you."

I sighed and set down my coffee. I haven't opened it, and I haven't seen the Ziploc bag up close, only on an x-ray."

"But—"

"I don't know why I say this, but I sorta think it's ash of some kind."

"Ashes?"

"Yeah."

"From a fire?" he asked.

I shook my head. "I don't know. No, not a fire. Abilene Cremation Services. They cremate bodies. That's what they're doing up there. And Dr. Death has an entire floor designated to R&D. What the hell kind of R&D would be necessary for a mortuary?"

"I think there are a few different cremation methods."

"Yeah, I remember the *Breaking Bad* episode where Jesse dissolved a guy with hydrofluoric acid."

"Maybe only slightly more legit than that, I read about something that's illegal in most states, and is not what they call fire-based cremation," he said.

"Chemicals?" I asked.

"Chemicals and water, I think. I'll have to look it up."

"Do you remember why it's illegal?"

"Sorry, no. Just that it's not used very often. I know there's something else on your mind."

"Well, yeah, of course. I'm trying not to get killed every time I set foot outside."

Jonas shook his head, not buying any of my diversionary tactics. It's okay, I did the same thing to him when he was stonewalling me, doing the guy thing and shouldering all the burden so others didn't have to.

"Something to do with our family?" he asked. "Is that what's bothering you? You think you're being targeted by Oleg because of me?"

"Not you," I admitted, and even that was more than I wanted to share.

Intrigued by our conversation, I spent the next hour reading about thanatology, the scientific study of death, and thanatology certification and master's degree programs. I found a surprising shortage of online articles on cremation. I'd learned about the manners of death while studying for my PI license and in an online criminal justice course I took. Mortuary technicians prepared bodies for cremation and only required a license in some states, where embalmers needed a license universally. Finally I found the technology Jonas was talking about: alkaline hydrolysis, which used both chemicals and large quantities of water to break down a corpse into its most elemental form. I read three different articles, cumulatively showing polarized feedback. Some of the comments praised its sustainability, while others disputed the disposal impacts from the chemical-laden wastewater.

I was about to Uber out to Jonas' parked car from last night when the doorbell rang. Thank God for peek holes. Lacy.

"Good morning." I held the door open.

"Damn, you look bad. What happened?"

"Fine thanks, and yourself?"

"I'm just glad you're okay. I brought a first aid kit. Is he being a good patient so far?"

"What do you think?"

"I picked up his car," she said.

"You're a saint. Wasn't there a saint named Lacy?"

"Not yet."

I left her with Jonas and was glad to be driving the Rav again, knowing I'd have to return this car sometime soon and Lacy's father would need his condo back. Now wasn't the time to confront big decisions about my future. I had questions that needed answering, and every time I answered one, twenty more emerged. What was Dr. Anders Ek doing in that huge building every night? Was it possible that he was involved in the illegal practice of alkaline hydrolysis to cremate bodies without burning them? But what did he do with the water? I tried to recall the property his building was on. It was dark and there was no telling how lush the vegetation was up there. Runoff from alkaline hydrolysis could result in either an overabundance of plant nutrients or universal die-off. I needed to go back there and look around, now that I knew what I was looking for. But was alkaline hydrolysis a controversial enough technology that it would require hiring unqualified, local security guards to protect the business entity from police exposure? There had to be more to it than that. I didn't know what Dr. Anders Ek was doing in that fortress every night, but I was gonna find out.

CHAPTER 23

In a way it was fun being up last night, sleepless and unsupervised in Jonas' house, taking advantage of his snoring by rummaging through his office drawers, looking at correspondence he'd told me was private. I'm so bad, but that's the way of brothers. Every family has a historian; for ours, that was Jonas. After college during the occasional family dinners, Jonas could always be counted on to finger through Mom's stacks of vintage photos and swipe one or two that would end up in his own stash. Lucky for me, I know where he kept it. The built-in bench at the kitchen bay window opened, typically for the storage of blankets and pillows, but for Jonas, his family photo stash. I don't know what I'd been looking for, so I wasn't very careful in my selection process, also not wanting to wake him in the next room. So I took the whole photo album and carried it out to my car.

I was dying to go to the ocean, especially being so close to the Santa Monica Pier. But that pier was too visible and I was a wanted man, after all. So I retreated to my borrowed home with its protective façade and sat on the windowsill with the photo album on my lap. There was one photo that I could see in my mind, even when I didn't want to. One photo that I'd dreamt about over and over, though I hadn't looked at it up close in a decade, maybe more.

I didn't even need to see it.

That photo, faded, folded, frayed on the edges, had haunted me ever since I saw the very same photo online in a Google search ten years ago. What was my family picture doing online? And naturally, I'd had plenty of time to think about it. Even now, when I pulled it out from where I'd last hidden it—behind another picture in a photo sleeve of Jonas' album—it still had that same power over me. My father, George Janoff, standing in what looked like a large library with tall ceilings, holding something under his arm, and flanked by four men, two on each side.

The image of my father was a profile, with him prominently standing closest to the camera, wearing a jacket my mother bought him on their second wedding anniversary and had been the most money she'd ever spent on him, as the story goes. Navy blue Brooks Brothers wool gabardine. So I'd verified that it was indeed my father in the photo. Scary thing was, the other four men were recognized members of a secret society...the Bilderberg Group.

I wrote a book report on secret societies my junior year of high school, in my AP English class, and one of the available topics was clandestine services organizations. Who wouldn't want to write about that? So while scanning through articles and imagery on the Illuminati, The Knights Templar, Masons, Skull and Bones, I read about Bilderberg, how it was originally, back in the 1950s, intended to foster US-European relations to prevent another world war, and had a secret agenda to develop a new world order with a singular world government.

But then, over the years, it had evolved beyond its small list of predominantly white male members to include a more diverse group of thought leaders from different cultures and verticals: royalty, politics, military, financial, private corporations, academia, and media. Through the Freedom of Information Act, group members were public knowledge now, including dossiers and countries of origin. My father, George Janoff, was not listed as a member. So why was he standing at a table in a library with four other known Bilderberg members?

Without coming out and asking him about it, I determined that his job as a CPA for the Department of State gave him access to all kinds of business and government leaders from different circles.

Maybe he was consulting with them, maybe the members in the picture were from private corporations with which my father did business. I wriggled the picture out of its sleeve, still safely resting where I'd last left it, silent in its incriminating implications. Once again, all these years later, I could barely breathe.

While broadening its constituency over the years, the group sought to create other areas of common ground besides just preventing another world war. Economic expansion, climate change, AI, cybersecurity, Brexit, space exploration, and social media. You know how someone can say something and it's not until hours or days later that the impact of their words shakes you in your shoes? When Jonas was telling me about the alkaline hydrolysis process of using water and chemicals to dispose of human remains, he mentioned the environmental impact. Something about that part of our conversation conjured up an almost instant image of this picture in my hand, my father with global leaders, heads of state, policymakers, shaping our world through their secret agendas, while holding some antiquarian artifact under his arm. Why did I feel like Oleg Kokov and his magic envelope had something to do with this picture?

I was able to reach Ray via text.
Can you talk? I wrote. While I waited for his highness to respond, I checked Waze to see how long it might take me to zip over there.
Call you 10, he wrote back.
Good. That gave me time to check on the laundry room. Of course I should be doing laundry right now, but since I barely had any clothes available, that could wait. Even so, I brought a small jug of laundry detergent upstairs so I'd at least look like I belonged. A young woman was crouched next to one of the dryers pulling out the last few articles of clothing. I waited outside and checked my phone. She bumped past me with her cumbersome plastic laundry bin.
"Sorry about that," she said.
"Morning. No worries."
I waited till I heard either the elevator or her footsteps on the stairs. Elevator. I closed and locked the door. Thank goodness the chair was still in the corner and, after a quick check, I saw the

envelope still hovering just above my head within the foam ceiling tile. When I opened the door again, the same young woman was staring me down.

"Why was that door closed?" Her voice sounded like a terrier first thing in the morning. There was fire burning from her green eyes. Barely twenty, bleached blonde hair, probably a student. God help me.

"Um...I don't—"

"Are you new here?"

"Yeah, I'm staying with my dad for a while," I lied. "Just wanted to do some laund—"

"And you forgot to bring your dirty clothes?"

Shit. I had one way out of this: to pretend to be transfixed by her beauty. I eyed the floor, shifted my feet, and wiped my palms on my pants. "Look," I started. "Could we start over? My name's BJ."

"Jenna," she said, rolled her eyes, and stormed off.

Whew, disaster averted. Now, if I was lucky, she'd chalk it up to another in a long line of clueless guys. The girl-variable I hadn't planned on. I laughed to myself and made note that she headed for the east staircase. My condo was on the west side. Small miracle.

CHAPTER 24

With several hours to kill before my second visit to Abilene Cremation, I had business to take care of. First, James. I texted him to ask if it was okay to go back up to "the hill", as he'd called it. *Same time and place*, he typed back. I assumed that meant hiking up from the tennis courts parking lot, climbing up the hilly scrub brush to the top of the Hollywood Tunnel and following the path. I didn't have a plan for how to handle Dr. Death and his soldiers. In the absence of Betty or a recording device, which they'd inevitably detect, it was just me, my grit, and wits. So be it. I wanted back up there in a big way, because the answer to my "why me" question lived somewhere in that building, I could feel it. I wanted to know more about the process he and his team were using to cremate bodies, assess whether it was illegal or not, and discuss why he was so determined to hide from the police. And then since last night, several new questions had been added to the list: What was the meaning of the sword on Dr. Ek's keychain, and was he or the million-dollar envelope somehow related to my father?

My deadbeat roommate never did call me back in ten minutes. Asshole.

"Hey, yeah, sorry, I forgot," Ray said when he answered.

"No problem. Can you check in on Jonas today? I don't want

him to be alone and I'm not sure how long Lacy's staying. He was hurt pretty bad last night." I let my words hang in the air to see if he picked up on the implication. Just silence. "Ray, are you still there?"

"Yeah."

"So…where the fuck were you last night?"

"Hey, man, Jonas told me to take off. So I did. What was I supposed to do?"

"Oh, I don't know, realize that you were tailing the freaking Russian mafia and stick around to give him some backup maybe."

"He didn't tell me anything about the guy, just the license plate and the car, man. That was my deal, just-the-car."

"Ray, do you realize what I just said? Jonas was hurt. Don't you care?"

He sighed.

"Okay, forget it. I'm heading out of town for a few hours and I need you to check in on Jonas. Can you at least do that?"

Silence, then another long sigh. "When?"

"Right fucking now!"

"Yeah, okay, I'll be there."

"And another thing. I want to meet you later to pick up Betty."

"Fine. Call me when your ready." And he hung up.

Next on my list: Kayla. I got the same surly imaging tech guy that I'd talked to in person, this time on the phone. I asked him about Kayla and reminded him I'd asked about her a few days ago.

"Kayla hasn't been to work in three days. I'm at the point of wanting to know who you are so I can report your name to the police. They're now looking for her as a missing person. Do you hear me?"

The guy was unglued. "I hear you, sir. Let's not get excited."

"Who are you and why are you asking for Kayla?"

Now I knew that the guy was her lover. I could probably find out his name online or on LinkedIn under a company search.

"I was referred by one of her colleagues in LA," I said, "and she was going to take a look at something on their behalf." It was a perfectly executed answer, my voice was completely calm. The guy wasn't buying it.

"Where do you know Kayla from and when did you last see

her?"

Definitely her lover. "I've never met her, sir. Never even spoke with her on the phone so she does not know me. Again, I was referred by—"

"She's-not-here." He hung up. Now I needed another connection to Jay Langley.

And I had no idea what to do about Miki Fine. She was a better investigator than I was, and she'd had none of the formal education or training that I had. I needed backup right now like I needed oxygen but calling and asking for her help was tricky. I needed a tactical plan, backed by a larger strategy. Miki. Geez. She had talent, too, for undercover work. One day showing up with her natural fine blonde hair and the next, long red dreadlocks. There was another thing about Miki that, as a guy, I couldn't completely ignore: she was stunningly beautiful, like the raw stuff nature gave her. Runway model bone structure, hair, body. And she had that rare, magical quality that made her utterly irresistible—she didn't care that she was beautiful. She knew, hell yeah she knew. And she was willing to use it to her or someone's advantage if she was paid enough. But unlike money, beauty had no meaning for her. One time she and Dax came over for burgers after a late-night stakeout. It was hot, August, and she just stripped down and took off her clothes, all of them. She apologized for the interruption and continued sitting there talking to us just like that. It's just skin, she explained. Get over it. I tried, believe me. Archie, well, he was more used to her odd behaviors. For now, I was putting Miki Fine on hold.

All this analysis made me hungry. The little market on the first floor of the building had what I called college food: ramen noodles, soda, pop tarts. It was enough of a meal to get me through the rest of the afternoon.

Back upstairs, I put one of the soups in the microwave. My phone rang. Shit, which phone was it? Oleg's. Did I need to answer it? I knew why he was calling. I knew what he wanted: something I wasn't willing to give. But if I didn't answer, he'd just find another way, and now he'd already hurt my family. I picked up.

"Hello, Oleg." I was deciding how to play it. Staying silent seemed like a good ploy for the moment.

"Okay. Let me make easy for you, Mr. Janoff. Yeah? Here's how we gonna play it. You deliver envelope to hotel like I pay—"

"Sorry, Oleg, you can't play that card again. I returned your money."

"Like-I-say," he said, slowly. He obviously didn't like being interrupted. "You gonna return envelope to hotel by six o'clock tomorrow morning. If you don't, I just text some picture that you might find interesting. Goodbye."

He hung up and there were no pictures. What in the hell was he talking about? Of course I wasn't returning the envelope. I had more important matters on my mind—lunch. Unfortunately, two bites into the ramen, the phone chimed with a text. My pulse quickened and there was a lump in my throat. My hands trembled slightly as I picked it up, silently praying that it wasn't another dead body. Had Oleg and his men killed Jay Langley because of what he had shown me? Who would be next? No. Please God, no. The phone showed three images: a woman pumping gas, walking out of an office building, and unlocking her front door. It was Lacy.

CHAPTER 25

Oleg said 6 a.m. Fine. It was just after six now, so that gave me almost twelve hours to figure out what the fuck was in that envelope. I started by retrieving it from the laundry room. I no longer cared about being seen by the busybody laundry fairy who caught me last time. I didn't even close the door. With the room empty and no machines on, I dragged the chair over, pushed up the tile a few inches, pulled it down, and stuck it under my shirt. I'd been ultra-careful not to squeeze the contents too hard, not knowing what kind of material was in it. I couldn't necessarily assume that they had Lacy, but they were watching her and that was enough of a deterrent. I started with Jonas.

"Hey."

"Hey."

"Feeling okay?" I asked.

"Sore but fine. What's up?"

"Oleg sent me three pictures of Lacy."

Silence. "Shit. When?"

"Now. I'm gonna call her but wanted to let you know first."

"Did he pick her up?"

"I don't think so, but he's letting me know that he's watching her."

"Did you call him? What did he say?"

"Said 6 a.m. tomorrow for the envelope delivery. He didn't even have to say or else. I know what he'll do."

"Alright. What can I do?"

"Nothing, but I'm calling Miki Fine. Just letting you know. Don't go out today, bro. Please, as a personal favor." I hung up before he could protest and talk about the many different urgent projects he had going that needed his personal attention. As long as he stayed home today, I'd be happy because it would be one less variable and one less thing to unravel my composure.

I forced myself to eat a few more bites of soup because I hadn't had a square meal in...I couldn't even remember. I decided texting Lacy was the best idea.

Hey Sunshine, are you around?

Busy.

Whew, she answered. That's really all I cared about right now. *No problem, catch you later*, I wrote.

Kk xo

I loved the fact that she added the xo in there. It wasn't typical for her, but now that I was doing dangerous shit, dealing with dangerous people, she wanted me to know what I meant to her. Kiss hug. From Saint Lacy.

Now, when it came to Miki Fine, I only knew of two ways to reach her – by text or going to her favorite hangout.

First order of business: financial meeting with myself. I knew Archie Dax had been paying Miki a shit ton of money for every job he hired her for, plus he took her to nice restaurants for dinner, sometimes out of town travel and, as I understood from Jonas, they never hooked up. Now, if she'd been in love with Archie all that time, that could explain why she shunned Jonas and me for the past three years, probably blaming us for his death. And if it wasn't love for Archie, it was love of money. The job I had in mind should, in theory anyway, be worth about $3-$5k, considering the urgency and sky-high stakes. I opened the Union Bank app on my phone, even though I already knew what was, or I should say wasn't, in there. $1784 in my checking account, even less in my savings.

Hollywood Billiards, the oldest billiards hall in LA, was conveniently located three blocks from the Griffith Park Observatory entry road. Looking for parking at Hollywood Boulevard and Taft, I remembered the Tommy's Burgers across the street. I sat in the drive-through and appreciated the time to plan my pitch. If I even found her, she'd likely be mid-game, and Miki was a pool shark who's played semi-pro before. So it was more than a game to her. All the times she refused to work for Jonas and me, we knew her main income came from billiards. Five-foot six and about ninety-five pounds, she covered her hair with a wool cap, wore no makeup, and with baggy clothing and a hoodie, could probably pass for a guy.

The burger smelled wonderful, but I just couldn't make myself eat it. Not when I thought of one of Oleg's men brute-stalking Lacy. I had a limited amount of time to do an impossible job. No fucking around, Brock, get it done. Okay. Here we go. I entered slowly, eyes peeled. It was the right time of day. Please let her be here.

Tending bar? No freaking way. There she was in the flesh, Miki Fine, no dreads, wearing makeup, earrings, definitely not looking like she'd been sleeping in her car. Did she get her penthouse? It wasn't crowded so there was no hiding from her when I walked in.

"As I live and breathe," she said with a flourish. The gapped, crooked smile shined back at me radiating genuine warmth. I wondered if she might walk around the bar and hug me. Nope. She motioned me in, though, and pointed to an empty seat.

"BJ," she said, biting her lip. She opened her mouth to speak but I jumped in, desperate to start this critical meeting off on the right foot.

"Hey. Miki. I want to start by saying that on behalf of Jonas and myself, we apologize for not contacting you sooner."

"Well, I told you both to fuck off last time I saw you."

"Yes, you did say that. Anyway, we should have checked in on you."

"And now you're here to check in and say hi? Or did you have some business to discuss?" She winked and poured me a Stella. I took a long sip. I loved Stella. Who didn't? Stella was the cognac of beers. Miki pressed her torso into the bar and her hands flat, sizing me up. Her face was saying *What are you doing here, BJ?* I continued sipping, reminding myself what time it was. Tick tick.

"Word on the street's that you're running with a rough crowd right now."

I smirked. "With? You mean from?"

Miki shook her head. "Not that crowd."

Her hair looked amazing. Clean, smooth, highlighted, and short enough to frame her small face. How could she possibly know about the other crowd, and did the *other crowd* mean British James? Jesus, it was like my life was televised live for the world to see. So then she probably already knew what I needed.

"Look. In the spirit of the awesome work you did for years for Archie, I need help with an urgent...project we'll call it, and I think you're the—"

"Right man for the job?"

"Exactly."

She disappeared around the corner for a few minutes, enough time for me to count the twenty-seven pool tables. The amount of money she'd made in this place years ago. Geez. Between that and Archie, she probably could have afforded a penthouse even back then. I saw her blonde head poking out around the corner, eyes wide. She pointed to a table in the back corner, a dark wood booth. When she approached the table with two waters, of all things, I saw her outfit of black skinny slacks, a slim white top, and short black jacket, an uncanny resemblance to a magazine cover juxtaposed to the gritty, malnourished con we'd known years ago. Maybe there was still a little con in her. One could only hope.

"How much do you know?" I asked.

She blinked back, tacitly reminding me that she was an informant and information was her currency. Of course she knew. "How much do I need to?" she asked. Smart question. The smartest.

"I need to replicate an envelope and its contents." I stopped to determine how much additional information was needed, if any. "I need it by 4 a.m. tomorrow morning." I added a buffer of two hours for quality control and transport to the Bonaventure.

Miki looked at her naked wrist. "I don't know what time it is but let's go."

CHAPTER 26

I suggested separate cars. She suggested we go to her place to talk about the specifications. I agreed. She'd lived literally one block from our office in Venice for the past three years and we never ran into each other. Was this even possible? She told me third floor, top of the stairs on the left. The building looked modest on the outside, but every visible surface inside looked and smelled brand new, everything gray or muted brown. I couldn't help being impressed.

"My humble abode," she said. "Make yourself at home."

She said she needed to change clothes and I couldn't stop my mind from wondering if it was hot in here and she might come out naked. Was it customary for the person pitching to take the sofa, and the receiver to take a chair? That seemed logical enough. I put the envelope on her glass coffee table and looked at it again, scanning for any nuances I might have missed. Miki returned a minute later in baggy jeans and a tight tank top. That looked more like Miki Fine to me.

"So that's it, eh?"

I nodded.

"FedEx, standard size. What's on the airbill?"

"Air bill?" I picked it up and held it out to her.

"One second," she said, and came back thirty seconds later wearing blue nitrile gloves. She took the envelope and examined the

113

writing on the shipping form.

"There's nothing on here. What's in it?"

I stared back, wondering how much she knew about this fated envelope so far. Oleg? Jay Langley? Kayla?

"Is it okay for me to handle it, like squeeze it, shake—"

"No. I'd be very careful."

Miki Fine sat back in the chair across from me. "So you don't intend to open this?"

"I didn't say that." I told her about the Ziploc bag and how I'd seen an X-ray of the contents.

"I heard about your friend."

Jesus. So she'd been living three blocks from our office and had been keeping tabs on us. Wow.

"Your dead friend, I should say."

"Jesus, Miki." I was losing it. I bent forward and ran my hands through my hair.

"You've been through a lot the past few days. What are you afraid of?"

"I'm afraid to open the contents in case it's some kind of bioweapon."

"Based on the texture that's palpable through the paper envelope, doesn't feel like it's in the kind of protective container that would be required to not only maintain potency in something like this envelope but also to prevent potential leakage. A Ziploc bag also isn't completely airtight, and there's air in the envelope. What I'm saying is I doubt it. It also feels a bit spongy, to my fingers anyway."

"Yeah, I felt that too. The images I got looked like pellets, sort of, in different sizes with slight variations in color."

"If it was heavier, I'd think it was sand with bits of shell and sea glass in it," she said.

She hadn't yet said a word about British James, Dr. Ek, or Abilene Cremation. And I was operating on a need-to-know basis. But it was our job to replicate the envelope and its contents and pass it off as legit to the reception desk concierge at the Bonaventure, such that Oleg was satisfied enough to leave precious Lacy alone. So be it.

"I think it's some kind of ash."

Miki sat back and placed the envelope on the table again. "It's very lightweight, but there is a weight to it. More so, it seems, than if it contained regular ash from like a fireplace or something. Is that what you're thinking? That someone burned something valuable and Oleg rescued some of the remains?"

Now I was getting into the NDA territory. I had to tell her enough to understand the gravity of this project.

"Maybe not something, but more like someone," I said, lowering my voice.

"Ah. So, not remains but cremains maybe?"

"Maybe."

"Well, that would account for some of the properties I feel through the envelope. Question: are you wanting to somehow open the envelope and remove the bag and replace it with something else and then reseal the original envelope? Or duplicate the entire thing and pass off the new contents and the new envelope as the original? And what about sensors?" she added.

"Sensors?" Fuck. I hadn't thought of that. "Inside you mean?"

"It's possible."

"I can't. I just can't fucking deal with one more potential catastrophe. Okay? My head's gonna explode."

"No problem."

"So let's just save ourselves the pain and suffering and, for now at least, assume there are no sensors that will go off."

"Got it. Operation Replica."

"Right. As for payment—"

She waved her hand. "Anything is fine. I don't consider this a real job anyway."

"Are you still taking real jobs? Like you did for Archie?"

She lowered her eyes to the coffee table at the sound of his name. "Hell, yeah," she said after a moment. "I'm using what I know. How do you think I can afford this place? Not on bar tips certainly."

"Still playing billiards?"

"Yeah, but just for fun. Some things have changed I guess."

"You look good, Miki."

"You too, I'm glad to see you."

We agreed on $1000, and she said it was the best gig she'd had in a while. The meat of the discussion rested on slitting open the bottom of Oleg's envelope with an Exacto blade or steaming open one of the other folds in the cardboard structure. Then we talked about the pros and cons of using a different envelope. We could certainly get that from a FedEx store, but we'd need to sufficiently age and weather it to look exactly like the original. We decided the heat from steaming open one end of the envelope could potentially impact the contents. I had an Exacto blade on the Leatherman in my pocket. I managed the lighting, and she did the slitting.

"Not the whole length, right?"

I considered this. "I think the whole length, yeah. If the slit is sized to the dimensions of the bag inside, it'll look more obvious. If the whole length is cut and then reaffixed, that would be harder to trace."

"Okay. And how do you propose to close it back up?"

"Don't worry about that right now."

I watched her steady hands, fingers, her breathing, and remembered watching her compete in billiards tournaments and how I'd marveled at her control. Not just composure under pressure but utter stillness. She made the cut, slowly, evenly, perfectly. Whew.

"Nice work," I said.

"Here we go." She let the bag fall out the bottom and onto the table. We both put rubber gloves on and lowered the lamp. First, the folded piece of paper, which was completely blank. Under Jay's machinery, it had looked like there was writing on it. I don't know why I was disappointed. I guess I hoped there might be a clue.

"They almost look like bone fragments. But they're not hard enough to the touch," she replied, pressing gently on one of them. "It's a little bit spongey."

"If this is cremains," I was just thinking out loud here, "is it possible that the body was subjected to some kind of chemical or chemicals that could have changed the bone composition?"

"Interesting question," she said, still inspecting the package. "I know chemicals are released during the natural course of decomposition." She watched my face. "But that's not what you're thinking, is it?"

I didn't answer. "How would you go about replicating this little envelope? We can't use sand because it's too heavy."

THE RIDDERS

"Well, I know of someone who might be able to help."

CHAPTER 27

"A third-party consultant?"

"You're not gonna like it," she said, narrowing her eyes.

I thought back to all the sketchy sidemen, informants, waifs, and cons Archie Dax used to use in his investigations before he landed on Miki. "Go ahead, I'm ready."

"Well, the way I see it, based on your business requirement for this project we need a landscaper."

I closed my eyes. "Please no. Ray?" I whined.

"It's a practical resourcing decision."

"He's a deadbeat."

"BJ, you came to me. Do you want my help or not?"

"I go by Brock now, by the way."

"Are you gonna grow a mustache, too? Okay whatever. Here's the thing: dirt has the right weight for this. Not only that, there are soil additives that have a sort of spongy texture and the fragments aren't typically uniform. Things like vermiculite."

"Vermiculite." I repeated the word because, much as I hated Ray, it reminded me why I was paying Miki Fine a thousand bucks for this project. "Fine, whatever. Call him," I said.

"You call him. He's your roommate and it's your project. I barely know the guy. Only that he's a landscaper and he has access to soil.

"You need to pay him out of your cut because I don't have

another thousand dollars. Besides, he still fucking owes me for back rent."

"Okay. Okay?"

I nodded. How many other things would I rather do than ask Ray for a favor? Here's how I did it: I was supposed to call him anyway about delivering my gun to me. I had him drop it off at Miki's place. She and I were discussing the problem of weight again in loud voices with the door open when Ray came up the stairs. I made sure he heard the word *dirt* echoing out in the hall. Ray's a vain, insecure, self-aggrandizing know-it-all so he'd never be able to resist the urge to make himself look smart.

"Knock knock." Ray's voice. I suppressed an eyeroll.

"Hey, Ray, come on in," I said.

Wrinkled clothes, bedhead, bleary-eyed. "What you got goin' on in here?" he asked and found Miki and me sitting on the floor of her living room crouched like gemologists over a lit-up glass table. "Playing with dirt?"

"We need some, actually," Miki said.

Ray snapped his fingers, hoping the synapses in his brain would fire enough for him to remember her name. I saw his brain trying to work it out, probably remembering Archie.

"Ray, you remember our partner Archie Dax. This is Miki Fine, she worked with Archie."

He finger-combed his hair and smiled, then stuck out his hand.

Miki looked at it, shook it with her blue-gloved hand, then changed her glove. OMG hilarious. Ray looked at the floor.

"What is that?" He pointed at the Ziploc bag on the table.

"Just some ash from a fireplace," Miki shot back. "Some guy's paying me to replicate this bag and the contents of it. I thought BJ might be able to help, and—"

"BJ, I'm the one who's a landscaper," he said, all puffed up and still fixing his hair.

Ray's brows were raised, indicating he was deciding whether to believe Miki's story or not. "Can I see how much it weighs?" He opened his hand. "Certain types of soil might work. Sand, peat moss, and vermiculite would probably give you the right weight, just from the looks of it."

"How about a color match?" I asked.

He nodded, crouching low to get closer to the lamp. "Pretty close."

"How quickly could you get your hands on those soils? "Miki asked, and I was glad she was the one who was asking. To him, a woman's interests would be more motivating than mine.

Miki ordered a pizza for delivery, and I paid for it. Ray left and returned thirty minutes later with a grocery bag of stuff. I noticed he'd changed into jeans, a clean t-shirt, and it looked like he'd combed (with a comb) his tangled mess of hair. Aside from an assortment of potting soils and soil additives, he also brought a postal scale. Genius.

An hour later we had a new FedEx envelope, a new Ziploc bag sized exactly to spec, and a duplicate contents package within one-tenth of an ounce to the original and nearly the same color. At eight feet away it looked the same and was nearly identical in weight. Up close, I'd be a dead man.

We set aside the contents, ate some pizza, and I went to work on the envelope. I had Miki run it over with her car a few times, I put it inside my shirt in the front and tucked into the back of my jeans a bunch of times, and I rubbed my hands on the pizza crust, which had a sort of flour-cornmeal dust on it and pressed it into the envelope. We set the contents inside with the folded sheet of white printer paper. I was ready.

Miki paid Ray half of her payout and I thought he might wet his pants or try to mount her right there in her living room. Now that I'd gotten my money's worth, and we had our decoy, the preeminent concern, of course, was getting the crime lab we used to agree to analyze the real contents and do it before Oleg's men found me.

Meanwhile, Jonas and Ray hired had a contractor to follow Oleg's latest car around town. So far, he'd traded in the 1970's primer Pontiac for a Mazda, Mitsubishi, Subaru, Buick, and most recently a Honda. What did they all have in common other than easy carjacking access? Dark tinted windows. Jonas was getting the play-by-play from the contractor via Ray. The plan was for them to lock pick their way into the trunk of Oleg's Honda and place the decoy envelope there and, at the same time, stick a geo sensor on the inside of the trunk so they could monitor him. Then I would call Oleg a little before 6 a.m., telling him to check his trunk. By then I would have also established the chemical breakdown of the real contents of the Ziploc bag, and the trip to the Bonaventure would no longer be necessary. The plan was nice and neat and looked good from a distance. Time would tell.

After Ray finally left, I decided to let Miki in. I told her I needed backup for more than just my little Oleg scam. I had a strong feeling that whatever ash was contained in that bag had a direct connection to whatever shady shit Anders Ek was developing on the second floor of his white tower. I'd do anything to not have to go back up there alone tonight. I had no more money to pay her, but I knew she was practiced enough to be able to meld into their operation easily, and wily enough to escape if things got hairy.

"You need to look the part though," I added. "You know, dress like you're still living in your car. Can you do that?"

A sly grin took form on her lips. "My homeless hippie name tonight will be Shasta."

"Love it," I said.

"You'll introduce me as someone you met on the street and my husband beat me; I ran away and needed a job. Text your friend James and ask him first if it's okay to bring me."

"Okay," I said, "though I'm sure it's fine because I think he gets a cut from everyone he refers." I felt instant relief from her willingness to help me, and yet terrified because I'd never mentioned James to her.

CHAPTER 28

I was feeling a little more comfortable with filters. At first, they'd felt false, dishonest almost, symbolic walls you erect around your heart to protect yourself from people whose interests ran counter to your own. Lacy wasn't in this category but Jonas, geez, where would I start? When my mother died, my father essentially vanished and Jonas became my surrogate mother, omnipresent in all my affairs, intrusive bordering on ridiculous, fearing of course that if our mother could die so young then so could I, potentially. So I pulled out the same defenses I used as a teenager, to preserve the freedom that was owed to me as a young man's adulthood transition. I had a filter for British James, observing his blind allegiance to Dr. Anders Ek and his willingness to defend his fortress no matter what. I could be wrong about that as I still didn't really know him. But I needed to be careful who I trusted right now, more careful than I'd ever been. And now Miki.

Here we were, exiting the car in the Vermont Tennis Courts parking lot, hiking up to the tunnel. She looked perfect in her homeless waif disguise, with me and my poor head exploding with the chaos of strategic decision-making.

10:15 p.m. Miki and me, I mean Shasta, made it to the top of the tunnel by 10:30, and by 10:40 we were in the yard, which served as the waiting room for contract jobs at the fortress. All the other untethered souls milled around in the dark, mumbling to each other, some mumbling to themselves, staring at the stars, two people sitting on the ground. But the majority were standing and lined up, hungry for a new opportunity, waiting for Dr. Ek's community liaison, Dmitriy, to emerge with directions about how many people they needed for tonight's work and with what skills. I'd explained all this to Miki on the ride over here, but she still had questions and seemed nervous, tapping her fingers on her leg and pacing. Or maybe she was just in character pretending to be a crackhead. In that case, she was even smarter than I thought. My phone buzzed.

Are you here? It was a text from James. I elbowed Miki, who was standing beside me. She looked up. I nodded. It was on.

After telling Jonas what I'd done last night and how Miki and I planned to go back tonight, he let us go only if we left an open phone line on while we were there. Now that we'd heard from James, I dialed Jonas and Miki dialed Ray. When they'd each picked up, Miki and I turned the volume up all the way and slid our phones in our pockets. Audio quality had evolved recently and there was at least some chance our experience tonight would record something of interest that could be heard on the other side. Worth a try anyway.

Yes, I'm in line, I typed back to James. *And I brought that friend of mine I told you about.*

"Hey."

I sucked in wind. It was James standing to my left now.

"How's it going?" I whispered. "This is Shasta." I gestured to Miki, who stood beside me, squinting her eyes, looking wary and standoffish. Perfect.

"Hey," Miki said. "Is there anything to eat up here?"

James shook his head a bit more emphatically than necessary. "No. There's no food up here. Just work. Are you okay with that?"

"Yeah, yeah. Yes, I mean. Yes. I can work." Miki's voice cracked, then she sniffed and wiped her nose. Damn, she was good. James looked at her, then me, and did that a few times.

"Are you guys hooked up?" he asked me.

"No," I said. "I met her today on the Metro."

"I'm not sure she's right for the guard job," James said, looking off.

I stayed quiet and was careful not to argue with him. "Are there any other jobs that she could do?"

"She's too small," James explained. "Dmitriy likes mostly men for the guard jobs and tall ones like you and me."

I was tall? I never thought so. "Okay," I said. "What other jobs are there besides security guard?"

James looked back at the fortress, also checking for anyone who might be eavesdropping. No one was around us. "You and I can be guards for tonight. Dmitriy might want her to be what they call a cleaner."

"Cleaning what?" I asked, almost scared to hear the answer.

"Mostly sweeping. Some of the experiments upstairs release something into the air that falls to the ground and gets on all the surfaces. Dr. Ek needs cleaners to wipe down all the furniture and equipment and sweep and vacuum the floors. Every night."

"I could do that," Miki said, listening in.

James considered this plan for a moment before moving. What was he deliberating about? We heard the rumble of a rollup garage door opening.

"That'll be Dmitriy," James said. "Stay here, both of you. I'll talk to him."

I read a text from Jonas that came in while we were walking up. *Oleg's car's been located again, and he's being monitored now*, he wrote. This was reassuring news because we needed Ray to have access to that car for the envelope drop tomorrow morning and to install the geo tracker. Wait. A second text from Jonas sent ten minutes later read, *Tracker installed*.

Nice work, I wrote back. *Love to hear a transcript.*

I'll be listening and will let you know if he says anything noteworthy.

James was coming toward us again. Miki had vanished. Fuck, not now.

My eyes were more adjusted to the dark. A small shape jogged toward me…from the front side of the Fortress. She approached me, grabbed my hand, and gave it two quick squeezes. I wasn't familiar with that code but it felt like an *I found something* message. Maybe wishful thinking.

"BJ, you're with me," James said, "on guard duty out front in that side of the property." He pointed to where Miki had just come from. "Dr. Ek isn't available tonight but he said to say hello."

"To me?" I took a step back. So I had made the impression on him that I intended. Good.

James gleamed back with a toothy grin. "Yes." He nodded. "To you indeed. He also said he'd like to continue your facility tour tomorrow night if you're free."

I nodded. "What about Shasta?" I looked at Miki.

"Cleaner duty. She'll be on the first floor with a team of five others." James turned to Miki now. "It's rigorous work, miss. Are you up to it?"

"Yeah, I'll be fine, and I'm grateful for the work."

James leaned down to take in her eyes. "If you can keep up, it'll be five hundred dollars at the end of the shift."

Miki's eyes widened. "Yes, sir. Don't worry, I'll make you look good for bringing me on." When she smiled, one of her front teeth was black. I laughed inside.

James liked that line. I was praying he would walk away for a moment so I could uncover what Miki saw out there. My wish came true.

"I'll be right back with the NDAs," he said.

I nodded, grabbed Miki's hand and squeezed it twice like she had with me a minute ago.

"NDA?" she hissed. "What the fuck? Forgot to mention that detail."

"I'm sorry. Just sign it Shasta Bailey."

"Bailey?"

"Madison Bailey? You don't watch *Outer Banks*? Never mind. Look, you're doing great playing the part. What did you find in the front of the property?"

"Five or six men, not military and not in uniform, but all wearing the same suit, sort of guarding the place. Waiting for something."

Black suits. "Did they see you?"

"No. And all carrying guns."

Fuck. "Well I'm a guard tonight so I'll find out soon here. Your phone's still connected, right?"

She pulled it out of her pocket. "Yup. How do we contact each other?"

I thought for a second. Words wouldn't work in case they stole our phones. "Top of the hour, let's check-in. 5 means all is okay, 4 means need help."

"And 3 means we're fucked," she added.

"Hopefully it doesn't come to that. Anything other than that we can catch up with when we see each other at the end of the shift."

It was gonna be a long night.

CHAPTER 29

I always loved the cool nights in LA. No matter how hot it got in the height of the noonday sun, there was something only a night owl could appreciate about the waning of energy when the sky turned dark. I'd been mindful about my clothing selection for tonight's recon mission; that's what it was after all. Sure, it was potential employment, maybe I'd make a little money to offset the major cash output I'd just given Miki for our envelope ruse. But that's not what it was about. I chose a long-sleeved utility shirt with the sleeves pushed up high and dark jeans that were closer to new than my ratty usuals. I wanted to blend in and feel ready for anything.

We signed the one-page NDAs without issue, Miki (Shasta) went inside with James to understand her cleaning responsibilities, and I was sent out to the "front line", as James called it. My phone was still on and set to the highest possible volume so Jonas, if he was listening, could hear what was going on here. There was no way to hold the phone up and narrate into it without looking like I was a reporter or something. I'd forgotten my Air pods but all the better because that too would look like an NDA violation. I was relegated to a roaming task, circumambulating the entire property, front to back, very slowly, and several times per hour. Once again, a fortuitous fitness workout.

Couple of interesting things about this place:

1. The black suits with guns that Miki described were nowhere to be seen. Were they hiding in the surrounding woods with sniper rifles aimed at my, or someone else's, head?
2. The grass was long. Very long. Too long to be accidental, judging from the copious attention this facility got. I mean like fourteen inches high and nearly covering my calves.
3. The facility had no apparent front door.

When Dr. Anders Ek described this fortress as no ordinary mortuary, I was starting to understand what he meant; there was nothing offered to the community here. No waiting rooms with soft-toned rugs and calming music to comfort grieving families. No reception area because the only people received here were dead. I kept a running notebook in my head of all my observations and it was literally killing me that I couldn't ask Siri to take notes on my phone. Not while I was connected to a call.

I was told there were five of us in my group of guards tonight. So, why was I the only one here? I'd just finished a whole trip around the property, starting in the front, which was the east side, the south side was where we all gathered, the west side had the bay doors and the only discernible property entrance, and the north side was an empty chasm void of anything but air. Wait. And humidity. The air felt noticeably cooler here and slightly moist. With a strange smell. Musty, dank, a slightly chemical smell. Gross.

Back around to the east side, my phone buzzed again. I'd already turned the brightness down to the lowest possible setting and I couldn't see any of the other guards out on the property. So it could be safe for me to take a look. The text could be Miki sending me a number, hopefully a 5, or it could be Jonas with a report from the listening device they had on Oleg. I was about to pull my phone from my pocket but where the fuck were the black suits and the other four guards? My heart raced, making me wish I'd skipped the can of Red Bull earlier. Was it Ek's directive to spread out the guards? I needed to see a parcel map of this property. I'd gone to Google maps and Google Earth to zoom in on the shape and dimensions of the building, but not the entire lot. My oversight. I could ask Jonas to do it, but if anyone caught me talking, who knows what might result from an NDA violation in a place like this. I steadied my pulse with a text to James first.

I don't see anyone else out here, I wrote. *Is that normal?*

Yes, he wrote back immediately. *The other guards are patrolling the road or at the out-buildings and other facilities.*

Out-buildings? What other facilities? I hadn't been privy to those details. The text I got had been from Jonas, not Miki, which made me wonder what exactly Miki was cleaning in the bowels of the fortress. Taking advantage of the long grass, I crouched low to read Jonas' text. The screen was too dark, I could barely make it out. I squinted instead of risking detection and raising the brightness. I gave my eyes a minute to relax and focus.

From Jonas: *One of Oleg's men said they found another Dr. Ek in Germany and they're arranging a meeting.*

I had no idea what this meant. Another Ek? Another Dr. Anders Ek, what, doing the same kind of research? Cremation R&D? Or were we talking cloning?

James had told me only to walk in one direction around the yard. Something about that felt contrary to common sense. How, then, would I be able to detect anything out of the ordinary? First I needed to determine what was ordinary for this place. My gut guided me to the north part of the property again. Interesting that none of the other sides had that same smell. From the East side, I kept my eyes forward but stepped back a few paces at a time till I got to the edge of the North expanse. The property was walled on that side by woods. The grass felt different underfoot here too, spongey almost. Heading directly north from the east side now, with still no one else in sight, I slowed my pace and dug my boot heel into the ground to see if I could determine what was under the thick grass. The brush was not only tall but vibrant green, I could see from the dim iPhone light, and the blades were thick. This looked like either artificial growth or else I'd been transported into a cow patch in Kentucky. But what my nose detected in this part of the yard was not farm manure.

It smelled, among other things, like ammonia. And smoke. And something else I couldn't put my finger on. Something was being dumped in this part of the property. That was at least one of the things that the guards like me and like James were monitoring: onlookers, photographers, law enforcement for illegal dumping.

I texted a 5 to Miki, followed by a question mark. Then I texted one word to Jonas, *dumping*.

K will look into it. See anything or anyone? Jonas texted back.

Still nothing. Like I'm the only one working here tonight. There are other buildings on the property, going to investigate those now.

How's Shasta? he wrote with a laughing emoji.

Haven't heard back yet, will let you know, I typed, and looked down at the phone to make sure the call was still connected. It was. Even so, I'd never felt so alone in my life. I sent another 5 to Miki with a *please reply*. Still nothing.

Jonas was typing something back to me, but my heart was in my throat waiting for Miki's 5. *Something else interesting from Oleg.*

Go ahead, I wrote.

What about the sword? Oleg asked that to the same guy who told him about the other Dr. Ek. The guy didn't reply.

Dr. Ek has a mini sword on his keyring, I texted back. *I saw it last night. Has to be related in some way. Assuming Dmitriy is one of Oleg's men, looks like Dr. Ek has a deep entanglement with Oleg Kokov.*

What are you thinking? Jonas asked.

I think the contents of the Ziploc bag is some kind of ash, or else a mix of materials from cremains.

What the fuck is he burning up there? Jonas asked.

I don't know. How's Lacy?

She's fine. Why?

Check on her for me. Just do it.

Roger that.

CHAPTER 30

I couldn't decide whether Miki or the other buildings on the property were a higher priority. There was nothing I could do for Miki at the moment and, in the absence of a texted 3, my logical mind had to assume she was fine and performing the job satisfactorily. I remembered I had one of those small Ziploc bags in my jeans pocket, from the table where Ray, Miki and I had been working when assembling the decoy envelope. I hovered low in the grass, pulled up a clump of grass, grabbed a handful of the mud below it, and stuffed a sample of it in the bag for further analysis. Now my hands were muddy, so I used the thick blades as a towel and wiped off the rest of the mud on my pants.

I heard a branch crack across the street. That must be where the additional buildings were located. So this operation had four floors of what looked like a 5000 square foot building and more buildings hidden out in the woods. What was Dr. Anders Ek hiding out here? Or maybe the answer was…who.

I stayed low in the tall grass peering across the street, listening for any new sounds. I tried Miki again, sending only the number 5, then a question mark as a separate text. Obviously she wasn't in a place where she could pull out her phone without being detected. Miki Fine was wily. She'd lived on the street for years, at least a decade, in and out of shady places with shady people, arm in arm with our old friend Archie Dax. What I would give to have either Archie by my side right now or, at the very least, Betty.

For a full five minutes, I remained still and stared out across the street at the dark expanse and saw no movement. No breeze, no crickets, no more branches crackling. This wasn't the right time, or the right night to be venturing off. I proceeded at my previous pace through the onion patch of toxic chemicals on the north side and stepped down the slight decline to the more open west side, with mostly dry dirt dotted only with occasional clumps of dead weeds. One of the two garage doors was open, I could see when I walked past on my regular patrol. I kept walking but made note of three men in white lab coats pushing a metal cart with three huge keg-sized reservoirs. I heard something sloshing around in there from a distance of about thirty feet. Concentrating on keeping the cartwheels smooth, they didn't see me. I kept going. No one in the yard on the west side, same with the east side; still no black-suited men, no one with guns, so I proceeded again to the north side. Same odd smell, spongy grass. On the west side again, there was no sign of the men or the cart now. I had to get in that building and up to the second floor again. A light flickered in the space behind the open garage door. As my father would say, it seemed like a sign.

I followed the flickering light, imagining it was some entity summoning me, maybe my genie again, reassuring me that answers to all my questions were stored somewhere in this fortress. And, for that matter, I should still have two wishes left. Last night, Dr. Ek and I had taken an elevator to the left of the open doors. Tonight I took another smaller lift on the other side. The doors closed and I pressed Level 3. If I wanted to investigate the second floor, starting at Level 3 seemed logical enough, and somehow I'd find my way down to 2. The doors opened onto a very different vibe than the second floor. Gleaming white floors and walls again, but the temperature up here felt about twenty-five degrees colder. Rows of white powder-coated shelving units lined both sides of the main room. I didn't walk through. Instead, I turned left into a different room with formed boxes on a long conveyor belt. A third room to the right of the main warehouse space had another conveyor belt with coffin-sized cardboard boxes in a single long row. When he'd said storage, what he really meant was cold storage.

My conscience nagged me. I knew I shouldn't be up here. But a more pervasive thought took root in my mind. Why was there no keypad in the elevator allowing anyone to just walk in off the street and enter the building? It didn't make sense. I checked my watch again: 3:15 a.m. Our shifts would end at six, according to James. On the far wall was a large blue arrow pointing left with the words Cryonics Lab over it. My heart thudded but I'd come this far. I need to know, I kept telling myself. I followed the length of the main warehouse all the way down, counting my steps. One hundred forty-five steps later, I was directly under the blue arrow. To my left was a door with a keypad, finally, leading to another large space, darkened inside except for a tiny blue light. I looked overhead and didn't see any cameras, so I returned my gaze to the keypad. It wasn't worth randomly trying access codes. But I did continue down the other row now, this time seeing an array of large, steel containers about eight feet tall and maybe four feet wide, with thermometers on the front and separate keypads. Oh my God, Anders. What are you doing up here? I tried to put the story together in my mind while fumbling my way back to the elevators. Dr. Ek was using society's expendables on which to conduct experiments—what kind I still wasn't sure—storing them in these steel containers and regulating their temperatures until he was ready for them on the second floor.

Jesus Christ, I think he's burning people alive.

I took a quick photo of the steel containers and one of the Cryonics Lab arrows on the wall and texted them to Jonas. *I may need backup here soon*, I typed.

On my way, he wrote back. I didn't think Jonas was healed up from his assault. I also knew nothing could keep him from a rescue operation, especially for me.

I had to assume that I was being watched. But there was more work to do here. I wiped my sweating palms on my pants, slipped into the elevator, and returned to Level 1. It opened into an empty cavern and, for a moment, I didn't know where I was. Wait, okay. I was on the other side of the building. Halfway down the first empty hallway outside of the elevator foyer was a staircase. I opened the door and closed it quietly behind me, leaning against the door just listening. Why wasn't there anybody here tonight? Last night on my guided facility tour with Dr. Ek, there'd been workers walking around everywhere like it was normal business hours. Tonight, no one either inside or out. I started up the stairs to Level 2 when I felt the buzz of my phone again. Please let it be Miki. I stopped and sat on a stair, surprised there was even signal inside a stairwell. Add it to the list of anomalies. Not Miki, it was from a number I didn't recognize.

Mr. Janoff, I know where you are and I'm the only one who can get you out of there alive.

I had a feeling it was neither Dr. Ek nor James. A stranger?

Where's Miki? I wrote back, realizing too late that I should've written Shasta.

She's here with us already. Get yourself down to the loading dock. How long will it take you?

Miki? Who took her?? Get your brain in gear, Brock. *Fifteen seconds*, I wrote back, *if no one stops me.*

No one will stop you. Go.

Why wasn't anyone stopping me? Why wasn't anyone here tonight? A feeling of dread washed over my whole body. Why did I somehow think they were all dead? I had to get to that loading dock. Now.

Go now. Do it.

Okay, I texted back. I breathed in and trusted this invisible stranger while opening the door to the hallway. I walked, not ran, down the white hallway to the open garage doors. They said no one would stop me. I stood in the open doorway, half feeling like someone was aiming a sniper gun at my head. On the ground below, a youngish, dark-skinned man motioned for me to follow.

CHAPTER 31

"Stay behind me three feet, no running," the man said. Strange accent, same as Dr. Ek's. Breath smelled like coffee. I nodded.

"Where's—"

The man whipped around and put a finger over his lips, pointing to the road ahead on the east side of the property. That was where I'd heard a cracked branch earlier tonight. Fine, stranger. I'll follow you; hopefully it's not to my fucking death. Even in the darkness I could see the man's brown pants and narrow gait in front of me, but so far nothing else. Wait. As we came around a slight curve, the outline of a parked van darkened the shoulder. Still three feet behind, I saw the man climb into the van. He offered his hand to help me climb in, and he pulled me into one of the backseats. I expected a heavy blow to the back of my head, or a pistol pointed at my temple. Instead, the man guided me in the dark to a soft bench seat and a woman, it looked like, pulled the van door but not all the way. The vehicle rolled silently down the road in neutral, taking advantage of the hill with no motor running. The man beside me whispered. "No talking yet. We'll tell you when."

"Is Miki okay?" I whispered back.

"She's fine."

"My brother's on his way here," I whispered.

"Stop talking. Not telling you again."

The van continued rolling down the hill on an unmarked dirt road about 10 mph. I didn't dare move but was dying to know how many people were crammed in this vehicle. Two up front, at least one behind me, and I could see Miki's legs behind the front passenger. Almost to the bottom, the driver started the engine and veered right toward Commonwealth Canyon Drive to North Vermont. I knew where they were going: down to Los Feliz, which spilled into Franklin Hills and the Hyperion exit onto Highway 5. Seemed like a roundabout way to get back downtown but they could take Highway 2 past Silver Lake and pick up 101. Then again, I was making the assumption that we were heading to downtown LA.

"Can I talk now?" I whispered to the man beside me.

He shook his head. I paid attention to road signs. Now we were on 405 headed toward Torrance, then onto highway 1 toward Wayfarer's Chapel. Ah, okay. My chest relaxed a tiny bit. I think we were going to Rancho Palos Verdes. There were a bunch of remote resorts in that area. I managed to stay quiet enough and caught a glimpse of Miki's face under a streetlight. I didn't like the dark vibe in her eyes. What had she seen in that fortress tonight?

Terranea Resort. Wow. I'd read about this place with its sweeping, panoramic ocean views, and $1000/night rooms. Why were we here? Because it was a brilliant cover. Any of Oleg's goons who showed up here would stick out like a sore thumb. The man beside me leaned close to my ear.

"We're gonna open the van door and all of us walk toward the open door of a house thirty feet ahead like little ducklings. Understand? No talking, yelling, asking questions, turning around, going back in the van. Just climb out and follow the person in front of you. Miki goes in front of you. Got it?"

I gave a clear single nod with my chin. Compliance, in this case, was likely to keep me alive. Both of us. For now.

CHAPTER 32

The temperature down in the valley was warmer, but I liked being closer to the water. Water had always comforted me. Not today though. My life no longer felt like my own. I needed to see Lacy, or at least hear confirmation that she was okay. There were still a couple more hours before Oleg's envelope was due at the hotel lobby. That meant I could keep telling myself stories of her safety and that Oleg's men weren't likely to harm her before getting their pound of flesh. Even still, it's funny how the heart speaks to you. The language it uses is not made up of words, or even conscious thoughts. More like a knowing that arrives in your soul, visible suddenly, and another knowing that whatever it is has been inside you all along. Stumbling out of the van and falling in the line of baby chicks to another unfamiliar location, I realized I'm in love with her. Maybe I have been all along, since childhood. I breathed in the night air and let the shock of this truth shatter my insides. It's okay, everything else felt already shattered at this point.

Miki in front of me, I followed her inside and was instructed to follow the man from the fortress through the house to the kitchen. Kitchen, okay. Another building, another room. How did I get here and what was this all about? I felt wobbly on my feet. My head swam like I'd had too much wine on a hot day, and my stomach burbled like when I forget the rule and drink beer before liquor. I didn't pay much attention to our captors, though I counted six of them, because I intrinsically believed that they had somehow rescued Miki and me from a dreadful, maybe cryogenic fate. They seated all of us at a large, oval-shaped table in a bright white kitchen the size of a basketball court. Someone had already placed a large tray with crystal goblets and a pitcher of water in the center. Normally I would have chosen the power seat with my back to the wall.

Tonight I took the one closest to the door to maximize my potential for escape, Miki beside me to my right. She poured water for both of us. When I took the glass from her, I turned to appraise her. She looked in no worse condition than earlier, but her eyes, once again, scared me. I don't know why, and there was no opportunity right now for us to talk. Just drink water at a strange table in a hollow house and wait for instructions.

The one woman in the bunch took the power seat—a tall, slim woman with reddish hair pinned back, just shy of forty, with what looked like an expert makeup job that was now two days old. The others, men of varying shapes, races, and sizes, filed in and sat between us. A heavy, older man in an expensive suit, a younger man in an ill-fitting jacket, and four other men—all young—in more casual clothes. It was the kind of group no one in their right mind would ever put together. Some had accents, including the man from the fortress.

Now that we were all here, the redhead started. She too had a strange accent. Not quite European. Scandinavian? It reminded me of Dr. Ek's accent. "You must have a lot of questions," she said, looking at Miki and me.

I nodded and glanced peripherally at Miki, who'd raised her brows with a WTF expression.

"They rescued us," I said to her, not caring whether our captors confirmed this theory or not.

"Very perceptive, Mr. Janoff," the woman said.

"And that's not even your best quality," Fortress-man added with a scant smile.

"I don't suppose I should even ask who you people are?"

"Correct," the woman said. "You can call me 'Excuse me' and everyone else here as well. If you need anything at all, get our attention and we'll do our best to accommodate you. You're in one of the premier resorts in North America right now."

"I'd just like to know why."

"Can I swim in the ocean? Miki asked.

"Sorry," the guy said.

"Pool?" Miki again.

Now the woman shook her head.

"Go for a walk?" Miki kept pushing.

"We can't leave. Am I right?" I asked.

"For the moment, yes. A few days, I suspect," the woman answered, sipping from her water glass.

"We're prisoners here," Miki said, "so you can protect us from —"

"No," I stopped her. "Yes they rescued us from whatever was happening at the facility tonight, but we're prisoners here because they need to know what we know." I looked at the woman, and the dark-skinned man to verify. But no answer came. Miki tapped her fingernail on the water glass. So I kept talking. "My brother, Jonas Janoff, I'm sure you know who he is, has been listening in on Oleg's conversation tonight through a tap on his car. One of his men said something about 'another one', another Dr. Ek tonight. What does that mean?"

I took a turn at the water glass and drained half of it at once. While I gulped, I watched a silent negotiation occur between the woman and the rest of the group, going person to person, looking for consensus to divulge whatever it was that brought us here tonight. Finally the fat old man in the nice suit, obviously the patriarch, nodded at the woman.

"Ridders," she said quietly.

"What's that?" I asked.

"Dr. Anders Ek is," she cleared her throat, "what we call a Ridder."

"What does that mean?"

"Um…" The woman shifted, came forward with her arms on the table to get closer to us, more intimate in her approach, then sat back and crossed her arms while she wrestled with her truth.

"There are more of them? Ridders?"

"Ma-ny more," the old man spoke finally. He had a thicker

accent. "Sixteen so far, and all over the globe."

I was careful in the planning of my next question, careful in my thinking, in my analysis and especially in my execution. "What do they care about, these ridders?" I asked, addressing my question to the old man two seats away.

"The future." The old man hunched forward. "They see a better way to conserve our natural resources, a more sustainable way of dealing with the dead."

"Isn't cremation already sustainable?" I asked, realizing I knew nothing about it. "It's an alternative to burial, right?"

"An alternative that requires heating to twenty-five-hundred degrees and the full cremation process takes eighteen hours."

Okay, well that was something I didn't know about it. "While I was patrolling the grounds tonight, I noticed the ground was wet and I smelled chemicals on the north side of the property."

"What do you conclude from that observation, Mr. Janoff?" he asked.

"Illegal dumping. I suspect that's what the guards are doing every night, patrolling to protect against being detected by onlookers or law enforcement. Am I right?"

"Yes," the man said. "I think you had an opportunity for other discoveries tonight, did you not?"

Jesus. So I was being watched when I went upstairs to the 2nd and 3rd floors; just not by Dr. Ek. I didn't respond.

"And how about you, Ms. Fine?" the old man asked her before I could answer.

"Shasta," one of the other men whispered and chuckled.

The old man snapped back a command that sounded something like *var tist.*

"I wasn't given any gloves," Miki said. "I was rubbing this oatmeal-colored, gritty powder off of everything in the room. It was still in the air, I could see it. It's probably in my hair. My eyes are burning and my skin feels tingly."

"Andrew," the old man barked. "Take care of the girl. For Christ's sake, what about normal precautions? Dmitriy should be handling these details."

"I'll deal with Dmitriy," the woman said.

One of the casually dressed men, late thirties with a sad, round face, rose and gestured for Miki to follow him. "Come with me, please."

I heard her voice, then the man's voice vanishing down a long hallway, then the sound of water. *Lacy, are you okay?* I asked her telepathically. *Where are you??*

"How about I tell you what I think is going on here, and you guys can either confirm or deny my theory. Okay?" I breathed and waited.

"Proceed," the old man said, obviously well accustomed to these types of conversations.

"I think Dr. Anders Ek is using some kind of controversial method for cremating bodies, dumping toxic chemicals onto the grounds of his facility, and using homeless workers to experiment on for his R&D research."

No one moved. I heard a fly somewhere in the kitchen buzzing from surface to surface to find a way out. I wished I could shapeshift.

"If you're right, Mr. Janoff, why do you think he's doing this?"

"I assume that's why we're all here," I said.

CHAPTER 33

When Miki came back to the table with the drone named Andrew, her eyes were even redder.

"Feeling any better?"

"I'll be alright," she said, but I could tell she was annoyed and wouldn't tolerate captivity easily.

"Ridders," said the old man. "I will explain this to you, Mr. Janoff, and to you, Ms. Fine, since you brave souls somehow found your way onto this perilous path. Ridders—" he looked at me when he spoke— "are environmentalists. Not just environmentalists but rabid in their approach, radical in their ideologies, and willing to sacrifice anything, life and limb, including their own in a few cases, to promulgate their cause."

"Which is what?" I asked. "Saving the earth? From what? They're polluting the earth with toxic chemicals."

"Not saving the earth from chemicals, Mr. Janoff. From people."

I considered this and considered the word they'd said. Ridders. "You mean population control."

The old man smirked and nodded. OMG. "Decreasing the world population by finding more sustainable ways to dispose of bodies?"

"In part, yes," the man said.

"I was reading about a process called alkaline hydrolysis that uses chemicals and large quantities of water to break down human remains. How is that conservation, if they're improperly disposing of harmful chemicals and wasting huge quantities of a limited natural resource to do it?"

"All excellent questions, Mr. Janoff, but you lack the perspective of the bigger picture."

"That's where we may be able to help," the woman added.

"So the Ridders are helping combat over-population by creating new methods of disposing of the dead that take up less space on the planet?" I asked.

"Yes," the old man moaned, "but not by alkaline hydrolysis." He looked at the red-haired woman and at the faces around the table. Then back to me. "Show me your envelope, Mr. Janoff."

"The real one," the woman clarified.

I was too tired for any more games. I rose and pulled the Ziploc bag from one of the lower pockets in my pants and set it on the table, then pushed it to the center.

"Do you know what that is?" Old man asked.

"No," I said, not having had time yet to bring it to be analyzed. "I think it's some kind of ash from Ek's experiments."

No one said anything. Another truth arrived in my head at that moment, a truth so unthinkable it burned. My head felt hot as I struggled the words out.

"Is Dr. Ek burning people alive? Is that what he's doing up there every night in that fortress?"

It felt like all the air was sucked out of the room.

"It's not a cremation facility at all, is it? He's taking unsuspecting people, holding them under false pretenses, and cryogenically freezing them before he subjects them to his experiments."

"Mr. Janoff, you—"

"No!" I banged my fist on the table. "Am I wrong? Is he getting permission from those people first? Who would ever give their permission for that?"

No answer.

"And just one more question: are they dead by conventional definitions before they're subjected to these experiments? Before they're frozen?"

All eyes stared back, wide and searching.

"So how is that any different from Josef Mengele during World War II? You people know about these human rights violations, practices that go against our most sacred ethical standards."

"We know about them, yes," the woman said. "Even some worse than that."

"All sixteen of these men, or women, these Ridders. Do they all have the same agenda?"

The woman nodded, staring at the old man. She drank two long gulps of water, then continued. "The process is called promession. You were right about cryonics. The bodies are first frozen, then they're subjected to a certain vibration that disintegrates the body into small parts, and those remains are cremated to produce what's in your magic envelope there.

"I'm just guessing here," Miki cut in, "but I suspect the remains after being subjected to cryogenics and high heat are no longer forensically identifiable at the end of the process."

"Very good, Ms. Fine," the old man smiled. "You've hit what we call the golden nugget, yes?"

"Ah," I nodded. "Hence the presence of the Russian mafia wanting to take advantage of a global team of crime scene cleanup men. Yes? So Oleg's making a killing financially, so to speak, and now he's just located another cash cow from whom he can make even more money in other parts of the world."

"Correct," the old man said. "Your father knows about it," he added.

"My father? Wait. How do you know my father?" I shot Miki a look. Maybe I hadn't heard him correctly.

"He's part of a group of European industrialists from which the Ridders originated, but now they've become too radicalized. The original group is distancing itself from them, working against them to shut them down for fear that they'll bring too much exposure and potentially threaten their many other global operations."

"Wait. No. My father's involved in—what exactly? Are you saying he's one of—"

"No. Your father, as you know, is a financial director, a CPA, for the US Department of State. As such, he's involved in many global operations as an oversight body, projects run by the United Nations and different committees and task forces. This group originated in the 1950s, with members from different countries promoting the idea of cooperative foreign relationships to prevent another world war."

"Ah," Miki said and smiled.

"What?"

"Bilderberg."

Again, all eyes widened around the table. "You've very informed, Ms. Fine. Both of you, for your young ages."

"Jesus." Miki sat back. "Your father's a member of the Bilderberg Group? Did you know?"

I hadn't heard that name since high school. "No," I said quietly, shaking my head, trying to fit all of these new pieces into a formation I could somehow understand. It wasn't working. "Why wasn't anyone at the facility tonight? I was there last night for a facility tour from Dr. Ek and there were workers on all three floors."

Miki glared at me with her red, watery eyes. "Based on the amount of ash up there tonight," she said, "I suspect they're all dead."

"And their bodies were...what...disposed of before I got there? Jesus!" I felt my eyes water, not from chemicals but from shock. What kind of Bourne movie had I stumbled into?

"No, Mr. Janoff. The facility workers were transported off-site to a holding location. I can assure you, they're not dead," the old man said.

"And Dr. Ek?"

"Escaped, I'm afraid," the woman said. "We, this group, try to stay one or two steps ahead of them, assigned as the sort of shadow group that watches the activities of The Ridders and reports back to the committee. But we can't predict everything, as you can see."

"Where will he go?" I asked.

"Dr. Ek will find the others and recalibrate their agenda to take up in a less conspicuous location, I imagine."

My pulse throbbed hard. "And my father knows about this?"

"He tried to stop it," the old man said in a more compassionate tone. "When he discovered what was going on, he threatened to expose it. So the primary group—"

"Bilderberg?" Miki asked.

"Yes, a specific committee," Old Man said. "The Steering Committee, which holds all the power, had only two choices: kill him, or apply pressure to coerce him into joining the cause or promising discretion for the higher good."

I nodded. Finally, I was hearing the answer to what I'd been asking all along. Why me. "I'm the wild card, then. I was brought in to get me so deeply involved that my father could no longer fight against the agenda without endangering—"

"Those he loves most," the old man finished my sentence and nodded. "Yes. Your father forced our hand, Mr. Janoff. Normally such measures would never be taken. But global discretion is a tricky and an ugly business."

"So why not just kidnap him? That would certainly get him out of the way, at least temporarily."

The dark eyes kept watching me, and his lips didn't move. Did that mean they'd already tried and he escaped?

"Who are the men in the black suits that I saw in the hotel? Do they work with Oleg?"

"Your father hired them to force Oleg's men to leave you out of the equation. He didn't want you involved and they tried to intervene before you were ever given the money, but things didn't turn out as planned. Your father promised to give The Committee whatever it wanted in exchange for your life and your safety, even offering his own in return. Perhaps you mean more to him, Mr. Janoff, than you thought you did."

"But why me and not my brother?"

"No reason, other than the fact that Oleg, for his own twisted reasons, chose you."

Wow. Did I really mean that much to my father? So that was the *why me* answer? To force my father to choose between what he believes in and my life. "What's the significance of the sword?" I asked, remembering the sword on Ek's keyring and refusing to get too emotionally tied to the story these strangers had just told me, prompting me to change the opinion of the man I called my father. Maybe what they said was true. Maybe it wasn't.

"It's their insignia," he said. "Each of the team of sixteen Ridders, or Promession Engineers—really they're biologists— learned the process from one teacher in northern Europe and they formed their environmental preservation agenda around this symbol."

"Is there an actual sword somewhere? A physical artifact?"

"Part of the Bilderberg Art Collection, a very exclusive collection of art from many different cultures. The sword in question is an 18th century Boateng Saber and it's one of the most expensive swords that's ever been sold."

"Who has possession of it now?" I asked.

Wide eyes again, another silent negotiation, deciding what to tell me and what to hold back. If we were playing chess, I would be winning so far.

"Dr. Ek stole the sword from the Bilderberg Collection as a sort of call to arms to formalize the radical agenda and announce themselves as terrorists—the sixteen scientists who would take on this fight, determined to make a controversial, fringe science a commonplace practice for a sustainable and environmentally-friendly method for processing the dead."

"Or the living, if they got in their way," I said, under my breath. "Oleg asked one of his men about the sword tonight."

"Oleg cares about money and only money," the old man said. "And if he can find who has that sword, it will bring a bright shine to his cold black heart. But he will never find it."

"Why not?"

"Because he's a thug with a purely tactical brain. He thinks only one step ahead. Dr. Anders Ek is a medical genius, a brilliant strategist, with the added benefit of patience and discipline from his military training. He's formidable in every way."

We took a break to stretch our legs, worn down by the gravity of our conversation. I showed the three pictures that Oleg sent me to the red-haired woman and my first order of business was to protect Lacy.

"She's protected," the woman said. Somehow I believed her.

CHAPTER 34

I laid down around 4:30 a.m. in the biggest bed I'd ever seen. Our hosts offered Miki her own room, but she wanted to be near me. So we lay there together, half-holding each other, minds buzzing with mental overload and emotional hypoxia. Back when we were working together, I was too young to be taken seriously by a woman like her. Even now, I think she still thought of me as more of Jonas' little brother than a grown man. Could the same be true for Lacy? I hoped not. My dreaming mind went to a scene from our childhood, where Lacy and I prepared breakfast for my mother when she was sick, while Jonas was the lookout man to ensure the impact of our surprise. She was still that same sparkly spitfire of a girl, just taller now. In my dream, I sent her a text that said *I dream about you.* Thank God it was only a dream.

Our captors hadn't asked for the envelope back, so I took it from the table and returned it to its safe spot in the cargo pocket of my pants. It almost seemed superfluous now, since we'd established the contents, and all but confirmed that Oleg only wanted it to sell as a sample to the highest bidder. I still didn't understand why those contents were such a commodity. Pretty soon it would be time to contact him with a directive to check the contents of his trunk for the envelope, albeit fake, which I hoped and prayed would actually be there.

When I got up to walk around the luxuriant space, I determined that four of the men at the table were plain-clothed security guards. Pit bulls with guns. The man who retrieved me from the fortress tonight was a decision-maker, probably equal in power to the red-haired woman. He and the woman were huddled in club chairs in an intimate corner of one of the three living rooms, not whispering but talking in low tones while the old man sat alone on the sunporch smoking a cigar vented by a side window. I could see all three of them, plus two of the four guards from my sneaky perch in the hallway.

None of them could see me.

In theory anyway, I could probably slip out the front door undetected, though Pit Bulls 3 and 4 were probably guarding the yard out front. Fact is, I wanted to be here. Though their allegiances weren't yet clear to me, they hadn't hurt us, they fed us and, in thirty minutes, they'd answered the thousand questions flooding my head over the past two weeks. I continued watching the two scenes: a smoking old man enjoying his solitude and the coffee klatsch in the living room, while I decided who to pitch my request to. I heard the woman call the man Minesh, likely an East Indian or Pakistani name, and he'd called her Ina, which could be a nickname.

First, I checked on Miki and brought a glass of water to her bedside table. Her phone buzzed when I walked into the room she'd taken. I decided not to look at it. I was a little surprised she'd been so quiet at the table tonight, only coming out with one or two insightful zingers. Having essentially been Archie Dax's partner for three years, I suspected a lot more was going on behind those sophisticated, survivalist eyes. What had she learned from him? I might wonder about that for a long time.

I decided on the coffee klatsch. I used the intel I'd already picked up while here to inform the style of my approach. I entered their space in bare feet, walking slowly with my hands clasped behind my back. Like a butler.

"Minesh, Ina. Do you have a minute?" I retreated one step and lowered my gaze. Like lions on the African plain. I was subservient, I was not a threat. But yes, now I knew their names and I was not stupid.

"Of course," Ina said, facing me and motioning me toward a grand, yellow sofa. Yellow, really? This was what billionaires wanted to sit on? Okay.

"Do you need something?" Minesh spoke this time.

"Yes." I could tell I annoyed him. Something about my face or my way, my rebellion, my upbringing, I couldn't place it yet.

"Please, speak freely," Ina said, inviting me to do that with her words but with her eyes she begged me not to be difficult, not to challenge her authority and force one of them to kill me. Who would decide my fate? Her?

"I need to find my father."

"Of course you do," Minesh replied. "It's natural to want to make contact after learning what you did about him tonight. You must be very upset."

This man, Minesh, seemed thoughtful, but I knew he didn't give a rat's ass about me or my interests, only his own. I trusted Ina even less. That said, they were both practiced negotiators and diplomats with likely five or six university degrees between them.

"My brother and I haven't had contact with him since our mother died. I could, like, call him. Ask to meet him for dinner or something."

They stared back with feigned compassion.

"Where's my father?" I blurted.

"He's missing," Ina said.

"Gone rogue might be a more appropriate characterization," Minesh added.

"But you make a good point," Ina said, thinking. "Maybe if you reach out to him, one of his beloved sons just wanting to reconnect with him after the tragedy of your family loss. That could work."

"He'd never reach him now," Minesh said to her. "He's been off the grid now for months."

"He would if he contacts him via a secure channel."

"Through us, you mean?" Minesh asked her.

She gave a single nod and checked my expression.

"Then he'd know that Brock was under our—"

"Supervision?" she said. "Yes, he would, and that might feel safe enough for him to answer."

"I don't get it," I said. "If he's running from you and he knows

I'm here, why would he respond?"

"People are complicated." Minesh shrugged. "He tried to come in a while ago, to be sort of re-resourced, as we call it."

"Meaning what?"

"Re-resourced means re-assigned to another committee or task force," Ina said. "Your father's an accountant, so that gives him sort of carte blanche oversight into the activities and finances of all of the Bilderberg committees. Everything."

"And he didn't want that?"

Minesh and Ina looked at each other, then searched the carpet for the right words.

"How could he have been involved with this? Miki told me Bilderberg's this sort of global organized crime ring trying to set up a single world government, single world currency, with only room for billionaires and paupers and no middle class. Is that true?"

"Your father got pulled in as a State Department employee," Minesh said, "because one of the committee accountants died and they needed a replacement as part of their rules. There are many people from the CIA and Department of State as members. Not everyone, of course, but it's easier to get in working for one of those agencies."

"So he never chose membership? He was forced?" I was asking Minesh, and Ina was deciding.

"Forced might be a bit harsh, but essentially yes," she said.

"When did he go off-grid?"

"After the—" Minesh started to say until Ina's hand went up. She moved her head very slightly left and right as if to say *no, he's not cleared for this intel.*

"What? A head of state assassination? A phony world war? What are we talking about here? Does he know too much and now he's in danger? Is that it?" I knew I needed to calm my nerves. It was just all too incredible.

"Lower your voice," Minesh warned.

"Brock," Ina said in her deep, feather voice. "Let's take it down a notch, okay? Why don't we return to your original question? We want to help you with that. I want to help you. Alright?"

That voice could calm Attila the Hun. I notched myself down and fell into the layered cushion of the absurd yellow sofa. Okay. A secure channel. "Yes, I'd like to contact him and I'd like it even more if he responded. I need to know if he's okay. I need to know what in God's name he's thinking."

And I suspected Ina needed to clear this new initiative with Old Man before anything was put into action.

CHAPTER 35

A thin, older woman I hadn't seen before knocked as she entered the bedroom. She set a hotel-style tray on top of a low dresser and left without a word, no eye contact, and I assumed did the same for Miki because I heard a knock at her door down the hall. The meal looked delicious. I picked at a few bites here and there, some kind of overly rich chicken and penne thing. Minesh came in at one point and advised us not to reach out to anyone while we were here because our location could be compromised. It was a preposterous excuse and I wasn't buying it. I was certain the walls in this unit had been reinforced with additional layers of firewall protection for their high-speed internet.

What are you wearing? I wrote to Lacy and snickered. It was a running joke going back to Mrs. Manning's eighth-grade class when one of the hoodlum Bower boys developed a crush on her and called her at night asking what she was wearing. Ever since, I'd text her during tense moments and ask her, always followed by her sending a laughing emoji. No response came to my text, and it was an interesting predicament because I couldn't ask our captors about Lacy without revealing that I'd breached Minesh's directive. I cared less about Minesh and more about why Lacy wasn't returning our standard texts back and forth.

Four quiet knocks on the door and Ina poked her tired face into view. "We're ready if you'd like to join us in the other room."

"Where's Lacy?" I couldn't help but blurt it out like that. Sure, I understood the bigger picture here, but my nerves were shot and every time I saw one of them I felt flooded with bitterness. I just wanted my life back.

"Wait here," she said and closed the door.

I positioned my ear right up to the hinge.

"He's contacted the girl," I heard her say, probably to Minesh because the sound came from the east side of the house where the two of them had been talking. Minesh mumbled something inaudible from here. I stood back six feet from the door even though she must know I'd be listening. It opened a few inches. "Come with me," she said.

She had that gloomy *I'm disappointed in you* look which, as a post-grad barely-adult, I'd grown accustomed to. She motioned me toward the yellow sofa again. Okay, maybe it was gold.

"Let's talk about Lacy," Minesh said.

"Look, I don't care that you asked Miki and me not to reach out to anyone. Yes, I breached that protocol and I texted Lacy. She didn't write back." There was a bite to my words now, no more playing around. "If she's safe like you say, why didn't she write back?"

"Mr. Janoff, I understood you were looking to contact your father. Did you still—"

"You," I said, "both of you, all of you have as much to gain from that communication as I do. You don't know where he is either, and you need to find him. I'll send the message to my father on a secure channel when someone tells me where Lacy is."

Ina sighed, raised her brows to show how explicitly put out she was by my demands, and pulled a phone from her pocket, pressed one button, and waited. "Where's the girl?" she said into the phone, then nodded.

"Sleeping," she said to me. "Do you require an affidavit? Photographs of her perhaps?"

"Why would she be sleeping? What time is it now?"

"5:45 a.m."

So of course she was sleeping. I texted her again. *Sorry to wake you. Are you okay?*

I should be asking you that question, she wrote back. *I'm fine,*

just doing what most people are doing this early. What's up?
Nothing, just busy doing research. I'll talk to you later.
Kk ttyl she typed with a heart emoji.
"Is that satisfactory proof of her well-being?" Ina asked.
"Thank you, yes."
"Alright then. We're sending your father an email that will have your name on it in the subject line only and sending on a secure channel through a cipher."
"What kind of cipher?"
"Like a version of Ciphermail but for government agencies."
"Gotcha." I knew that Ciphermail was an email encryption Android app that could S/MIME encrypt messages and then decrypt attachments.
Ina's face revealed that she knew she shouldn't have said that.
"So is there some kind of code name or secret message I should include or just write something natural?"
Ina had her fingers on the keyboard, opening whatever secure sandbox her server had set up for encrypted email. "You're not writing," she said. "It's an audio message. Is that a problem?" she asked to my confused look.
"Am I gonna like read a script or something?"
"Just think of it as leaving a casual voicemail."
"To your parent who you haven't talked to since your other parent died? Nothing casual about that, sorry." I said it to inspire guilt, but Ina kept clicking her keyboard, Minesh looking on beside her. I also no longer smelled cigar smoke in the house, so I suspected the old man and his pit bulls had left us here with our two chaperones.
It took two tries, and they told me not to mention anything about where I was or any of what had been happening. Just that I wanted to see him.
"Hey, Dad. Um, it's BJ. It's been too long, and I'd like to see you or talk or something. Hope you're doing okay. I've got a different phone number now."
Apparently, when he heard the prefix of the new number I was using, he'd know where I was and what was happening. Holy shit, this was hard, lying to my father to bring him in and risk both our lives.

"Good," Ina said. "Now we wait."

"How long?" I asked.

She looked at Minesh for the answer.

"Give it a day or two," he said. "If there's no response, plan B is to assign an asset to one of the Bilderberg committees to ask around about the sword, posing as someone from the insurance company that insures it."

"Oh, right. Like that hasn't been done already?"

Ina allowed a crinkle of a smile. "Do we have anyone at Sotheby's?" she whispered.

Wow, these people. They were asking whether they had any intelligence agents posing as Sotheby's brokers.

Minesh nodded. "One. Someone at Sotheby's International. Head of Strategic Relationships and Venture Capital."

"Wait, no. I want to be the one to go in. He's my father."

"Meaning no disrespect," Minesh said, "you have no experience at this."

"Maybe not, but so far I think I've been doing just fine with the cards I've been dealt. Or at least I'm not dead. That's something."

"Certainly is," Ina said. "The issue is that you represent your very specific age group, cultural attachment, and personal style, which are unfortunately not aligned with the group's typical membership."

"So train me. He's my father. I want to do this."

They were silent, deciding how to sell the idea to the old man, I was sure.

"If not me, then, what about Jonas? He's older and more refined than I am."

The look on their faces told me there were bigger implications here than just pulling my family back together. Maybe global implications.

CHAPTER 36

5:50 a.m. I texted Ray to make sure the envelope was implanted in Oleg's trunk. Check. And at 5:55 a.m. I texted Oleg: *I will not be at the hotel at 6:00. The envelope's in your trunk.*

Oleg's huge ego would be bruised that we were able to breach his vehicle, and just wait till he realized the envelope wasn't really *the* envelope. I felt pretty good about the decoy, and I'd brought in the right experts for the job—Miki's street-smarts and Ray's soil expertise. The weight and color of the envelope's contents were a near-perfect match to the original cremains from Dr. Ek's Frankenfortress. Oleg will see it eventually, though. And his first thought will be Lacy. I'd covered that more than once with my captors, and by communicating directly with her myself. I guess until I could see her in my own space, my heart won't rest.

My body couldn't help but rest, though, in the ginormous pillow-top bed. My limbs felt heavy, too heavy, and my head felt swimmy like it did with an illness. But I wasn't ill. Was I? Something didn't feel right with my body, like the controller for my movements was out of sync.

I dreamed again, but now back in time by twenty years. One of my dad's famed camping trips that he planned months in advance ended up with my mother stranded on a sandbar, Jonas hobbled by a broken ankle, and my dad and me struggling with our oar blades through rough waters to row our little skiff into shore. We'd gone on a morning jaunt to one of the Florida Keys on summer vacation; nothing on the weather tracker predicted a squall that day. I argued with him to take the front because I didn't know what I was doing.

"No, you ride shotgun because I can steer us better from the back."

Out of nowhere, we found ourselves paddling through a washing machine spin cycle. Every wave, it seemed, left an additional gallon of water in the boat. By some miracle, we'd ended up with a child's sand pail in the bottom, which I used to scoop out the water while Dad tried to steer us to safety. It wasn't working. After another few minutes, it seemed like we were actually further from shore. I could no longer see my mother on the sandbar and my arms were about to fall off. The bad thing was that she couldn't swim well with her impaired lungs. Wiping seawater from my eyes, I detected the shape of Jonas onshore standing on two legs and waving at us with one of his crutches, shouting an inaudible message.

"Are we all gonna die out here?" I asked my dad at one point. I don't even know how he heard me over the racket of the water and wind. But he did. He spoke to me at that moment in a different voice, like at the end of Indiana Jones *The Final Crusade,* when Sean Connery says quietly, "Indiana...let it go."

In our vulnerable, gyrating, inadequate boat, my father said to me, "Look for a sign."

Being a bean counter, George Janoff was the farthest thing from new age. So this esoteric, almost spiritual guidance felt otherworldly to me, and I wasn't even certain I knew what he meant. But I'd heard him. I listened, and I kept watch for something out of the ordinary that might ping something deep inside to help us get to shore.

"Dad, we're sinking. We're taking on too much water."

"I know," he said. "Keep at it," meaning with my bucket.

The dark sky cast a greenish tint to everything. But a tiny patch of sun bled through the wall of clouds and came straight down into the boat from above our heads, nearly blinding me with a sudden light. How could that *not* be a sign? Of what, I wasn't sure. But I took that to mean something. "Dad, look!" I said.

"Good work, BJ." He rarely used those words, so I knew we

were up shit's creek. "Switch with me now…slowly," he said. "I'll take over with the bucket in the front because I can go faster, and you climb back here and just keep digging that oar in as deep as you can. Left, right. Left, right. And keep your eyes straight ahead onshore. We'll get there."

We did get there. Dad had to jump out and pull my mom into shore and I had to paddle myself. It was too much for my underdeveloped arm muscles and I felt like a superhero when we got there. Jonas' smile told me I was now in a different category in his heart.

I felt as though I was out in that water again during a life-threatening storm, struggling against rogue waves and currents too strong for me, the threat of death for myself and others imminent, not even able to see shore anymore. Dad, help me. Send me a sign.

⸺ ⸙ ⸙ ⸙ ⸺

Someone, thank God, had made a full pot of coffee early. Not only that, someone brought in clean clothes—correctly-sized—to Miki and me while we were asleep. The first cup of coffee did nothing for my lethargy. Maybe some evil person had made decaf. Or maybe I'd been drugged.

I was on coffee number two when the first sign came in. Russian crime boss, Oleg Kokov had our decoy envelope, and it appeared that it failed the first hurdle. A text came in from Oleg's phone a little after six that read simply, *Delivery received, not original*. I'd gone into Miki's room and we drank coffee together in a nook by a large, picture window. I brought her up to speed on the audio message to my father.

"I can barely move this morning. I'm wondering if I'm sick. And lucky for you, you slept through all the fun last night. How are you feeling?"

Miki looked at me like I was brain dead. "Hello…"

"What?"

"They drugged us, of course. That's why you're feeling lethargic and why I slept like the dead."

"Why bother? I mean why would that be necessary if we're guarded by six able-bodied adults?"

Miki's phone buzzed and I remembered it had when I came into her room earlier. "Something urgent?"

"No, nothing. Just my sister. She can wait. Anyway maybe it's an extra security measure."

I saw the bitterness on her face.

"Which of them is up now?" she asked.

Thing is, Miki Fine didn't have a sister. So now she was lying to me, too?

"Actually no one," I said, "not that I can see, though I'm sure one of the pit bulls is outside patrolling the yard. We need to get out of here."

"What do you have in mind?"

Miki spent thirty minutes checking all the windows in the east wing of the house where they'd stationed us, for outdoor patrol. No one was visible either on foot or in cars parked on the street. I even climbed up on furniture to check under the windows. Where were they? We both checked for cameras—none visible. I closed the bedroom door, then we ducked inside the closet and closed that door. If there were listening devices positioned throughout the house, they'd never record us in here. There was just enough room for Miki and me to crouch on the carpet under a rack of satin clothes hangers. I looked at her with a question in my eyes.

"Do it."

I dialed Jonas' number, knowing my phone, or my clothing could be bugged. Hell, these people could have surgically implanted a tracking device under my skin for all we knew. It was worth the risk.

"Naturally. He's not picking up."

"Hang up," Miki said. "He'll see that you called and we can send a text."

"That says what though?"

I laughed at the irony of our situation, and still felt the effect of tranquilizers slogging through my veins. I moved to sit more comfortably on the carpet, my body still not quite feeling like my own.

"Vanilla." I smirked.

"What, that's the text?"

"We need an extraction, right?" I stared at her.

"Vanilla extract, okay. That's cute."

"Something we've used a couple of times."

I typed the word Vanilla as a text, with a capital V and a period at the end. Hopefully he'd write back with a link to latlong.net, which would tell me he'd understood my message and was asking me for the latitude and longitude coordinates of our current location so he could reverse geocode them to get a fix on us.

"Come on." I opened the closet door and helped Miki up. "I think we both need more coffee," I said. "Can you do that? I want to check something."

"Sure."

Next, windows. They had no bars on them, nor were they installed with alarm sensors. The front door and sliding glass doors had alarm sensors, I noticed when we came in. The bedroom window was a horizontal slide. I lifted the lock mechanism and it opened easily. The screen was the same kind Jonas had in his house and could be popped off. Windows, check.

Miki brought me coffee #3. "What's the plan?" she asked. I told her about the window and pointed to the credenza she could crouch on to get through. She looked through the blinds at the jump and surveyed the yard. "Pretty exposed here. I don't like it."

"It's still early," I argued.

"Nothing from Jonas yet?"

"No. If we don't hear anything in ten minutes, I'll get us an Uber and have them meet us down the street."

I picked up my phone to raise the volume and Jonas' text came in as expected. "Here we go." I pointed to the phone. "Latlong.net. Thank God." I clicked the link in the text, entered this address and it spit out the coordinates, which I copied and pasted into a text.

Terranea, impressive, he wrote back. *Twenty minutes.*

I sent him back a thumbs-up emoji and told Miki.

Do you have backup? I texted him.

Yes.

Let us know when you're here. We'll be ready.

I grabbed Miki's hand and held it. Her warm skin and steady pulse calmed my nerves, though it was me intending to calm hers. "If we run," I told her, "we won't be here to receive a message back from my father."

She looked at the floor. "He'll neither see nor hear that message."

"What do you mean?"

"They never sent it."

CHAPTER 37

Hearing this brought up a hundred new questions. Why had they deceived us, and how did Miki know? And how she had known before me that they'd drugged us? I still wasn't completely certain I'd been sedated, though it certainly felt like that. No, I stopped myself, don't do that. Don't go turning on everyone. Not Miki. Not now.

Ten minutes had passed. We were in my bedroom now, the door mostly closed, Miki peering out from the crack to check for movement in the house. We neither saw nor heard any movement, felt no vibrations or signs of life here. Were they gone, sleeping, or were they all dead?

Fifteen minutes passed now since my text exchange with Jonas. Miki quietly closed the bedroom door. We lifted the credenza so it was directly under the window, and she coughed when I popped off one corner of the screen. The other four corners peeled off nicely and I dropped it on the patch of grass below us.

I felt the vibration of footsteps in the house, a door opening, mumble of voices, and the word 'no'. Ina's voice, a high-pitched no. Pleading. I turned but Miki was already going to the door to open it.

"Don't," I hissed.

Without checking with me first she opened it, looking out, searching, paranoid like me about our narrow life expectancy. And here's me crouched on top of the credenza next to an open, screenless window. Time felt slowed-down, thicker somehow. Minesh, standing against a wall opposite the bedroom door, now wore a gun on a shoulder holster fully visible from his stance, not by accident I suspected. Miki was in the doorway threshold, her gait frozen by the sight of him. Minesh's hand was on his belt, just two inches above the grip of his gun. Miki was closest to him but he kept his dark eyes fixed on me, his mouth contracted, jaw tight. With one shake of his head back and forth, he broke the moment.

"Just-give-me-a-reason," he said, in an icy tone.

Miki twitched her head back toward me. "What do we do?"

"Tell your brother to arrive on schedule and walk in through the front door." Minesh, now in the bedroom, coming toward us in slo-mo. "If he does anything else, they'll kill him."

They knew I contacted Jonas. This was important intel. This also seemed like a different version of Minesh than I'd seen before. Was this the real Minesh, badass Minesh, assassin?

"Tell Jonas what I said. If you don't, or if he doesn't follow directions, they'll kill him in front of you to make a bigger impression. It's what they do. And then you two will be loose ends. The Commission hates loose ends."

What the hell was the Commission?

"They?" Miki asked. "You mean you."

"If you value your brother's life, you'll text him, Mr. Janoff. Now."

I climbed down from the credenza, closed the window. *Park out front and walk in the front door,* I wrote to him.

WTF?

Do it. They'll kill you, all of us if you don't.

I heard a car out front and went to the window, my heart pounding. I didn't recognize the car but saw Jonas and Ray. I turned and nodded to Minesh. He started speaking but not to us, though I couldn't see any visible audio device in his ear. We heard the front door open, footsteps on the front walkway. It looked like one of the black-suited men from the fortress. So that had all been a big story? Ina and Minesh told me they were hired by my father to retrieve the envelope from the hotel to supposedly save my life. The guy looked blocky and athletic, tall, probably Special Forces. His jacket was buttoned, gun at his side. Oh. My. God. I ran back and grabbed Miki, dragging her out of the bedroom to the open front door. The suited man walked around the car slowly to the passenger side and raised his gun…at Ray's head. Oh no. Jesus! To Jonas, he motioned with his hand for him to exit the car and come toward him.

"They won't kill Jonas," Miki whispered. Her hand pressed into my shoulder. "They need him." Logical as ever.

I could barely breathe. Jonas dutifully walked around the front of the car, careful to only look at the man and not me. But I know he saw Miki and me in the doorway. The gunned man pointed to the front door. Jonas took several steps and looked back just as the man held the gun with a silencer up to the window and fired. A bullet plunged through the glass at Ray's head. His body slumped down onto the driver's side seat. Ray. Holy. Fuck.

Like pausing a movie and advancing it frame by frame, Jonas lowered his head toward the ground and kept walking toward Miki and me in the front entry, one foot in front of the other. I detected Ina's grass-scented fragrance behind us without looking. In a split second, Jonas walked through the door, I grabbed him, turned back to make sure Minesh or Ina weren't also pointing a gun at our heads, and then turned back to the street.

No car, no Ray, no gunned man. They'd all vanished. I gasped for breath.

— • -◇-◙◙-+-◙◙-◇- • —

Suspicion is sort of like poison. It enters the body, assesses the environment and sets a strategy for the most efficient distribution. It grows. It explores, free-associating one thing to another when, eventually, you start thinking like a conspiracy theorist and *everyone's in on it* becomes your general way of looking at the world. And then everything in your mind, your heart, body, begins to change.

I smelled cigar smoke again when I closed the front door behind Jonas. The old patriarch must be back. I placed my hands on my brother's shoulders and took him in with my eyes. He looked hollowed out.

"Dean," I said, summoning our *Supernatural* personas.

"Hey, Sam," he whispered.

165

"Vanquish any demons lately?"

"Not enough, apparently."

"They never sent the audio message to Dad," I said. "Or that's Miki's theory anyway."

"Miki," Jonas said and nodded.

She nodded back, watching everything with her android-like, calculated eyes, absorbing all the details, calibrating and re-calibrating every second.

"In here please." Minesh motioned with his hand toward the living room. It was not a suggestion.

Miki followed him. I gestured for Jonas to go ahead and I stayed back a few paces, doing something I should have done in the first place, maybe three years ago. I made sure no one's eyes were on me and I sent a message to my father. I didn't know what to believe about him now. So I told him the truth and told him what I wanted:

Hi Dad, I really need your help. Jonas and I both do. We're being held by some people who have told us things, crazy things. Where are you?

Minesh left us there when we'd all been seated, the three of us, while he went to gather the others for whatever macabre showdown they had planned, to either get rid of us or deploy us on the scent of my father. One of the pit bulls was stationed just outside the living room now, his gun visible.

"Who brought you here?" Jonas asked.

I pointed to the other guy. "That same guy, name is Minesh. Don't know who he is, any of them. They positioned themselves as some sort of shadow org or watchdog tracking the activities of all the Dr. Eks and their shady research."

"They had a lot to say about your father," Miki added.

I jumped in and added all the details of our father's opposition to the promession research, and the cryonic chambers I'd seen in the fortress last night.

"They said Dad is in hiding and pulling strings from some remote location to try and stop the doctors. They call them Ridders."

Jonas blinked back listening. I knew that expression. He was deciding something, negotiating something within himself.

"Yeah, he's in hiding," Jonas said. His voice cracked.

I moved a few inches closer. "You know where he is? Have you always known, all this time?" It was betrayal that I saw in my brother's face now, eyes weak, brows contracted, heart in turmoil.

He shook his head. "No. I don't know where he is. But I know why he's in hiding. Might not be why you think."

Now Miki leaned in closer to Jonas, the three of us perched on the ends of furniture, whispering over the coffee table. "They said they're reining him in because he possesses dangerous information," she said.

Jonas widened his eyes. "Have you heard anything about an antique sword?" he asked both of us.

"Dr. Ek had one on his key chain. Our captors here told us a tale of an antique saber that the Ridders use as their sort of mascot or symbol of rebellion."

Jonas looked at the table waiting, it seemed, for us to catch up. And only then did I start to reframe everything I'd learned, all the people I'd met, seen, heard, listened to. Funny how knowledge arrives sometimes. I swallowed the lump in my throat. My God.

"He stole the sword?"

CHAPTER 38

Moments ticked slowly, like fat rain droplets peeling away from towering eaves and falling to the ground. We'd huddled into one of the bedrooms, cowering, it seemed, letting the dust settle, waiting. Not one of us moved. Our captors were just rooms away, monitoring our sounds and movements I was sure. We used nonverbal communication to reach a consensus. Our father, mild-mannered accountant, diplomatic statesman, George Janoff, had done the unthinkable. He'd somehow stolen one of the most valuable and controversial artifacts from the Bilderberg Art Collection, the Boateng saber. He'd done it to send a message to the global community of Ridders to cease and desist their apocalyptic agenda of homicidal practices and come back to reality lest a public and political shitstorm would cancel them even from the dimmest shadows of society.

The door was open a few inches, and I couldn't see our captors anywhere. I leaned into Miki and Jonas. "He stole the Bilderberg sword."

Jonas nodded. "So they say," he said, all of us sort of nodding it into reality.

"Why, though?" Miki now.

"Through a friend I was able to access some classified intel that he went rogue six months ago," Jonas whispered while barely moving his lips, all six of our eyes staring down the hallway. "He apparently started taking out members of what is called the Brotherhood of Ridders," he said, turning his head toward me. I nodded. "Scientists, biologists, who are involved in pushing the practice of promession on influential, industrialized population centers."

"Taking out?" I asked. "What does that mean?

"Killing, Mr. Janoff." It was the old man now, a burning cigar spilling a thin tendril of smoke into the bedroom from the hall where he loomed. "That makes your father, say, an assassin."

I shook my head. "No."

"Oh yes," he argued, stepping one pace closer to the door and opening it slightly. "An assassin, and analysts nowadays put them into categories, is someone who kills people, sometimes a lot or a succession of people, for a cause, for a political ideal, and is willing to sacrifice their own well-being for that cause. That's what he is. That is what your father has become."

My mind could not process this inflammatory slander.

"Ina," the old man said, snapping his fingers. Then he motioned us to join them in the living room. What did we have to lose at this point?

Ina, whose face showed the heaviness of sleep, leaned down and placed three photographs on the coffee table. I filed in first and lowered myself to the sofa, Jonas and Miki beside me. I saw Ina's light skin and slight cleavage in the v-opening in her blouse when she pointed to the first photograph.

Light-haired, youngish man on the ground, face-up, with his head turned to the side and a visible bullet hole on his left temple. I shrugged. This could be anyone.

"Anyone could have killed this man," I said.

The old man raised his head toward Ina, who pointed to picture number two; the background was dark but it was unmistakably the face of my father, George Janoff, holding a gun and looking at the ground, where he'd presumably just shot the man in the previous picture. Again, this picture in no way proved that he had actually fired that gun at all, let alone at the victim lying on the ground. No. No way.

Picture three showed another man, this time an older man, much heavier, with the same shot in the temple. Dead. I felt sick.

The old man, watching me, sat in the armchair directly opposite me. "The way he sees it, your father I mean, these people are mass murderers. As you so eloquently described, freezing and cremating live humans without their consent and getting paid millions of dollars for it."

"Millions of dollars?" Miki asked. "You mean Dr. Ek? Who's paying him, paying them?"

"Organized crime syndicates," Jonas mumbled like it was obvious. "Oleg," he added and waved his hand in a circle.

"Very good, Mr. Janoff." The old man smiled, showing the space between his two front teeth. He looked a bit like the actor, Ernest Borgnine.

"It's the ultimate crime scene cleanup," Jonas said.

Jesus. That's what the guards were keeping a lookout for. They, we were waiting for organized crime thugs to deliver bodies that needed to be eliminated in a way that didn't leave any forensic evidence. I felt a sour taste in my mouth.

"And who are you?" Jonas addressed the old man in an irritated, bitchy tone. "Your team. What's your interest in this sordid business?" Jonas studied him, then Ina standing with her arms crossed leaning in the doorway, Minesh in the hall ominous with his shoulder holster.

"I don't know this gentleman's name," I said to Jonas, pointing at the old man. "His team," I said, "Ina," I pointed to her, "Minesh, they're supposedly from Sotheby's. They're the insurance company that insures the Boateng saber, the priceless stolen sword. That's their interest."

◦ ⸱⸺⸻✦⸻⸺⸱ ◦

I don't know how I knew this. I just did. The way all the pieces came together, it felt only logical that this, the insurance angle would be why they had such an interest in finding him. So Minesh plucked me off the grounds of the fortress to bring me here, have the old man tell us the story of assassins, show some provocative photographs. But then what? I wasn't seeing the end game. No one spoke for what felt like an hour, though it was probably three or four minutes. Minesh drifted into the living room, entering the vortex I had unwittingly created with my epiphany. He didn't sit. The wind had begun to howl and the sky darkened. Symbolic, wasn't it? Branches on trees scratched at the windows.

No one had refuted my claim yet, so I had to assume I was correct.

"Well, what say you?" Jonas asked the old man, using old-world language. "Is he right? Seems like you people sort of misrepresented yourselves to my brother and our associate, Ms. Fine. Are you the insurers of the sword?"

"Nothing was misrepresented, Mr. Janoff," the old man said, "as we had not yet gotten around to formal introductions. But that said, contracted out as a third-party, essentially yes. We're part of a security firm that conducts independent audits of organizations with important art collections. Not private collectors, mind you, only organizations."

"Bilderberg," I said. "Seems like they're a bit more than just an organization. More like an institution. And you believe my father stole that sword?"

No answer came to that one.

"Okay, let's try another question," back to Jonas now. "Auditing what, exactly?" he asked.

"Exactly what you would expect," the old man said with a shrug. "Comparing the line item titles and descriptions of each piece with the actual artifact, confirming the name and identity of the collection curator, verifying the locations of each artifact, inspecting their condition."

"Authenticating?" Jonas asked.

"No. We are not art authenticators. They could all be fakes for all we know. Not our particular expertise."

"Where and when do you believe it was stolen?" I asked this time.

"We are not at liberty to reveal any details," the old man said, leaning forward to flick his cigar ash on the floor. Expensive Berber carpet in a luxury home. That was noteworthy. He rose and left the room, mumbling something to Minesh on his way out.

Ina was in the next room on the other side of the wall now. "So where does this leave us?" I asked her.

"I think the one commonality is that we all want the same thing," she said.

"To find my father? Sure, for different reasons maybe. What are you going to do with him if you find him?"

"You mean when we find him. Well..." She paused to think. "The truth?" She moved closer. "All we care about is restoring the missing artifact to its collection. Once we get that back, there will be no retribution from us in any way. Interpol, that's another matter."

I kept thinking about her low-cut blouse. She wasn't the least bit attractive by my normal standards, and she was at least fifteen years older than me. I was very sensitive to scent, but that wasn't it either. I guess maybe I felt a duality in her that drew me in, good and bad, strong and weak, powerful yet vulnerable. Some part of me sensed she was out of her depth on this one and might need protection.

"We need to work together to find your father and bring him in via protected channels to make sure nothing happens to either him or the artifact," she said.

Now it was my phone that buzzed in my pocket. I didn't dare move. Could it be Lacy, and what the hell would I tell her? What could I tell her? Was it safe to share any of the details I was getting, share our location, safe for her? Of course not. I checked the number. *James.* My God, I'd nearly forgotten about him. I checked the text.

Where are you BJ?

I inhaled and answered him. *I'm here.*

What did you do?

I looked at Miki.

"What is it?" she asked.

"James," I whispered.

She leaned into me on the sofa to read the text.

What do you mean? I typed back.

They're all dead.

CHAPTER 39

"Ina," I bellowed into the hall. "Ina!"

"What happened?" Jonas asked.

I'd jumped to my feet holding my phone. My hands were shaking. Minesh appeared first.

"Get Ina," I said.

He stared back, reminding me of the chain of command and the gun in its holster.

"Ina!" I shouted.

I heard a door open, then her soft footsteps. "What's going on?" she asked.

Ina's skin looked paler every time I saw her. I held out the phone so she could see the text exchange. She looked at the floor and swallowed.

"You told me all of the guards and homeless workers at the fortress had been 'moved'—" I made air quotes. "Or is that another lie in the long string of them you've told me already?"

"It wasn't us," she said softly, raising her brow, seeming to imply that if it wasn't them, maybe it was my father.

Jonas was behind me now in the carpeted hallway. "You think our father did this?'

"He would never kill innocent civilians," I said. "If what you've told us is true, his whole crusade was intended to protect those exact people from the Eks of the world."

Jonas shook his head. "Then who did this?"

I went back to James, asking for clarification. I should've called him, but I couldn't bear to lie to him about where I was and what we were doing, and thereby risk him thinking we were somehow part of it. But he already thought that.

Who do you mean? I typed.

Bodies everywhere, he wrote back. I showed it to Ina.

"They might be drugged. So it might be temporary," she said. "There's a memory wipe drug, lots of them nowadays but one that was used in the MKUltra project and is still used by underground groups."

"Like who?"

"Organized crime? Jonas asked.

Ina widened her eyes. "If Dr. Ek smells any scent of law enforcement or possible exposure, and he's on the run or in hiding —"

"Then Oleg's got a big cash flow problem," I said. "But what would his operation have to gain by memory wiping the fortress workforce? And is that even possible?"

"We've got a ground crew tracking Ek right now," she said. "But our top priority is finding your father so we can restore the artifact, and of course bring him to safety."

"I seriously doubt you care about both of those things," I couldn't help saying.

"What do you have in mind?" Jonas asked her.

"Switzerland."

＊ ⸗⬦⧺⬦⸗ ＊

The short, nameless, gray-haired woman returned with another tray, this time tea and scones with jam on what looked like a solid silver platter placed on the living room coffee table. It landed in a weighty thunk right on top of the photographs, after which she shook out her hands.

"Tea, foranyonewhowantsit," she said in one long syllable. The 'it' went up in pitch, the accent Irish, possibly English. Like flies to sugar, most of them gathered around the tray. Clinking bone China, the clang of spoons, miniature knives rounded at the tips for spreading jam. The food tray frankly looked like another opportunity to be drugged. Besides, how could they possibly eat at a time like this? British James was standing in a landmine filled with what were probably dead bodies. I asked Ina, the reasonable one, to have someone pick him up and bring him here, but her eyes simply landed on Minesh, like she would have no say in the matter. Had anyone called the police? Had James? It'll be seen as mass murder, or possibly a suicide pact, which could start the authorities on the hunt for another Jim Jones or David Koresh. Meanwhile, I watched a silver knife spread a large wad of bloodred jam. I ran to the bathroom.

To say I felt lost was an understatement. We were in jail—okay a very nice jail but jail nonetheless, unable to go home, work, or resume the natural rhythm of our former lives. The raspberry jam must be fresh because I smelled it in the other room. I heard the word Geneva in the tearoom but I had another agenda. I moved freely around the bottom floor searching for cigar smoke, Minesh trailing me ten feet back like a tired shadow. I found him in the west end of the house on the sunporch.

"Mr. Janoff, come in. Or out, I should say. I don't suppose you smoke cigars. Not even old people like me smoke them anymore."

I pushed open the door and joined him.

"It used to be that men, even women enjoyed subverting the wishes of their doctors. Drinking too much…my God the amount we drank in the sixties, it's a wonder any of us made it to forty."

I tried to laugh. I did find him interesting, even amusing. But there was something foul going on here and nothing felt comfortable.

"You have something on your mind."

I nodded and pulled the old photograph out of my back pocket, the photograph I'd been carrying around of my father since stealing it from Jonas, and the one I'd been carrying around in my heart for much longer. I took a moment alone with it, choosing a seat away from the old man while he tugged and plucked at his stogie.

He'd been handsome back then, my father with his chiseled features and deep-set, brooding eyes, almost apologetic in their shape, like a lost dog that everyone wants to help. Was that how he'd gotten so far in his career—adding to it his education, wits, looks, and guile? What else did a government diplomat need to exert quiet influence all over the world? Who was this man who had been the head of our family? I no longer knew what to believe. About him or anything else.

I handed the photograph to the old man, who put up his palm and made me wait while he extinguished his cigar on the edge of a plate of cookies. Better than the carpet.

"I've shared this picture with you. So now I need to know your name. Fair trade I think."

Two adversaries in a staring contest, him doing a personality assessment, wondering which of the enhanced interrogation techniques were most likely to work on someone like me, while I performed a predictive threat analysis. I saw a lifetime of deception behind his stern, brown eyes.

"*Soglasovano.*"

"Sorry?"

He smiled and dipped his forehead toward me. "Agreed. Andranik Dvali. I'm Armenian on my mother's side, and my father was Georgian. I spent part of my childhood in Ukraine, I loved it there. But most of my life here in your country."

I shook his hand but refused to smile because this introduction wasn't intended as a pleasantry. It was a security measure on my part. Truth is, I liked Andranik Dvali so far. But the other truth was that he was intending to kill my father. And maybe me as well.

CHAPTER 40

"Now, let's see," Old Man said, carefully pinching the photograph in the bottom corner like he was touching an expensive piece of art. Good protocol. I liked that.

"Oh yes," he said, dreamily. "This is a very old photo, which I haven't seen in a long time."

"But you have seen it?"

Andranik Dvali looked up at the skylight and seemed to lose himself. "I took it myself." He shook his head.

"Where was it taken?"

"The library at the Bilderberg Hotel. Oosterbeek, Netherlands."

"Who are these other men? Are they business associates? What were they doing there?"

"Of course." He nodded. "You must have many, many questions, Mr. Janoff. And maybe someday I will tell you the identities of these other men. For now, all I can tell you is that they were all spies."

"For—"

"You know, various countries." He shrugged as if photographing spies was a commonplace occurrence. "And sometimes their allegiances changed depending on where the money was coming from."

I reminded myself to breathe and tried not to jump to any irrevocable conclusions. One breath. Two. He hadn't specifically said that my father was one of them—maybe just that he was in the company of spies.

"What's the book my father's holding?"

"Ah, yes. The fateful book. It's a rare, first edition of *Theory of Games and Economic Behavior* by von Neumann and Morgenstern. Ever hear of it?"

"I took economics in college, but no. An old book?" I gauged the significance this would have had on my father. I don't remember seeing a book like that in his own collection growing up.

"In this picture—" he pointed— "is the original 1944 edition written by a mathematician and an economist." He sat back and smiled, crossed his legs, his face full of energy. "This book had as much influence on the modern world as Einstein's theory of general relativity. Think about that. It launched what later became known as game theory, which is the study of human behavior in high stakes, strategic settings."

"High stakes, strategic settings," I repeated. "Like politics?"

He smiled. I could tell he'd been a teacher at some point. "This book is still required reading at the FBI Academy, CIA training programs, and yes, your father used and loved this book."

"And as an accountant, did he have many opportunities to apply something as esoteric as game theory?"

"Oh no, not esoteric in the least, Mr. Janoff. Don't you see? Game theory applies to everything. It's about power, politics, business, negotiation, statistics. The entire human experience. Your father was an accountant by trade and education, yes. But what he brought to his work wasn't just bean-counting, as you Americans call it. No. Game theory was his passion! The lens through which he looked at life. It was his secret edge."

My attention was rapt, hearing an important man talk so reverently about my father. I was also hearing voices in the other room.

"The State Department used him to investigate all kinds of government fraud," he went on, "of course they would. But somewhere along the line, as he studied this book and other books like it, he became something more—a gifted tactician and strategist who was sought out by many different countries, as well as military, government, and civilian entities." Dvali's eyes widened.

178

"Bilderberg."

"Eventually, yes. He started as a consultant brought into the fold just for accounting oversight, and that went on for a number of years. But later, he knew so much about their activities, their global agendas, and their members that it was too dangerous for him to be on the outside any longer."

"Was he coerced into joining?" I asked.

"In a way. He was an unofficial member of the most powerful Bilderberg committee: the Steering Committee. They eventually forced his hand by insisting that because of his knowledge of certain black programs, it would be against the rules for him to not agree to formal membership. They threatened to slander him and his family with a phony embezzlement charge if he didn't go along."

I got up and paced across the thick carpet to gather my thoughts. I thought about being in that boat with my father years ago during that storm. Would a skilled strategist have told his son to look for a sign? Seemed esoteric, new-agey almost. But what was becoming more and more clear every minute is that I hadn't known my father at all.

I heard the word Geneva again and my stomach growled without warning.

"*Spasibo*," I said, and stood in front of Old Man Dvali, gently pulling the photo from his gnarled fingers. It was the only Russian word in my limited vocabulary.

I worked my way back to the other side of the house. The vibe back in the living room felt different now, energized by their lively discussion and over-caffeinated tea. I poured some into the remaining teacup and took stock. For some reason, it was Miki's face, again, that was of greatest interest to me, her quiet, secretive way, her repeated text messages from a mystery-sender. Suspicion again was feeling like a war in my head that I was destined to lose.

"What are you guys cooking up in here?" I asked, purposely using the word *guys* to make myself look at ease in this context. Of course it was the farthest from the truth, but was I starting to think more strategically? Like a spy? Like my father?

"A plan," Miki said, with a sly grin.

"We've been learning about freeports." Jonas motioned me toward an empty chair. I sat and waited.

"Art galleries located in an airport; not all airports have them of course, and they never exhibit art."

"Go on," I said.

"Their security rivals supermax prisons." This was Jonas, now, speaking for all of them.

"And the purpose, then, is to avoid paying duties and foreign tariffs?" I asked.

"Yes," Ina said, taking over the instructor role, "but that's not it. They constitute a sort of region or zone outside of any specific country. Not the freeport structure, specifically, but the art housed within its walls."

"Like maritime law?" I asked.

"No, admiralty law," she corrected, "is very complex but extremely prescriptive. Freezones are more nebulous because they remain even now somewhat under the radar and off of existing law enforcement jurisdiction grids. There are very few rules governing how the art is received, stored, and retrieved. There's also very little case law available when it comes to theft prosecution, and it almost never happens. So freeports are a haven for private collections that are in limbo, in transit—"

"Or stolen?" I added.

She nodded.

"Cool. What's the plan?"

"We think a freeport," Ina said, "not just any Freeport, but Geneva, one of the largest, is a likely place for your father to have stored the Boateng saber."

"Do you think he's living in Geneva?" I asked.

"Not knowing what his long-term plans are, it's logical that one would want easy access to such an artifact, should an opportunity arise for him to retrieve it for some reason, such as to transfer ownership."

"Even though he doesn't actually own it himself?" I asked. "Never mind. So when do we leave?"

Ina stood. "Three of us will go. I suggest myself and you two," she said, pointing to Miki and me. "Jonas, you'll need to remain here until we return. Minesh will st—"

"Hold on," Jonas objected.

The doorbell rang. Everything stopped. Minesh slipped into one of the bedrooms, presumably to look out front.

"All good," he said and moved to the door. He opened it and quickly ushered two people inside. It was—oh my God. A security guard clutching Lacy's arm. I ran to her. I couldn't help it, in an unbridled, cinematic display. I lifted her up and buried my face in her neck, then put her down all in a quick second.

"Oh my God, I'm so glad you're okay."

Jonas grabbed her. "Where the fuck did you come from?"

"Crawling around the back of the house," the security guard said. "Like a little scavenger."

Lacy untangled herself from the security guard's grip and Jonas' arms.

"How did you—"

"Tracker," Lacy said, "on your shoe." A grin spread across the face that was etched on my heart.

"Sly fox you are."

Ina eyed the security guard and blinked a command.

"Arms out and spread your legs, please, Miss," the guard.

"Do it," I told her.

Jonas and I stepped back. The security guard patted her down on the front and back.

"She's clear," he said and disappeared through the front door.

"I'd suggest Lacy and I come with you, Ina. And let Miki go."

"Miki Fine, it's been years," Lacy said.

"Not enough, apparently. Can I go?" Miki asked Ina.

CHAPTER 41

As if the day hadn't been uncomfortable enough, it got worse when Ina refused to let Miki leave.

"No one's going anywhere right now," was all she said and then disappeared back into her room at the end of the hall to recover from the strain.

Then there was the problem between Miki and Lacy. They had some kind of sordid history, though each was as tight-lipped about it as the other. A man? No doubt. One of us, meaning Jonas or me? God help us. I didn't even want to think about it. For the moment, they were in separate rooms and that was as good as we were gonna get right now.

Honestly, when it came to Miki, my mind failed to untangle itself from our old partner, Archie Dax. What a traumatic day. We had all been working the same embezzlement case of a bank CEO and we'd staked out one of the warehouses he used to traffic his train of stolen semiconductor equipment. Someone, we learned later, had rigged the building so it would explode after someone entered the security code on the upper level. Archie was on point inside the building, downstairs, I was tech, and Jonas was managing com. I was in the van with Jonas, and Miki was positioned outside doing perimeter watch like she usually did on Archie's jobs, assuming the role as his sort of unofficial guardian angel. Well, that day, anyway, it didn't work because when one of the CEO's goons tripped the upstairs lock the whole building went up in a ball of fire. Our van was thrust backward about thirty feet and we lost critical equipment, but we were otherwise fine. Archie's body absorbed the magnitude of the explosion and, when we pulled him out, he was alive but bleeding and barely conscious. "Take this," he'd said, handing me his Beretta .9mm with what looked like his last ounce of strength. Miki, out of her mind with fear that he would die, stayed with him. Jonas and I ran back to the van to get our phones to call for help. It took a minute or two to get the van door to open after being thrown back from the explosion and, naturally, it took a while to get 911 to answer, then we had to stay there answering all their questions. Ten minutes later, when we got back to Archie, both he and Miki were gone.

The story we got from Miki was that she drove him to the hospital herself because she'd come in her own car, and they pronounced him DOA. There was a funeral of course, and closed casket which wasn't surprising, given his injuries. But I always wondered, and I think Jonas did too, whether his body had actually been inside that polished, walnut casket at all.

Minesh hadn't said two words to us all day, relegated to patrolling the hallways and monitoring movement outside. Ina was making arrangements for the trip. Luckily, my Georgian/Armenian ally never refused food. So he let me get GrubHub delivery and we ordered a spread of Mexican food that consisted of enchiladas, chile rellenos, quesadillas, and carne asada accompanied by Mexican Coke.

Miki, aloof now after my shameless display of affection to Lacy and obviously chapped by Ina's refusal of freedom, hung out with Jonas. I brought Lacy up to speed with everything that had happened leading up to our extraction, and then what I'd just learned about my father. She laughed at first, then apologized.

"Sorry, this whole thing is the farthest thing from funny."

"No, seriously I've been having the same thoughts as you, thinking back, looking for evidence, for *signs*." That word again. "Just hard to picture, I guess."

"Not really, though." Her voice was dreamy now, her head leaning on the edge of an armchair with her legs dangling off, her typical pose. It was just the two of us in one of the many sitting rooms in this gigantic house. Unsure of our future, I felt like bolting the door closed to time-capsule this moment.

"What makes you say that?"

"Well…" She sat up now on the edge of the chair. "Your dad always seemed too laid back to be a spy." She smiled with half of her face.

"Maybe that's what made him so good," I said.

"The spy profile doesn't really fit, until you tell me he's a freaking world-recognized game theorist. Now *that* fits."

"Really?"

"Remember how adept he always was at breaking up fights?" Her face brightened.

"No. Was he? Between the three of us? Oh, yeah, I guess so."

"Between anybody. You and your mom, Jonas and your mom, neighborhood squabbles. He was a master. He'd casually end up at the head of the room with his probative questions and he'd get people talking to each other again."

I listened, nodding.

"Remember in ninth grade when that guy Matthew Feroli asked me to the junior prom and I was mortified about telling you?"

"The Ralph Macchio guy? Why were you mortified?"

"Never mind. I'm actually relieved you don't remember; it's an adolescent-girl thing. Anyway, I assumed you and I would be going together. As friends, you know…"

"Of course," I nodded, struggling to keep my face neutral.

"I talked to your dad about it because he found me really upset one day alone on your back porch. I told him about the dilemma—"

"I still don't see what the dilemma was—"

"And he white boarded me!" She laughed.

"What do you mean?" I asked.

"He had this rollaway whiteboard in his office and did a visual analysis of all the different possible outcomes of going with Matthew, going with you, or not going at all. It was dizzying but it made sense. Who did I end up going with?"

I raised my palm. It was the best night of my entire adolescence.

"That's right." She nodded. "And that was…"

"Because of my dad?"

"He was calm, clear, and masterful. He was a brilliant strategist. He used game theory on me."

I considered all that while Lacy ate. I wasn't hungry, so I continued my phone research on freeports to educate myself about Customs and Border Patrol and the nuances of domestic status, zone restricted status, privileged and non-privileged foreign status. What was most interesting, though, was how unregulated they were and what could and couldn't be placed in such a zone. When I caught sight of Ina emerging from her room to look for extra towels, I asked her about Geneva. Her face looked like a deer in headlights.

"I'm sorry, I didn't mean to startle you," I said. "I know it's been a long day."

"It's alright. What do you need?"

"Well, you mentioned the Geneva freeport. I've been doing research on freeports all afternoon."

"What about it?"

"Well, you're right, it's the largest freeport in the world—"

"And the oldest," she added.

"Why Geneva, though? There must be another reason. There are lots of them closer than that."

"We've got a team tracking Dr. Ek; you know him obviously." I nodded. "Well, looks like this morning he purchased a ticket to Helsinki."

"Okay. What's the significance of Finland, and why—"

She raised her shoulders, thinking. "It's an old spy trick to hide out in major European cities and get to them by way of Scandinavia. We think he's going to Helsinki because he intends to then go to Geneva. We want to be there when he arrives."

My mind worked through the details. "And you suspect Dr. Ek's going to Geneva because he thinks my father stashed his sword in the Geneva freeport?"

"Yes, but you need to understand something. The sword does not belong to Dr. Ek. The sword belongs to the Bilderberg Art Collection. Dr. Ek stole the sword as an iconic symbol for the group of Ridders, using that and their practice of promession as their rallying cry for environmental conservation."

"So my father's stolen a sword that was already stolen."

"A technicality, but yes. That technicality unfortunately won't stop him from being prosecuted."

"Maybe it will, maybe it won't."

"Look, Mr. Janoff, I'm tired. Your father is said to be in possession of something that doesn't belong to him and is purported to be the most valuable sword ever sold. I represent the Bilderberg interests in this matter and my actions are sanctioned by Sotheby's Security Division. We will get this sword back. As for your father, what will happen to him is up to a tribunal and Interpol."

Clean towels in hand, Ina rolled on her dainty heel and returned to her lair.

CHAPTER 42

I was learning some interesting new terminology through this ordeal. Examples: freeport, Boateng saber, etc. I especially loved our captors' use of the phrase "a car". That apparently meant that a car would magically appear that wasn't registered to them, was presumably untraceable, with a driver who'd been screened and vetted but who the captors didn't know personally. As such, a car arrived at 6 a.m., picked up Ina, Lacy and me and brought us to LAX to board a flight to Geneva, on a private jet no less, connecting in Paris. Lacy and I both felt very cosmopolitan, giddy with the excitement of luxurious travel accommodations on a global treasure hunt, despite the fact that we'd been kidnapped and forced to travel with our captors to another country. We kept making eye contact with impish, twelve-year-old snickers, knowing we were out of our depth and excited by the prospect of trouble. No doubt our silliness came from misplaced fear and exhaustion. Unfortunately, the reality was less glamorous when you considered a sword locked up in the equivalent of Fort Knox and hunting a man who clearly didn't want to be found.

We were each assigned our own security detail and not allowed much time together, oddly. Lacy was seated in the front, me in the back, Ina in the middle of the twenty-seater, which flew smoothly through the air despite its small size. Then again, weight could be a factor, as there was marble on every surface.

I could tell Ina was tiring of our barrage of questions. "Is it true 61% of people living in Geneva speak English?" I asked her.

"Don't talk to anyone," she said, without looking up from her magazine.

"Will we be given weapons?"

"No."

"Will we be working undercover?" Lacy this time.

No answer.

"What about currency exchange?" I asked.

"Your security detail will pay for whatever you need. Note I said need, not want."

After that one, Ina directed us to text her our questions and she'd answer them during the flight.

They at least allowed us to eat together so I could continue debriefing Lacy. She was such a stabilizing force right now. For whatever harm Ina and her team had caused us, I now had a chance, albeit slim, to see my father again. A flight attendant took our lunch order and returned five minutes later with warm, microwaved panini sandwiches. Not terrible, but far from good.

"You look sad," Lacy commented when I'd been staring out the window. "Thinking about Ray?"

"Yeah."

"I was too." She grabbed my hand and squeezed it. Ray. Jesus.

"I feel so bad now about the things I thought and said. He was my roommate. I'm having a hard time processing the fact that he's dead because of me."

"I never trusted Ray," she said.

"Why though? I mean, I know you never liked him, but you never said anything about trust before. That's different."

She was holding something back.

"Just that kind of face, or you're not into people who don't bathe? See, I just did it again."

"Both, I think. Well, there was this one thing when we first met," she said. "For a while there, every time I'd come over before you got home, Ray would pump me for information."

"About what?"

"About you and what you'd been doing, and also about us, like our friendship."

"Of course he was. He was wondering if you were up for grabs."

She shook her head. "I never felt the come-on vibe from him. It was something else. Almost like it was leverage of some kind, him fishing for details about you, or us, that he could use against one of us later."

I was in a window seat now, Lacy in the aisle, an empty seat between us. I can't say our strange conversation made me feel any better about Ray, maybe worse. I kept watch outside, I guess to make sure we were actually headed east and then north towards Paris like I wasn't certain we were going where Ina said we were. The flight attendant cleared out our lunch trays and we both opted for more coffee. I could tell it had been freshly brewed, and it was surprisingly strong. Lacy let out a loud sigh.

"What?"

"Oleg's million-dollar envelope scam. What the fuck is that all about?"

"It's genius, in an evil sort of way," I said, the final details only becoming clear to me right now. "Whoever Oleg gets to agree to his job and take his money, that person is on the hook to keep delivering envelopes to hotels for him for the rest of their life—under penalty of death. It's how he ropes people into his operation and how he manages his resources."

"Hard to believe," she said. "But who's supposed to be the recipient of all these envelopes, and do they all have the same contents?"

I thought about this and glassed the layers of clouds out the window. "I would guess yes, same contents. And it's a good efficiency measure for his operation. Oleg's getting samples taken from the promession process, by his army of Dr. Eks."

"Meaning what exactly?"

"So after a body is frozen, subjected to the high-frequency vibration and then after those remains are cremated, Oleg packages up a small sample of that final stage material to have someone forensically test it to see if they can determine the person's identity from the cremains—and they can't." I smiled; I couldn't help it. This

189

part of the plan was both sinister and genius. "It's like his business card for crime bosses all over the world who need to sanitize their operations and prevent legal exposure. He leaves an envelope for them with a tiny Ziploc sample of the "cleaned" cremains for prospective buyers who are thinking about investing in his cleanup services all over the globe."

"Pretty sophisticated for a thug though, as you describe. What does he charge for this service?"

"Jonas told me $500k per person."

"Whoa. That's a lotta cabbage."

We changed seats again and both slept on and off. The pilot announced we'd be landing in Paris shortly to refuel and then we'd be underway to Geneva. The landing was surprisingly smooth. I heard normal plane sounds while we were on the ground preparing for our next leg. I could see half of Lacy's face five rows up from me, and Ina—wait. Lacy had been two rows in front of Ina last time I looked. Now she was directly in front of her. Had she moved? What a sneaky fish. Ina was speaking with someone on her phone, and I could see Lacy had slumped to the side of her seat, eyes closed, simulating sleep. What a little faker. How long had she been listening? I was careful to keep my eyes off of them and my head aimed down toward the phone in my lap where I was playing Candy Crush using the micro-USB phone chargers in the seat dividers.

I couldn't help it. *Did you think she wouldn't notice you moved your seat?* I texted Lacy.

She looked down at her phone and stayed in that position for a few minutes. I thought maybe she'd fallen asleep again, but her next move was pure theater. She jerked upright, deep exhale, rubbed her face and looked around the cabin. "I must have dozed off. Hope I wasn't drooling," she mumbled to no one in particular and headed toward the restroom in the back. Sure enough, my phone buzzed with a text as soon as the restroom door locked.

Something bigger's going on here, she wrote. *Here's what I overheard from Ina, word for word: 'Lazarus, she said it several times, standard subnet mask, we already have an ARP in place, so they won't detect us. No idea what that means. I've got to go. The guy who just entered the cockpit isn't our pilot.*

190

CHAPTER 43

Get out of the restroom. You should get back to your seat, I texted back.

Honestly, this feels safer right now, she wrote back. *What about the rest of it?*

ARP is an address resolution protocol that lets you penetrate another person's network but appear as if you're an authorized network host. And a subnet mask covers up an unauthorized IP address.

Who are they hacking? she asked.

IDK yet.

That's okay, she wrote. *We may not make it off this plane so it might not be relevant. What's Ina doing now?*

I looked up to check. *She took her laptop out and she's typing something, with one Air pod in, talking softly.*

You can't hear anything?

I was too far away. *No*, I wrote. *Here comes one of the security guards, probably to make you come back to your seat so we can take off.*

I was right. "Seatbelts on, please," the man said to me on his way to the back of the plane.

Different security guard than when we took off. And shouldn't the flight attendant be checking my seat belt?

The guy knocked three times on the restroom door. "Miss," he said. "Please get back to your seat now."

Thank God the door opened immediately. I watched Lacy nod and walk back to her original seat, two rows in front of Ina. Maybe Ina hadn't noticed. *Lazarus*. I planted the word in a file in my brain.

The pilot, whoever he was, announced a fifty-five-minute flying time and we took off like a Harrier jet and seemed to reach cruising altitude in about ten minutes. I'd had this shoe-drop panic in the marrow of my bones ever since I watched one of Ina's security guards shoot Ray through the window. I was dying to investigate what happened to that car. And, only now for some reason, it occurred to me that there was no blood splatter on the window when Ray was shot.

Thirty minutes into the next leg of our flight, Ina got up and approached me. "Do you two prefer two rooms or one?" she asked. Very clinical in her approach, neither accusatory nor presumptuous. I looked at Lacy and considered this very serious question.

"One room, two double beds?" I asked.

"I'll see what I can do. You can't leave the hotel once we check in," she said, eyes wide, staring me down.

"Why are we here exactly?"

"Strap in, we're landing soon."

I texted Jonas the moment our rubber wheels hit the tarmac, leaving out the parts about Ina's phone conversation, Project Lazarus, as I was calling it, and the other pilot. *Landed in Geneva*, I wrote, then randomly remembered the book I'd taken from his house. It should still be in my backpack, which I had with me.

Did you see the book Mr. Bergman left for me? You know I took it, right?

Glad you're ok. I'd forgotten about that book. Something about insects?

The Wasp Factory, looks like a novel.

What about it? he wrote.

There was a note stuck in the pages, a crossword clue, cold beetle. Mean anything to you?

No, but interesting that you mention them. I haven't been able to reach them for two weeks. It's like they just vanished, suddenly no

longer interested in their missing daughter.
    Maybe she came home?
    Maybe, he wrote. *But seems like the press would have covered the return of a mission heiress.*

Amazing how relaxing it is to fly to Europe when you're not contending with queues and waiting and noise. We still had to filter out through a smaller Customs and Border Patrol office, show that we had valid passports, and state the reason for our visit. Ina had given us no specific directions about this, so I took a gamble. The patrol officer was a youngish man. He spent a full five minutes scouring every molecule of my passport.

"The purpose of your visit, sir." He said it as a statement rather than a question.

I ceremoniously looked at Lacy, then turned back to him and smiled. "Honeymoon," I said with a giddy smile. Ina wasn't watching but was within earshot. The man's face was stone.

"You don't have many bags. A short honeymoon?"

"The trip was a surprise from my mother," I said, and looked at Ina. Her face went white, hilarious. Lacy tried to hide her amusement. I looked back at her again. "I love her, what can I say?" It was the most truthful thing I'd uttered in a month.

"Aren't you funny now," Lacy said on the way down a long hallway to the street-level services. "Ina said there'll be a car waiting for us."

Another car. With another driver. And what was all that with the pilot? We'd gotten here safely. Hadn't we?

"So, is Ina supposed to be my mother or yours?" Lacy asked.

"Mine, I assume, since we have the same skin color."

"Did you also arrange for a honeymoon suite?"

"One room, two beds." I stopped walking, this time, to check her expression. "Okay?"

She shrugged. "Fine. Like camping in the backyard when we were kids."

The gamble, here, was that I'd now gotten Lacy to start thinking about me in a different way, or what I presumed was a different way. The hazard, of course, was if sleeping with someone who's been your best friend since childhood would obliterate that friendship.

Some things in life were worth risking.

We were in Room 317 of Geneva's CitizenM Hotel, a ten-minute drive from the famed Geneva "free port zone" as it was called, with two goons at the end of the hall, and Ina three rooms away on the opposite side. She'd tried to get adjoining rooms and if you could have seen the sour expression on her face when that didn't happen, a mother insisting her children needed supervision. Funny.

"I'll text you with further directions from the 735 number," she said and watched us enter the room. I was secretly elated that Ina crammed us both in the same room together, careful to feign indifference. Like a gentleman, I took the bed near the window and gave her the one closest to the bathroom. I opened my backpack and pulled out my laptop and plugged it into the charger. Shit. No 220V adaptor.

"How the fuck did you get a laptop in here? Does Ina know you have it?"

"Uh-huh."

"So?"

"I didn't touch it after I got to Terranea."

She wrinkled her eyes.

"The resort we were staying at."

"Oh, right. So you faked her out, making her think you cared nothing about the laptop?"

"Exactly."

"Nice. And now that we're here..."

"We...make a fort?" I asked, which prompted a sudden jumping-up-high-five like ten-year-olds. Another speck of lightness under a cloak of despair. "Man, the forts we made as kids," I said.

"Jonas was always such a planner." She pulled a small bag out of her backpack and put it in the bathroom.

"More like the architect. He had drawings and shit."

"No way."

"Well, he had no social life so he had time to do things like that."

"Um, I'm the only one of us who had a social life, because I was the only one who was cool."

"Fine, I won't argue. How do you want to do it?"

CHAPTER 44

I won't say we were delusional. We both fully grasped the danger we were in—the sting of our confinement, and the potential danger my father was in at the hands of our deadly captors. That said, forts were serious business.

Lacy's parents both worked and were never home, and she was an only child. So without the structure and constant parental presence, she was considered to be "latch-key" and ultimately at-risk. And since they lived next door, that meant, to my mom anyway, that she was also our responsibility. So she ate with us a few nights a week, slept over on the downstairs sofa bed more than sometimes, and came on every camping trip I could remember. In between all that was a rich culture of forts: inside forts made out of blankets and pillows. The outdoor forts were more elaborate and diverse, and dirtier. Empty cardboard boxes. Spiders. Large, wooden shipping crates. Bags of sand and potting soil. And up until I was eleven, we had an awesome Army surplus store walking distance from our house, where we could always find fort-building staples like tarps, twine, and wooden stakes.

We walked around the room in silent vigil for a few minutes, assessing the structure, knowing Ina and the guards would be very curious about what we were doing in here if we made too much noise. She motioned me toward the entry and opened the sliding closet doors.

"There?" I looked inside the empty cavern. "It's pretty big, actually."

"If they've bugged our room, it would probably be hard to hear us if we were talking or whispering inside the closet with the doors closed."

"Mmmm, good point. So I declare this region Command Central for our duration."

We brought in every available pillow and blanket, for both comfort and sound insulation, which left little room for us. She was right, of course they would bug our room. That's probably why they made us wait so long to check in. Bastards. I pulled her inside the closet and crouched down. "We need to have a steady stream of what sounds like normal human conversation between two friends while we're here or they'll suspect something."

"Good idea. Keep the TV on with the volume up, at least till bedtime."

"Even though it's in French?"

We closed off one of the closet doors and only entered and exited through the other, so they wouldn't hear too many closet door sounds and get suspicious. There was just enough room for us to sit side by side with our backs to the rear wall, my computer on my lap. We got an adapter and an extension cord from reception.

"Are you on WiFi?"

"Yep. And TOR is up."

"You're running VPN?" she asked, surprised.

"TOR isn't technically VPN, but I'm sure someone, somewhere is trying to track our browsing history, probably from our phones as well. That's the whole point of TOR, browsing privacy. And that's what we need right now."

"You're crazy. What are people buying on the dark web these days?"

"Stolen credit card numbers are big. Bitcoin lottery tickets, fake college degrees, plastic explosives, poison."

"Lovely."

"What's really popular right now is what's called the replica market, so...counterfeit luxury goods. Hacked government data, uranium."

"Uranium?" She laughed in disbelief. "Like in what preparation? Mailed through the post office in shrink-wrap?"

"I'm not planning to buy any weapons. Just want to keep our browsing private while we're here."

"Okay." She put up her hands. "You're the IT guy. So what's our list of priorities? We don't know how much time we have. Wait, do we have a phone in here in case Ina calls?"

"In my pocket," I said, while my fingers raced through a series of commands. I accessed a gateway site and brought up duckduckgo.

"What's that?" she asked, eyeing the screen.

"The dark web equivalent of Google." I started with Lazarus, which was the word Lacy heard Ina saying. Then I deleted the word."

"What are you doing?"

"It's not gonna be meaningful unless it's in the context of Ina and Minesh and their organization. Here, let's start with something easier." I opened a Notepad document with the list of terms I wanted to research and turned the screen so Lacy could see.

- Dr. Anders Ek, promession, Abilene Cremation Services
- Oleg Kokov, Russian gangster
- Ina, Minesh, Andranik Dvali Georgia

"Who's Dvali?" she asked.

"The old man who told me about—"

"Game theory," she nodded.

- Bilderberg, Boateng saber sword, and George Janoff

Next, I added Lazarus and Project Lazarus to the list. Then Lazarus Files, and The Wasp Factory.

"Hey, can you get that book out of my backpack?"

"Sure."

Lacy disappeared, and that made me wish I'd showered and brushed my teeth. Never in my life would I have cared about something like that around her. Was it all changing now? Had it already? I felt this strange calm on the outside, but a hot terror was growing in my chest as she crept back in the closet next to me and handed me the book. She was way out of my league, and I honestly wasn't ready for this.

"Can you take the paper out? It's near the back. I think it says cold beetle on it."

She held the note up to the light of my screen. "Crossword: Cold beetle. That's interesting."

I added that and also Sten Bergman, Estelle Bergman, and Anastasia Bergman to my list of terms.

"What else?"

"What did you see when you went upstairs in the fortress the other night?" she asked.

It seemed like so long ago now. "Cryogenic chambers."

"So maybe cryonics in the context of Anders Ek and Abilene?"

I added that to the Notepad document.

"If you want to start running these, I'm gonna order room service." She winked. "I'll tell them your mother's paying for it on the same card the room was booked under."

I nodded but didn't answer, because I was quick-scanning search results. I also felt a momentary tinge of pain at the phrase 'your mother', for obvious reasons. Lacy and I hadn't ever really talked about that, so it wasn't a common topic for us. Back to my list, I went last to first.

Cold beetle brought up a European cocktail, a raunchy porn site, and the Upis beetle that apparently loves forest fires. Why would that come up under cold beetle?

Next: the Bergmans. Nothing under Sten or Estelle, but this was interesting. Their daughter, Anastasia, whom Jonas and I had already started searching for, was actually their… granddaughter? "I was right."

"About?"

"Nothing," I mumbled, reading something pulled from a university journal article. Anastasia Bergman wasn't wayward or a crack addict. She was a world-renowned biologist. My eyes scanned down the page—an award-winning researcher living in Stockholm. Ah, here we go: she and her father pioneered the controversial promession process, an advanced, environmentally conservative cremation technique. Whoa.

It was hot in here, too dark, and my left leg was cramping. I crept out into the room with the laptop, stretched, and put on a short-sleeved shirt. I turned the TV up and spoke in Lacy's ear, telling her about Anastasia Bergman, and the cock and bull story her grandparents had told Jonas and me about her disappearance.

"I knew they were full of it."

"Well, what if what you read is true and she's still missing and they're still trying to find her?" she asked.

I climbed onto one of the beds and resumed reading the article. "Maybe. Wait a minute."

She stood a few feet from me, looking accidentally beautiful in baggy pants and a cropped top. "I was reading about the phrase cold beetle and there's this beetle that actually likes forest fires and eats charred wood pulp," I said under my breath.

"Okay...."

"And I just realized I saw another word in that article besides fire. Anti-freeze."

Lacy plopped onto the other bed and sighed. "Meaning what?"

"Let me check. How long till our food delivery?"

"Twenty minutes."

I crept back into the closet, careful to not bang things around too much, this time putting my back against the side wall and stretching my legs out. Upis beetle, it was called, not only liked eating fire-charred trees but it could apparently withstand freezing temperature to the extent that they could be frozen, and then completely thaw again without impacting performance of their biological systems. What? I knew that capability wasn't possible with humans yet, despite all the advances in cryonics with other biological life forms. If Anastasia Bergman was the world's premiere promession guru, using cryonics and high-frequency vibrations, what if she was also doing research on freezing and re-animating frozen subjects? I crept out of the closet again and gave Lacy the lowdown now that she'd fully taken possession of the bed by the window.

"How does it do that? The freezing thawing thing, I mean without dying in the process. And that's assuming what you read on the internet is actually based on fact."

Okay, so there was that.

"I mean, what's the biological reason the beetle would have developed this feature? Does it have a certain protein or something that—"

"It's not a protein," I said. "It's a molecule, called xylomannan. It's naturally occurring in its blood."

She nodded, evaluating this new information in her big brain.

199

"What's her motivation?" Lacy asked of Anastasia Bergman. "Is she a cryogenesis expert, is she a bio—"

"She's a biologist," I cut in. "But more than that, she's a rabid, no, maybe even a fringe environmentalist determined to find more sustainable ways to decrease the space needed to store our civilization's dead."

Lacy was shaking her head. "That's still not answering my question. Why would she care about freezing people *and* bringing them back to life? I thought the whole point of her technology and process was to break down a body to its smallest constituents after death to conserve space on the planet."

A knock at the door pulled us back to reality.

CHAPTER 45

Lunch consisted of five types of sausage and ten types of cheese, including a flight of three fondues in little chafing dishes. Beautifully presented, well-prepared small portions clearly intending to kill us off before we're thirty.

"Can we turn the French television down while we eat at least? It's giving me a headache."

I left the volume up because I knew we'd still be talking about the keyword search.

"Nothing much came up about Bilderberg," I said, "other than what I'd researched already. They apparently have many artifacts like swords in the Bilderberg Art Collection, and there's nothing about any thefts."

"Oleg?"

"The name is the regional equivalent of John Smith. I'll keep digging."

I watched her chewing, struggling to chomp through a mystery-sausage. She paused to wipe her mouth before speaking. How could she be such a tomboy and so dainty at the same time?

"What about Lazarus?" she asked.

"Couple of things." I held up my index finger. "Zombies, gaming, and a 2008 movie. So I kept the capital L in Lazarus and added a word after it and kept the rotation going to see if anything

201

came up. Lazarus promession, Lazarus Anastasia Bergman, Lazarus Oleg Kokov. Nothing yet but I can refine my search parameters."

I got up from the tiny, round table in the corner and started pacing. My hands buzzed with energy, with the nervousness I felt about the swarm of questions in my head. What the fuck did Lazarus mean? Was it the name of a secret project? I couldn't help but think it had some connection to Dr. Ek and his promession research, seeing as the word Lazarus had become synonymous with resurrection and death was the commonality. Like two things should fit, but they somehow didn't.

I returned to the closet and tried another search round. I remembered Jonas telling me the Bergman's daughter was a Swedish heiress. So I entered Dr. Anastasia Bergman Sweden. The search took a minute. The duckduckgo search page wasn't resolving for some reason. I refreshed the page, same thing. I felt something, somewhere, in my body. Anastasia Bergman. I tried again. Dr. Anastasia Bergman, Professor of Biology. *Bingo*. Uppsala University Faculty of Medicine. Now, Dr. Anastasia Bergman promession.

An article came up, written in Swedish, no translation available, but the search showed the title: Ethical Disputes on Controversial Swedish Cremation Method, Professor Banned from Prominent University.

Okay, that was important. Why? Because she was fringe now. An outlier dispatched from acceptable mainstream. I kept digging, different variations, looking at arrest records, legal history. I brought Lacy up to speed as my phone buzzed with a text notification. "Must be Jonas," I said, grabbing it. "Shit."

"What is it?" Lacy asked.

"Jonas. He said Anastasia Bergman's dead. Her parents, I met them just the other... Wait, he's typing again. Now he says...oh for fuck's sake." I paused to process the words. "Anastasia Bergman died six months ago."

I collapsed on the bed and buried my face in one of the soft pillows. So everything the Bergmans told us was a lie. Nothing felt comfortable or even real right now. And in the few minutes we'd been talking after lunch, I watched Lacy's face gradually change. I knew that face so well, her pre-cry face.

"What's the matter?" I asked.

"What are we doing here, BJ?" she whined. "I mean, are we under house arrest? Like we can't even leave this room?" She laid back on the other bed and stretched out her arms and legs.

"She never said that. We can leave the room. Just not the hotel. Problem is, we're visible."

"And?"

"I don't know what Ina's real agenda is. And without knowing that, we don't know what our potential exposure is if we're seen."

Lacy bit her lip, which she did when she was editing her thoughts. "And you don't trust the story she told us? About chasing the sword?"

My phone buzzed again. This time I didn't recognize the number.

"Who is it?"

"I don't know." I moved to the desk and turned on the lamp, holding my phone under it. My hand was shaking. Lacy was beside me.

"Oh my God," she said, reading the words:

Pack up your backpack, take your computer and charger. Wait for instructions. You have five minutes.

I looked at my watch and remembered I don't wear one. The time on my phone read 4:45 p.m. Geneva time.

Who is this? I wrote back.

I saw the status dots showing they were writing back.

Lazarus.

So whoever they were, they had a camera in our room and knew about the laptop, probably audio surveillance, too. And I suspected they weren't working with Ina and her team of phony insurance adjusters. I blinked at Lacy and gestured toward the closet. I unplugged and packed up the computer, zipped it into my backpack and stood inside the door, waiting.

"Time check?" I asked.

"Two minutes."

"Pack up."

"I did," she said, then I noticed her bag was already inside the door.

"What-is-this?" she asked, with her don't fuck with me face.

"I think it's a jailbreak."

"Time?"

"It's time," she said.

I texted a message to the same number. *It's five minutes*, I wrote. *Who are you and what do you want?*

Do you have headphones or an earpiece?

Yes, why?

Call this number and have your earpiece in.

I showed it to Lacy and wrote back. *WTF?*

You'll need the earpiece because you'll be running.

Why?

There's a bomb in your hotel.

⊹ ⧼⧽ ✦ ⧼⧽ ⊹

"Holy fuck. What do we do? Let me turn off the TV."

"Leave it on," I said. "Make it seem like we're still in here. Okay, I'm calling the number he sent. Are we ready?"

"Do it."

I dialed the number exactly as he'd typed it, starting with 41, the country code for Switzerland, securing my iPhone headphones tight to my ears. I wish I'd brought my Air pods.

"That you, Mr. Janoff?" A deep, male voice, slightly familiar.

"Yes."

"Listen to me carefully. Leave your room but stick the Do Not Disturb sign in the door like you're holding it open for someone."

"Got it."

I exited into the hall, Lacy followed. The sign stuck out, visible.

"Done."

"Turn left, walk quickly down the hall and take the stairwell on your right, one floor only."

I pointed left to Lacy, then right to the stairwell using hand signals.

"Done. Now what?" I asked.

"Exit the stairwell and turn left to walk around the elevator shaft. Keep turning left till you see another stairwell. The door will be on the right. Tell me when you've seen it."

Lacy and I were jogging, exactly what he'd told us not to do. But he'd just told us a bomb was about to go off in the building. "Got it,"

I said.

"Take the stairs to the bottom level. You'll find yourself on the Housekeeping floor."

We were running now, the frantic pitter-patter of steps on the concrete stairs, one level, two levels, three and that's where they ended. I tugged on the steel door.

"Yeah, the door's locked," I said, into the phone.

"Knock three times with your fist."

Bam. Bam. Bam. I rammed the fat part of my hand into the steel so hard my bones shook. A man in a black suit opened the door for us, motioning us through. Without speaking or making eye contact, he scanned the large warehouse space while holding his arm out straight to block us.

"Now, follow the man in front of you."

After a two-second delay, the man looked left, right, and started jogging straight ahead toward the back wall. Still connected to the phone, I sent Lacy in front of me and I followed them past rows of floor-to-ceiling metal shelves, rolling carts filled with sheets and towels. The man opened a door and immediately turned right.

"You still there?" I asked the man on the phone.

"Keep going. I see you. Follow him out of the building."

I see you? How the fuck was he seeing us?

"Twenty seconds," the phone said.

"Twenty seconds," I shouted ahead of me so both Lacy and the black suit would hear me, assuming we had twenty seconds to live. We sprinted down a darkened corridor, still concrete under our feet, now with dirty windows high above our heads. Another door, another corridor.

"We're in another building," Lacy said.

"I know; it smells different." It smelled musty, and there was no sound.

The black-suited man kept running. "Gonna get real dark here," he said. "Don't stop running. It's a straight shot forward. Listen for the footsteps. There's a door fifty feet ahead of us. Go now."

I kept my eyes on Lacy and had to trust that the man who called himself Lazarus was trying to save us, and not the opposite. Where the fuck were we? I tried to calm my nerves and make my body cooperate with the unexpected exertion, not to mention a growing pain in my side. Everything felt heavier with my backpack on my shoulders, my laptop ramming into my spine with every step.

"Lace, you still there?" I asked. But I didn't need to. I could hear her footsteps. Feel her energy, sense her silky presence right in front of me.

The door opened; the man was right. Amazing how someone had actually told the truth for once. I could see now, twenty feet, fifteen, Lacy was through the door, ten feet, just me left running across a dark warehouse alone now in complete darkness. Why was the floor moving under my fee—??!!

CHAPTER 46

The force of the vibration heaved my body into the air. I half-landed on Lacy, who was running out into a fenced parking lot outside the warehouse we'd just come from. The black-suited man was nowhere around.

"Are you there?" I asked the phone man, Lazarus. No response.

We'd ended up in a heap with my head crammed against a concrete block wall and her on her side. I think I'd crashed down on her hip. "Lace, you okay?"

She rolled out from under me and stood, brushing herself off, and checking me out. "Can you run?"

"Yeah, I'm fine," I lied. I was the farthest thing from fine. I'd be surprised if I could walk.

We moved past the parking lot entrance heading down a dark street in sort of a limping fast-walk. Behind us, I heard an alarm, Then a fire truck sounded about ten blocks away. Police cars now.

"Where are we going?" she yelled back to me.

When I opened my mouth to speak, I heard the screech of rubber tires behind us. My God. What now? We walked faster, closer to the block of brick buildings on the right, hoping for some kind of alley to slip into, finding only the cruelty of exposure and peril that was waiting for us. By the motor, I could tell it was an older car, not well maintained, rolling faster and faster, trying to cut us off before we got to the end of the block.

"You okay up there?" I shouted.

"Who's in the car?" she asked.

"No idea." We were a hundred feet from the end of the building, uncertain what was around the next corner.

"What do I do?"

"Go straight," I said.

"Mr. Janoff," the voice on the voice spoke again finally. He startled me. "Turn right, stop, and wait."

"Lacy, turn right and wait," I said before I even had a chance to evaluate the directive.

She slowed and turned toward me. I pointed to my earpiece. We both peered at the screeching car, moved around the corner and collapsed panting on the hard ground. I looked up into the mottled gray sky, my view distracted by stunning architecture and the smoke and chaos of the explosion someone set in the building from which we'd just narrowly escaped.

I leaned against the smooth, white concrete of what looked like a bank catching my breath while the car haunting us from behind pulled up and parked. The back door opened.

"Get in," someone said. A man. The man on the phone.

Lacy's face was a mess of emotion.

"Where else are we gonna go?" I asked her with just my eyes, alone in a foreign city. "We can't outrun them. We don't even know who or what they are."

I went in first, instructed toward the rear bench seat in a dark limo, Lacy pulled in beside me. The door closed and the old man, Andranik Dvali, leaned down and smiled so we could see his face.

"Um, what the actual fuck was that?" Lacy shrieked.

The old man closed his eyes, I was sure his old age made it difficult to hear that language from not only a woman but a young woman. Wait till he found out she was also a lawyer.

"Was that explosion meant for us?" I asked.

"Go," the old man said to the driver. The car rolled ahead, slowly this time. "Not you specifically," Dvali said. "Someone who was coming to meet you."

"No one was coming to meet us. Ina told us to—where is Ina?" I asked. Oh no.

"You are traveling in dangerous circles, Mr. Janoff. All who pursue the things that we pursue understand the risks."

"Jesus Christ. How many more people will—"

"Will die for your cause? Is that what you were going to ask?"

"I feel sick." I lowered my head.

"I do not know yet if Ina made it out. I will know soon."

"Who was coming to meet us?" I asked. I sat and looked at Dvali's face. "My father?"

No answer.

"Did he make it out?" I asked. "Answer me!"

Dvali shook his head. "Your father is a wise man," he answered. "He was requested to meet at your hotel, and I'm sure he had no plans to comply with that request. Or not without sending someone in first."

"Someone who might be dead now? Another dead? How many have to die, Andranik, for whatever this is?" I was almost screaming, my voice like gravel, real tears in my eyes, nose running. I wiped them with my dirty hands. "Is it really a sword we're chasing?" I asked more calmly now. "You don't actually think we believe you work for an auction house, do you?"

Lacy leaned her head back on the seat in opposition. The old man looked at her.

"And you, young lady, what do you have to say?"

"Nothing."

"Because you don't care?"

Her famous eyeroll with her ultra-long eyelashes. So glamorous.

"Or perhaps because you do?" Dvali asked, looking back at me now.

"I think you and your team of government goons are full of shit," she said, finally. "BJ has a theory that I think has some merit." She looked at me now, tacitly asking for permission. I bit my lip and shrugged.

"BJ?" Dvali repeated, amused. "This is what people in your world call you? Brock is maybe the name your older brother calls you? Or your father?"

I nodded at Lacy, ignoring the old man.

"I'm sure you'll neither confirm nor deny this," Lacy said.

"Go ahead," Dvali said. "What is this theory?"

"BJ believes all of this has nothing to do with the Boateng saber, and everything to do with Anastasia Bergman."

Lacy and I stayed glued to the man's face, looking for an eye movement, twitch of the mouth, something involuntary, a tell. Anything. The face didn't move. That *was* the tell. I remembered the book that Sten Bergman gave me, to me personally, with a note stuck in the page that he himself had written to me, so I could somehow pull it together and stop this runaway train to hell.

"I think you've got a significant financial interest in several works of art," I said, "and I'd bet my life that those art pieces are stored in containers far larger than their dimensions," I pointed, "right here in the Geneva Freeport."

I leaned in. It might be my imagination, but it seemed like Dvali sank back in his chair an inch or two in response. He didn't protest or negate my words. Just sat there in silence with a cloud of dread surrounding him, eyes wide and waiting.

"Stop the car," I said. "I'm getting out."

"Let him out," Dvali said to the driver. The car stopped. Dvali opened the door. I stepped out and paced, the door still open, my arms wrapped tight around my body. I needed some way to hold the strands of my life together right now, and it wasn't working in that car.

"Please, Mr. Janoff. Let's be civilized here and talk. Come back to the car."

"Cold beetle." I said it out loud now so I could actually hear it. "Anastasia Bergman's dead, isn't she?" I froze, Dvali leaning out of the car to watch me, Lacy sitting back. "She died six months ago. I don't know how she died, but I suspect my father had been following her, possibly working with her, for a long time. Just a theory, I know, but maybe she trusted him, and he was working undercover for her, as one of her scientists, learning her trade, learning promession. And then, one day, she shared her secret with him."

"What secret?" Dvali snipped back. "You know nothing about this." But he sounded scared.

"Cold beetle," I said to him now. Lacy's mouth opened an inch. "I think Anastasia Bergman was experimenting on humans to use a molecule found in the blood of an Alaskan beetle, xylomannan, that lets beetles freeze, thaw, and still go on living. I think like Dr. Anders

Ek, Anastasia Bergman was freezing live humans and subjecting them to the promession process without their consent and cremating them to refine her process, make changes, improve her efficiency, R&D with live humans." I paced again, out of breath and trying to pull it all together.

"Mr. Janoff...please..."

"And all of the biologists who studied under Dr. Bergman, like Dr. Ek and the other fifteen biologists across the globe, started using her horrifying, unethical practices to freeze and kill live humans without their consent. That put those doctors at risk of exposure, possible legal action, and potential prosecution and license revocation. And what if Dr. Bergman found a way to make those doctors disappear for a while, to keep them from being exposed or prosecuted?"

"What are you talking about, Mr. Janoff? It's cold. Get back in the car, please," Dvali whined.

"Shut up, let him talk. Keep going," Lacy said.

"I think with Dr. Bergman dead, there may be only one person left on earth who knows how to bring those Swedish promession scientists out of cryonic stasis without killing them. And I think that person is my father, George Janoff." I shivered when I said it. Dvali was right, it was cold. I got back in the car and closed the door behind me.

"What about the sword and the Geneva Freeport?" Lacy asked now, Dvali sitting quietly beside her, deflated of his usual bravado.

"I think they're hiding the frozen bodies *in* the Freeport and disguising them as crates of modern art sculptures...or possibly an ancient sword."

CHAPTER 47

"**Well done, Mr. Janoff.**" **Dvali clapped.** "**You're only** twenty-five but you show great promise as an investigator. You're on the right track, yes. Your father, your family I should say, goes way back with the Bergmans. You see, your father was close allies with Sten Bergman, Anastasia Bergman's grandfather."

"Bilderberg? They were both members?"

"Bergman, yes. Your father was a consulting accountant at that time and not yet a full member, but yes, essentially. He was studying Anastasia's craft because—"

"Because he was in love with her?" I interrupted.

Dvali narrowed his eyes. "Is that what you thought?"

"Growing up? Yes, that's what we both thought, Jonas and I," I said. "So did my mother."

Now he shook his head more emphatically as if I'd insulted him or something. "Nothing like that. Nothing. He traveled with Anastasia, yes of course. But he was learning her craft because he knew about her human rights violations even in the beginning, how she was using promession as a way of ridding the world of indigents, a sort of post-modern civilization-cleansing. Your father wanted to shut her down, and the only way to do it, in his mind, was to get close enough for her to trust him with all her secrets."

I considered his monologue. "He told you all this?"

"He didn't have to. I knew what he was doing."

"Did it work? Did she share those secrets, in particular how to protect people from prosecution by freezing them and storing them in a Swiss art museum? It sounds like a bad sci-fi film."

Dvali smiled. "You're a sharp young man, Mr. Janoff. And yes, your father got what he needed from Dr. Bergman."

I leaned forward and put my head in my palms and stayed there for a moment, preparing myself. "Did he kill her?" I looked up. "Did my father kill Anastasia Bergman?"

Dvali didn't answer me, which had to be a yes.

I grabbed Lacy's hand and held it against my chest. She moved a little closer in the backseat and we stayed like that while the driver took the freeway onramp.

"Where are we going now? I asked him.

"To the source."

— ◦ ◦ ❦ ✠ ❦ ◦ ◦ —

I didn't know what he meant by the source, but I was exhausted and becoming less efficient with my questions. I asked him about James.

"You're worried about him, yes?" the old man asked. "You want to take care of him. That's an admirable trait in a man. Compassion. Useless, but admirable."

"What about him and the other workers there that night? At the fortress, he said they were all dead, lying on the ground. What happened to them?"

Dvali looked out the window. "That was Minesh's project. Sometimes he goes too far. But—" he looked into my eyes— "I suspect they were only drugged. We are not in the business of killing people as a general rule. Sometimes, yes, this is necessary. But it's messy and the risk of exposure is too great."

"For you and your organization? And what organization is that, exactly?" I asked. "Interpol, CIA, MI6, FSB?"

"I am old, Mr. Janoff."

"Does that mean all of them?"

"Old men need to rest. Maybe young men do, too."

I originally thought we were going to the Geneva Freeport, so I couldn't imagine why we'd been in the car for so long. It was supposed to be a ten-minute drive from CitizenM Hotel. We'd been driving an hour. I looked out the window. It resembled the area around our hotel, where we'd been an hour ago.

"What's going on? We're going in circles."

Lacy had been resting her head on my shoulder. Her hair smelled faintly of cinnamon.

"Yes," Dvali said.

"Why?"

"Because you don't walk straight into the Geneva Freeport and ask to see an ancient artifact." Dvali closed his eyes, but I saw him smiling at something. He was waiting for me to catch up again.

"Let me guess. Game theory."

His mouth spread open to show a lower row of stained, gapped teeth and his admiration of my powers of deduction. "It's a somewhat new game theory strategy. Timing. Small adjustments in timing can tip the scales and change what we call the equilibrium point, giving advantage to one side or the other."

"So then we're waiting for, what?" I imagined my father and me, in that moment, in that small boat. Waiting for a sign.

"I think you reaching that conclusion *is* the sign, Mr. Janoff. See if he's there now," Dvali said to the driver, who made a screeching, perilous u-turn in the middle of the street. I rolled down my window and smelled smoke in the air, a reminder of what had happened here, of our narrow escape. I was still afraid to ask him about Ina.

We arrived at what he'd called the source, driving in through a gate. Dvali said a few words to an armed guard, whose eyes scanned him, me, Lacy, and the driver before he let us through. Someone had taken great care to control the flow of traffic here. One single lane, two others blocked on each side, led down a straight path to a five-story building. By the entry back here, I couldn't tell if this was the main entrance or the rear. But when we drove past it earlier, there was no front entrance.

"Get your identification ready," the driver called into the rear-view mirror. "After I park, follow me in through the door that says Documentation."

"Nyet." Dvali shook his head. "I will take them in myself."

"Yes, sir." The surly driver held a *whatever* pose on his face. I hoped Dvali knew what he was doing.

We followed him, but not through the door the driver specified. Andranik Dvali marched in there like a cowboy and ushered us to a set of elevators, ignoring everyone in his path. Guards holding machine guns saw his formidable face and took a step back to let him pass. It was getting more interesting every minute.

We proceeded to the third floor. Everything was light gray. No papers needed, no passport checks. Lacy and I hung back while Dvali spoke in hushed tones to a well-suited woman, pointing up with his finger, and gesturing toward us. He motioned us forward.

"Yes," he said. "Yes, today. No more than an hour. But we'll be back with someone later, and we will need to be here for a day or so, and at that time we'll be needing complete privacy. It has all been pre-arranged."

"Of course," the woman said almost in a shrug, like she got similar requests all the time.

"What the fuck is this place?" I whispered.

Lacy was soaking it up. Her big brown eyes were tiny computers, assessing, tracking, calibrating scenarios, calculating odds.

"A shopping mall for white-collar, organized crime?"

I raised a brow, ever amused by her thumbnail sketches of humanity. She was right, in a way. Freeports were for storage, holding cells for expensive artifacts. But the fact that they were off the radar of law enforcement and virtually unregulated created an environment for all kinds of things.

Dvali motioned us toward another elevator now. We exited onto the fourth floor and were ushered into a sort of holding room while Security assessed our space. Here we were, the three of us, Andranik Dvali of MI6 or Interpol seated on one side crossing his legs, Lacy standing with arms folded at a window.

"Why's it black?" she asked of the window. "It's still light out."

"It's an interior window to a warehouse," Dvali said. "The warehouse lights are off, that's all."

"You said Security's preparing our space. How many spaces do you have here?" I asked.

He nodded. "Okay," he said, slapping his palms on his thighs. "Let's have all your questions. You too, young lady. Come. How many spaces? Fifteen. Sixteen actually."

"Why sixteen?" I asked.

"I like how you asked about the number of spaces even before you asked what's inside them, Mr. Janoff."

"Glad to provide entertainment value for you, sir." I smirked.

"We know what's inside them," Lacy said. "Brock already told you. The fifteen scientists who worked under Anastasia Bergman. Dr. Ek is the sixteenth. Right?"

"Razor sharp." Dvali nodded and smiled. "Keep going."

"What is the cost of one of these spaces?" Me now.

"Eight hundred thousand including Security," he said.

I gulped. "US dollars?"

"Per month," he added.

"Times sixteen, right?"

"Times sixteen."

I sucked air into my lungs, processing this information. "So this facility—"

"There are two, actually," he added. "This one and another just like it, a little smaller, near the airport fifteen minutes away."

"So, they're like a cross between a Catholic confessional and a construction company," Lacy said, "that custom builds an infrastructure for you to hide all your sins."

"Or your valuables," Dvali added. "You're right, though, hiding and storing."

"I suspect it's pure economics," Lacy said. "You're so desperate to find Brock's father so he can provide the secret ingredient to thaw your test subjects to save you the cost of the rental payments?" Lacy asked, but she'd already drawn the conclusion.

"Crude word for it, thaw, but true," Dvali said. "Defrosting a subject from the cryopreservation state takes time because you're bringing them from below zero to ninety-eight degrees."

"It's pure science fiction," I said. "It can't be done, not with humans."

"It can and it has."

"And my father knows how to do this?" I asked.

"Your father has the magic serum that will allow their bodies to intelligently do the work themselves. The Bergman technology. And more importantly, if something were to happen to that fragile serum, your father knows how to recreate it. The hazardous part is that he is now the only person on earth, that we know of, who has successfully done this."

That, and the costs involved, was starting to explain why someone might blow up a building over this.

"Why am I here, Andranik?" I asked.

Dvali regarded me with his cautious, calculating eyes, running his tongue over the front of his teeth. I liked calling him by his first name, not because it was casual and, therefore, more welcoming but because I knew he considered it to be disrespectful. I couldn't help feeling played by these people, surveilled, deceived, kidnapped, coerced, and now dragged around the globe, my mounting resentment spilling out at unexpected times. What would be the tipping point?

"You, Mr. Janoff, are here so you can understand your family, and see what your father has been doing. What he has been learning, engineering, and ultimately planning to sabotage all these years. That's reason number one."

"Jonas is older than me, though. More experienced, probably more stable in my father's eyes. Why wasn't he chosen?"

The old man shrugged. "Maybe he thought you were more likely to buy into all this."

I didn't believe him, but I pretended to go along because pretending was becoming my most marketable skill. "And number two?"

"To suss him out, of course. We've been trying unsuccessfully to do that for months. You, we believe, will have a powerful effect on his decision-making."

Game theory. Leverage. Whatever. "And he's not dead?" I asked then shrugged. "Practically speaking, I mean."

"It's a logical question, but no. He was seen recently. Today, in fact. And you—" he pointed to Lacy— "are here for one reason, my dear. Can your keen mind guess what that is?"

Lacy was perched precariously on the edge of a modern, white chair by the window, again purposely isolated from the main seating area, planning our escape path.

"It's too sinister. Do I have to?"

"Please," he said.

She sighed, rose, and chose a similar white chair opposite Dvali. But she sat and looked directly at me when she spoke. "I'm his insurance policy," she explained. "I'm the pressure point he intends to press, if needed, because he thinks I'm your weakness." She glared at the old man now. "I'm not, you know. It's not like that. We're best friends. We grew up together."

"Maybe so," the man shrugged. "Regardless of your history, Mr. Janoff is indeed in love with you and, we suspect, will do anything to protect you from harm."

Oh. My. God. I wanted to burrow myself into the floor. He'd said the words I hadn't been able to. I was actually two or three stages away from being able to say it. I didn't move, twitch, breathe for at least thirty seconds, during which time Lacy's eyes blinked at me and the old man, deciding whether to trust him or not. A guard appeared in the doorway.

"Tu peux entrer maintenant."

I knew *maintenant* meant now. Dvali rose.

Our point of no return, I think the saying goes.

"Are we ready?" he asked.

I ignored him and moved to the door to stand behind the guard. I resented the old man's brazen security leak of my highly classified information. Since when were my personal feelings a point of leverage? Anything goes in game theory, was that it? Fucker. I did feel that way, though, the point of no return. A security guard of unknown origin, me, the five-foot-seven Darth Vader directly behind me trailed by Princess Leia. I felt like Han Solo in *The Empire Strikes Back* when he was captured by imperial soldiers about to be frozen in carbonite.

Frozen?? A white terror cracked like lightning through my chest and belly. Was that what Dvali had in mind for me? And for Lacy? Were we about to be cryogenically frozen? Was that the real reason we were brought here?

CHAPTER 48

I texted Lacy while we were all walking in a line following the guard down a series of tall, echoey corridors. Dvali was no more than three paces behind me. I could send her one word.

Carbonite, I wrote, hoping she'd remember the scene, the movie, the Star Wars mythology we grew up on. I hoped she was even talking to me after that unthinkable breach. She had to be almost as mortified as I was.

Us?? She wrote back with the screaming-in-fear emoji.

Need a plan.

Dvali's old, was her reply.

That was true. I knew where she was going with it, that we might be able to maneuver him into one of the chambers and freeze him instead. If he didn't have a gun, that is. While I contemplated that substantial *if*, I noticed the line was getting shorter. The guard in front of me took slower steps, forcing me to come up behind him. Dvali followed close. When I turned my head to check him, his head was turned toward Lacy. We needed to act fast, but there was nowhere to run. I tried one last thing.

Dad, help, I texted to the last known phone number of my father, the secret agent, Brock George Janoff. *Geneva Freeport, me and Lacy, upper floor, about to be frozen. Where are you?* I didn't stop to check my spelling errors; I just hit Send and kept walking, trying to think of a happy memory to take with me into cryogenic death.

My phone buzzed. OMG. Dad? I literally almost cried picking it up. *Right in front of you is an ally*, he wrote back. *You might recognize him.*

Could that have actually been my father texting me just now? Or was it a trick? Ina, Minesh, one of Dvali's many goons? I took him on his word for now and thought I heard the buzz of another phone. The guard in front of me. Who was he? I watched the man now, watched him look down at his phone. That walk looked familiar, though he was wearing a uniform and cap. I knew that walk. The guard turned back toward me.

"Come, Mr. Janoff."

I could see half his fa—

"We're almost there now."

The man spoke perfect English, and with a slight New York accent. OMFG. Breathe, Brock. It was our dead partner, Archie Dax.

⁂

Shock ran through my body; I was surprised I could still walk. Heart pounding. I felt sick. The accident, the explosion, the building where it all went down. Archie's half-broken body lying in a crumpled heap on the dirt, Miki Fine sobbing and screaming at his side. Jesus. What kind of trickery was this?

"Man behind the curtain?" I asked, still behind him, in a loud enough voice so I was sure he heard me. My tone was snide, to say the least. No answer. "How many curtains are there?" Still no answer.

The Geneva Freeport security guard known as Archie Dax turned and grabbed Dvali's elbow. "Right this way, sir. Everything's been prepared for you."

I saw what he was doing—pulling Dvali in front of us so he and I could communicate freely. Now Dvali was attended to by another guard unlocking a set of double doors ahead of us. Archie turned toward me, seeing my red eyes, evidence of my broken and now frozen heart. He leaned down toward my ear.

"Asshole," I said. "What the fuck is this? You're, like, not dead."

"Disappointed?" he asked, still walking.

"Fuck you."

"Listen." He slowed and turned. "Miki's escaped; Jonas will call you. Don't tell him anything. Don't talk to anyone. No one. About me or anything else. It's for your protection."

"And you're Lazarus, I presume? You used a pitch modification app to change your voice. Aren't you funny now."

"Yes," he said.

I turned to Lacy, whose hand was over her mouth. She, of course, knew Archie as well as any of us did. Her questioning eyes probed me for an answer. I nodded and wrapped my arms around her frail, shaking body.

"I cried at your funeral, fucker. And many times after that."

"I'm sorry," he mumbled. "It couldn't be helped."

"Where's my father?" My voice was like black ice.

"Here," he whispered.

I looked around the cavernous corridor. "Where?"

"In the building."

Dvali finished talking to the other two guards, whom he escorted out of the room and closed the door behind him. He gave a sober glance at Archie with a faint nod. Omg, did that mean what I think it meant?

Our spatial arrangement in the room seemed noteworthy, Dvali just inside a set of doors, Archie two feet from him, and Lacy and I two feet from Archie. Dvali's eyes looked large and dark as he stared at Archie with some telepathic imperative. I felt the vibration of his impatience, waiting for Archie to kill us, probably with a syringe of some kind. Time slowed. I breathed in and out. I grabbed Lacy's hand and walked three steps to Archie's right, so now all three of us were a foot or so from Archie, whose gloved hand was still in his front pocket. I decided playing dumb could be a worthy diversion.

"What are we waiting for?" I asked. "Mr. Dvali said he had something he wanted to show us up here."

"Yes," Dvali said. "This way. I'll take you. And then I need to tend to some operational business in the finance office a few floors down, but that shouldn't take long. Everything is done, I just need to sign a few forms."

Dvali facing us in the open doorway, a breeze chilled my skin from an adjacent room. Dvali turned his head for two seconds to look

221

into the other space, during which time I whispered the word "Scarlet" into Lacy's ear. I loved our long, shared history in this way, decades-old references to books, games and movies that we could still use to communicate secret, insider messages.

She immediately understood the ninth-grade reference to her role in our high school production of *Gone with The Wind*, in which she had played Scarlet O'Hara's fainting aunt. Without a second's hesitation, Lacy's knees buckled and she let out an "uhhhh", collapsing butt-first on the polished floor into a bent-leg, half-rolled-over heap. Perfect.

Even before I got a chance to launch my feigned concern routine, a guttural moan emerged from Dvali's mouth and he crumbled to the floor. Archie Dax had his hands at his sides, one of them holding a syringe. Had that serum been configured for Lacy and me, either to produce instant death, or something even worse? We stood there, the three of us, awkwardly stationed in the open doorway between two areas of an upper floor of the Geneva Freeport, waiting.

"Is he dead or tranqued?" I asked Archie, who put a finger to his mouth and shook his head.

"There," he said, pointing at Dvali's face, "watch him. Once the eyes are closed we're good."

"Dvali's not dead?" Lacy asked.

"No," I said because I knew what Archie had just injected, and I knew it even before I saw Dr. Anders Ek emerge into view.

CHAPTER 49

"Nice to see you again, Mr. Janoff. You never did get part two of that facility tour."

Au contraire, I thought, except it was self-guided. I nodded, amazed at his calm demeanor.

"Ms. Diaz, pleasure to meet you. Your reputation precedes you."

Lacy shook her head in disgust. "So does yours, 'doctor'."

"Would you two like to come with me?" Ek said, while eyeing Archie. "Do you have the support you need to take care of Mr. Dvali?"

"I do," Archie answered him. "Will be along shortly to join you in the atrium."

"Very well," Ek replied, a Dr. Mengele disguised as a gentleman. "First, let's get properly suited up." He pointed to a closet with the doors open, pulled down a plastic bin, and handed us plastic face masks. "Put these on, please," he said and put a pair on himself.

"Did you inject Dvali with the same substance you were using on the homeless people down at the fortress?"

"Fortress?" Dr. Ek asked. "Abilene?"

He knew what I meant.

Dr. Ek clasped his hands behind his back, a bold move with vivid symbolism. Another game theorist manipulating me by pausing and feigning submission as a means of tacitly exerting control. I was tired of games like this. I longed for my normal, boring life. If I ever got lucky enough to find my way back there, I'd never complain about it again.

"That's right." Ek gazed at the ceiling. "You did finish the tour, but you did it on your own the following night. So you've seen the cryonic chambers."

"Interesting that you use that word, Doctor. You see, I've been doing some reading on the technology and learned that cryonics only refers to the freezing of the dead, whereas cryogenics refers to technologies that lower the body temperatures of living humans. Which brings us to an interesting ethical question."

"Dude, why go there now?" Lacy asked me. "Seriously, what's the point?"

"Please." Ek had his hand out now. "I'd like to hear your point of view."

"How were you able to justify experimenting on live humans?" My voice cracked. "I mean, without their proper consent, subjecting them to freezing and thawing practices only to lose the majority of your subjects?"

"How could you possibly know what the—"

"I saw them!" My sudden scream echoed Cathedral-like off the walls and tall ceiling. Ek snapped back an inch. So did Lacy. "I saw all of the—"

"Oh, but I did have their permission," he countered. "The NDA that you yourself signed, don't you remember?"

"It was dark, too dark to read the fine print. I'm not even sure I'd understand exactly what I was signing."

"I would have," Lacy said.

"Yes, but you're too smart to get yourself into situations like that," I told her.

"Well, I'm here aren't I? So much for that theory. However, if you forced staff members or even volunteers to sign a legal document without adequate lighting to give them an opportunity to read it and without verbally outlining the terms to which they were agreeing with their signature, the NDAs could very well be ruled invalid in most civil and criminal courts."

Ek was deciding how to respond.

"Oh, you didn't know she was a lawyer?" I smirked.

"No," he said, hands clasped behind him, eyes on the floor.

"Dvali?" I asked him again.

"Eight hours. He'll be fine."

I breathed in and held the air in my lungs for a moment.

Footsteps echoed from the other room as Archie rejoined us. "It's time," he said to Ek, who nodded.

"You'll want to see this," Ek said to me.

Like a museum curator, Dr. Ek led us down another long hallway into a locked room, and a locked chamber in the back that had a tall, steel door the thickness of a bank vault. An electronic keypad outside it matched what I'd seen on the third floor of the fortress. Smart lighting flicked on as we moved through the space, responding to our movements it seemed, low lights on the floor and a few tiny spotlights in the ceiling. Alexa for freeports?

"Oh my God." Lacy gaped at rows of what looked like metal coffins with modules on the outsides of them, literally something out of Star Trek. Dr. Ek moved with Archie to the back end of the room, where one such vessel was positioned perpendicular to the others—head of the table, so to speak.

"Is he dead?" I asked, scrutinizing the features. My chest tightened. I could see my father's face even before it came into view. Was it possible I felt him, felt his frozen energy, from three feet away?

"No," Ek replied.

"I've been bringing him out slowly," Archie said.

"Where is he right now?" Ek asked Archie.

"Ninety degrees."

"Okay, how does this work?" I asked. "I assume you've found a way to freeze people and bring them out again without harm to their biological systems." Ek nodded slowly. "By using some form of xylamannon from the Upis Beetle?"

Archie stared at Ek, then me.

"We've developed an eight-hour serum and a thirty-day version, both of which have worked so far with no exceptions."

"According to what?" I asked. "Your extensive published case studies, your multi-arm clinical trials?"

"Joking, of course," I added to Lacy.

"It's not funny," she said.

"Maybe not FDA-approved clinical trials, but clinical trials nonetheless," Ek retorted. "I am a medical doctor."

"Tell me, Dr. Frankenstein, how many died in the development of these two serums?" Lacy asked. "And I don't mean rats."

Dr. Ek shook his head. "That's not relevant when you look at the bigger picture."

"Humor us," I said. "Since we'll never make it out of here alive." I watched what happened on their faces, Ek and Archie, when I spoke.

Ek cracked a smile, then quickly returned his mouth to its former scowl. "Sure, in that case I'll be happy to share that data with you. Eighteen or so."

"What are you doing?" Archie asked him, arms at his sides now like he was corralling us somehow. "We had an agreement. They are not to be harmed. That was the deal."

"I have—the serum!" Ek held a syringe in his hand filled with a gold-colored liquid. That hand was trembling now, his eyes wild. "I spent years, decades, developing it." He started pacing, breathing heavy. His voice sounded strained from emotion, face sweating, like something had just snapped. I was watching the man unravel right in front of us. I kept my breath even and held onto two of Lacy's fingers, watching. Waiting.

"You're alarmed at that number, young lady, aren't you? Eighteen?" He laughed, a full, toothy, throaty laugh that distorted his tortured face. I looked at it now with new eyes, the shape, the form, lines. He was so controlled, too much so. He couldn't sustain it anymore. He'd suffered. I could see it now. What, ridicule from colleagues? Lack of acknowledgment of his contributions, bullied on the schoolhouse playground, child abuse?

"If eighteen throwaways died, that's what I call them because they are—" he paused and bent forward at an angle to breathe— "I died seventeen times! Don't you see?" His face looked shiny now. Tears? Was he not actually made of stone? No one moved, Lacy and I standing frozen together, Archie by the door, ready to improvise.

"Every time we lost one, we had to try again."

I blinked while my mind tried to process his convoluted logic. I shook my head, not getting it.

"Your father…" He pointed at me wiping his eyes. "He refused!"

His voice cracked. "So who else was there to do the hard science? I had to go under. Your father froze me—seventeen times! That means seventeen times he successfully thawed me, using my serum."

"And you're fine?" I asked. "That's what you're saying?"

His head bobbed up and down, his face contorted into a laugh/cry.

"Because you don't look fine, Doctor. You don't *seem* fine at all."

While Ek had Lacy and me in his sights, Archie slipped a syringe out of his lab coat pocket for us to see, then slipped it back in. I was careful to not look directly at it. But I'd seen it. And I understood suddenly, what was about to go down.

"Ek has the freeze serum," I said, in a normal tone.

Lacy turned toward me. "Like freeze for eight hours or—"

"I'm afraid not, Counselor," Ek said to Lacy.

She moved to take two steps toward Ek and again, while his attention was locked on her, Archie pulled a second syringe out of his other pocket. I read this to mean that he had the thaw serum in one pocket and the freeze-forever serum in the other, likely meant for Dr. Ek. Better not get those mixed up.

"I just have one question." I took one step forward to match Lacy's position, which pulled the three of us—me, Lacy, and Dr. Ek, together in a sort of cluster, giving Archie a little more space to plan. We were in the front of the long room, now. I quickly turned to glance at the back of the room. The cryo-chamber was open now... and empty. "Where's my father right now?"

"I did the hard science. Your father refused to let me put him under and threatened to report my human rights abuses to the Steering Committee if I came near him." Ek's hair was fanned out Einstein-style and saliva sprayed from his lips when he spoke.

"Bilderberg," I said.

"But he agreed to stay on with me, learn the process, and administer the nanowarming serum to me, along with him," Ek pointed to Archie, his gnarled finger outstretched, face contorted by rage, tear streaks making shiny lines from his bloodshot eyes. He wobbled on his feet, gait too wide, feet not firmly planted on the floor. Step by step, moving toward an empty corner of the room.

"What is he doing?" Lacy asked.

Dr. Anders Ek was distancing himself. He placed his hand high on the wall and turned back, like he was planning to leap from the closed window.

CHAPTER 50

Some things you just know in your heart, without the need for intellectual validation. I knew, for example, that everything in my life thus far had in some small way been preparing me for this moment, this lawless facility, this scientific ego war between innovation and criminality housed in a *Stranger Things* upside-down. Anders Ek, Overlord of Rogue Medicine, freely admitted to Lacy that he'd killed eighteen people in the course of his unregulated clinical trials for the sake of research. And only here, on this white, polished floor did I begin to realize his motivation.

"My God," I said to Lacy. "That's where Archie's been all this time. Working with my father."

"What's happening to him?" She pointed to Ek, now huddled in the corner like a wounded animal.

"Calm down, Doctor," Archie said. "We're fine here. Everything's under control." He turned to us. "It's a process of using nanoparticles to uniformly heat the bodily tissues."

"Xylomannan, I read about it."

"An antifreeze molecule contained in the blood of several insects. We studied it, replicated it, and were able to create a synthetic form that we've incorporated into the serum to control the degree and speed of cooling and to create a bottom, sort of, which makes it easier to safely thaw tissue and maintain normal physiological processes."

Since when had Archie Dax become a medical doctor? I sensed someone in the adjacent room, probably the other guard Archie had spoken to earlier.

"Dr. Ek," I called out.

"You have no…idea…the magnitude of these experiments. Do you?" he asked me, head shaking.

"I guess the part I'm fuzzy on is why. You began your career as an environmentalist, not a doctor. So I know conservation is more than just a professional pursuit for you. But then it seemed like evading the law made conservation a secondary objective, so you could focus on hiding your controversial promession techniques by freezing your practitioners, that is if they disagreed with your desired endgame or if they were becoming too visible."

"No!" His voice bounced off the walls and tall ceiling.

"What about Anastasia Bergman?" I asked.

The doctor raised his fingers to his face and dug his fingernails into his forehead above his brows, acting like he was in agony.

"Was she getting in your way, refusing to cooperate with the direction you were taking the research? I guess maybe that number is now nineteen, then?"

"You don't understand," he moaned, emerging from the corner to take two steps toward me. He was leaning over, mouth open and snarling, breathing heavily, swinging his torso like a rabid dog assessing potential prey.

"Look at him," Lacy said.

I compared this withering creature to the man who'd shown me around his formidable lab less than a week ago. "Or is it ego?" I asked, "wanting desperately to be known and remembered for doing something—"

"That's right, something that no one else ever did. Ever conceived of!" He shouted his retorts now, shaking his head when he spoke. Nobody moved.

"Yes, but you're tricking nature, don't you see that? You might get away with it for a while, with a few, but the human body wasn't meant to withstand cryogenics." Then I got it, like a bolt of lightning hitting the top of my skull. "Nobel. Is that it?"

The snarl on Ek's face softened at the word. He stretched his spine and stood tall, breathing in the cool air of the room, somehow elevated.

"Are you looking for the Nobel Prize in medicine? Is that what all this is? Did the Bilderberg Group support your research and promise you something? Like a Nobel nomination, maybe, if you could create a more sustainable method of dealing with the dead than burying them in tombs?"

"Bilderberg's had several Nobel Prize winning members," Lacy said.

"Not only that, a few that were on the Nobel Prize nomination committees," I added, nodding at my own epiphany.

"Where'd you get that idea? Nobel?" Lacy asked me.

I shrugged. "I don't know. Sweden, I guess." I turned back to Ek. "The problem isn't with your idea, Doctor. Believe me, you win the innovation award hands-down. The problem is choice."

He turned his head left and right, the maniacal eyes wide and fixed.

"Your victims, I don't think it's inaccurate to call them that, don't consciously decide that they're willing to take the risk. You're not disclosing when you freeze them, that they're actually signing up for a risky experiment and, if it fails, they'll be subjected to promession cremation to hide the scandal of your repeated mistakes."

"A one-way trip?" he asked, then nodded.

I paused for a few seconds, assessing our positions on the game board, envisioning the takedown in my mind first.

"You're sick, Doctor," I went on. "We can all see that. Let us get you the help you need so you can continue your research."

Somehow I'd come three steps closer to him, though I couldn't consciously remember taking those steps. I felt power up here. There was something fortifying me in this building, this space. I took one more step and kept my voice low, gently cornering the sadistic killer disguised as a wounded animal. Did he have something to prove, still, to a childhood squelcher, a teacher, or another student? Was that the emotional engine driving him, the baggage he hadn't yet reckoned with?

"You're suffering, Doctor, we can all see it. Come with me now. You need help."

"He's dying, actually."

I didn't need to turn my head to know who had spoken, but I did all the same. I'd know that voice anywhere. It had probably been the second voice I'd ever heard in life.

"Oh my God," I said, and exhaled at the same time, then ran to him like a child lost in the woods and rescued. I couldn't remember the last time my father and I embraced. He held the back of my neck, pushing my head down into his shoulder, a pose designed to hold and comfort. His body felt thin. His clothes smelled like smoke. Three years of emotion and uncertainty compressed into five seconds. I'll take it.

The hug was a good distraction for everyone because in those seconds Archie was able to get within a foot of Dr. Ek. I pulled away from my father and looked back just as Archie raised the syringe. It got within an inch of Ek's neck when the doctor squirmed away and wriggled on the polished floor. His eyes were on Archie and that syringe.

"There's no way out," Archie said. "Don't you realize we're trying to—"

My father was able to slip behind Ek and grab him around the chest, clasping his fists over his ribcage. The doctor's legs dog-paddled on the floor without making traction. It took five more seconds of this painful display for Archie to get the syringe injected finally into the top of Ek's shoulder.

"Which syringe?" my father asked Archie.

"I'm not sure, actually. In the struggle…" He reached his hand into his pocket and pulled out the other syringe.

"Die or not die?" I asked.

"Not, and we've got about eight hours before he regains consciousness. But we need to lower his temperature. Now."

Lacy and I stepped away and watched Archie and my father work, first carrying Dr. Ek across the hall into the room with the cryo chambers. She and I trailed behind, keeping a lookout down the corridor near the elevators. But there was no one here. That's how they'd gotten away with this, all this time. Absolute privacy, the whole floor. You could do anything up here and never be detected.

Archie pressed a button on a module, which opened the top of one chamber. I watched him and my father fold the doctor in on his back and position his body in the chamber, banging the back of his head so hard I was sure he'd have a concussion. If he ever woke up.

Lacy squirmed watching the awkward display of elbows, knees, grunts, and shoes scuffing on metal.

"The poor guy," Lacy said. "I know he's a madman but that was grotesque."

Five minutes later, they had him positioned properly and secured for the next eight hours, with his body temperature and consciousness slowly climbing down a ladder. My father did the honors injecting a syringe full of clear liquid into Dr. Ek's neck and closing the top again. A burst of smoky air filled the chamber, then cleared after a few seconds. Ek wasn't moving.

"How does it work?" I asked. "How low will his body temperature get?"

"Eighty degrees or thereabouts," my father said. "But the rest of them are a much higher priority right now." He roved his finger around the room to the other chambers.

I counted. Fifteen. "How long have they been in there?"

"Clock is ticking and we don't have much time left to bring them back."

"All of them?" Lacy asked now. "You're gonna bring them all back out at once?"

"Why?" my father asked.

"Will they know where they've been?" You could have heard a pin drop.

"Mutiny?" I asked her. "Is that what you're thinking? Some kind of uprising?"

"They've all gone through this a number of times and did it willingly," my father said.

"But why would they willingly freeze themselves and lay here in stasis?" Lacy pushed hard. "I mean, aren't these men and women some of the top scientists in their countries? Presumably, they have critical work and deadlines. It's not making sense to me, logistically speaking."

"I suspect the authorities were onto them," I said, waiting for confirmation. But my father was at one of the chambers now in the front of the room, adjusting them one by one.

"When can we get out of here?"

"Will they even let us go?" Lacy asked, and I assumed she meant my father and Archie Dax, two people who should certainly be considered our allies. But right now I wasn't sure of anything. We were far enough away from them to be able to talk discreetly.

"We first need to help them get those scientists back to a waking state. Otherwise, the alternatives are pretty grim. Maybe for all of us."

CHAPTER 51

We watched them unfreeze one man, a Doctor Maeda, with a syringe injection in his neck, literally the equivalent of a Star Trek hypospray. It's not like I expected him to leap out of the chamber, but I stood three feet away and saw his eyes open in less than thirty seconds. How could that be? And more importantly, how could this possibly be safe for the human body?

They went through a list: Archie holding a file folder reading off names. Falk. Mondragon. Oberman. Nielssen. One step at a time, Lacy and I backed out of the laboratory realizing we had a gap of unsupervised time to look around this place. I kept one ear peeled toward the lab.

"Who are they on now?"

"Winchester." I stood guard while she slid in and out of rooms, turned on lights, looked for anything resembling documentation, file cabinets, books, folders. I heard her footsteps at first, but now nothing.

"They're on the next ones," I called into the hallway.

"Names?" she asked, to show me she was still within earshot.

"Oberman and Nielssen."

I heard something that didn't sound like Lacy's voice. I padded down the corridor listening. It was her voice. "Who are you talking to?"

"Inventory," she said. I followed her voice into the second to last door on the left. The door was open. Lacy stood in the center of the room and said it again. "Inventory."

A spot on the same wall as the door moved, made a long whrrrrrr and then thunked.

"Wow." A file cabinet emerged from inside the wall. "What are the chances it's unlocked?"

I pulled on the top-drawer handle. "Pretty good." We quickly split up the task of going through them—her on the top drawer, me on the bottom.

"Well, I asked for inventory and that's what it looks like," she said. "It's odd, though."

"What?"

"Why would a place like this, wired with smart home technology, contain paper documents? I mean to what advantage would that be? Especially with all the shady shit that goes on here. Paper's just—"

I laughed.

"What?"

Brilliant. "A decoy. Of course. Those are the fake files, with dates and actual inventory, weights and dimensions of artwork, storage reports, shipping manifests, contact names—"

"Meaning phony contact names?"

"Of course. With fake phone numbers and fake residence and email addresses."

"Why?" she asked, the incessant litigator. "This place is so under the radar I'm sure it doesn't fall under any kind of regulated inspection schedule. So why bother?"

"For appearances. To demonstrate a visible system of documentation and a level of rigor that inspires trust and credibility, so people like Antonin Dvali continue to pay $800k for a cryo storage unit."

"Per month, don't forget. Close," she said but the file cabinet didn't move.

"Maybe it requires French commands?"

"I said Inventory," she countered, "in English and it showed me a file cabinet."

I jogged twenty paces back to the laboratory.

"Last one," Archie said. "You got him?"

All the cryo chambers were open now, tops off, my father and Archie standing aside. Waiting, it seemed.

"Are they not waking up?" I asked.

Then something weird happened. Archie glanced nervously at my father, who seemed to purposely avoid his gaze.

"It could take a little while," my father said, Archie staring at him.

"What are you not telling me? Are they dead?"

"Certainly not. The process has been perfected. Ek perfected it himself, crazy bastard."

One man, the inhabitant of the first chamber, sat up, slowly set his feet down on the bottom and climbed out with Archie's help.

"Dr. Falk," Archie said. "How are you feeling?"

"Where's Dr. Ek?" The man glassed the room, pausing on each of our faces. Short, balding, with a round face and a nose two sizes too big.

"He said he would be here when I woke up. Who are you people?" There was an accusatory tone to his voice; of course there would be. The level of trust required to commit to being frozen seemed unthinkable.

"Dr. Ek's detained, and he's asked us to process you upon waking."

That lie seemed to satisfy him. The man nodded. "Is there a room I could rest in? My body temperature's still coming back up. I feel very weak and a bit dizzy."

"Of course," Archie said, my father looking on silently. "Lacy, would you mind escorting Dr. Falk down the hall to the last door on the right? It's a lounge. And could you please bring him some water?"

"Of course, Doctor," Lacy answered in a rare moment of compliance, getting in her sense of humor because Archie Dax was the farthest thing from a doctor. Or last time I saw him anyway.

Three others started rising up from their chambers. They all just seemed too agreeable to me, comfortable with the idea of being temporarily frozen and then just waking back up and resuming the shopping list they'd been working on, or getting back to their emails, or their research, eating, drinking, working. Now four more men sat up, attended to by Archie and his tall stature and calming voice.

Why were they all men? I watched my father working the room, tacitly playing the solid, comforting presence to counterbalance the obvious uncertainty of Ek's victims. I sidestepped to within a foot of him and asked my question.

"We tried," my father mumbled, barely moving his lips. "I pushed for a more diverse group of scientists to provide a broader data set for research. We were looking for volunteers. There were no women who volunteered."

"But they were paid of course, right?"

"Not enough incentive I suppose."

"Ek doesn't give a rat's ass about research," I shot back.

"Not proper, recognized methods at least. All he cares about is getting his name on a headline."

"What's the plan for getting them all out of here, and thereafter?" I asked.

The corners of his mouth pulled up. He had a plan at least. Thank God someone did. "The thereafter will be to transport them to the Observatory facility so we can perform post-stasis tests on their biological functions."

Archie had the scientists in three stages throughout the room— some still supine in-chamber but awake, others sitting upright and coming back slowly, and several who were quicker to recover huddled in the front of the room, mumbling together, staring at my father and Archie like a middle school clique on the playground. I felt the energy of their murmured conversation. Archie's serene demeanor wasn't working.

A noise in the hall started small, like a group of motorcycles far away that eventually drowns out every other sound on its approach. Two men talking in French. One of them sounded familiar. Dvali?

My father stepped beside me and lowered his mouth toward my ear. "Exfiltration in progress."

Vanilla, I thought and smiled. I knew what exfiltration meant. Officially it meant extraction of an asset, and I wasn't sure these scientists were necessarily assets to our operation. Sure, I'd read about spycraft lore, including terminology, since I was old enough to walk, thanks to a nerdy older brother who cared nothing about immature constructs like popularity.

Jonas! That was the familiar voice.

"*J'ai juste besoin de trouver ma fête et je vais les escorter,*" I heard Jonas say out in the hallway.

"*C'est très bien. Par ici.*"

Must be one of the guards with him. I needed to let Lacy know to get back in here. I pulled out my phone but there wasn't time. Jonas and the guard appeared in the doorway.

"How'd you do that?" I asked my father.

"Leveraged available communication channels."

Jonas had his stage face on now. He was a lifelong introvert. But sometime while he was getting his MBA, maybe giving frequent presentations, he'd cultivated a sort of flip-switch to turn on his extrovert persona. I recognized the raised brows and feigned grin. Sure, bring it. I was ready for anything.

"Professor Janoff," he bellowed to my father across the room. "How is your tour going today?"

My father, not missing a beat, moved to the center of the room and waved his arms around our "guests", then pointed to acknowledge Archie. "We're just about finished," he said to the guard, then looked at Archie. "Yes?"

"Fifteen minutes or so," Archie replied.

Funny watching Jonas' face when he saw Archie. I'd had the same reaction. But he stayed in character. The theatre of survival.

The guard, now. Moving deeper into the laboratory, roaming from chamber to chamber. "My job is to explain why your... guests...were not on the attendance manifest from this morning," he said.

"I bet I know what happened," Jonas cut in. "One of the Cantonal Gendarmerie Officers left early today due to an illness and, on top of that, there was an unscheduled shift change for the afternoon security detail. In the confusion, it's possible some visitors entered without signing in because the signup sheet probably wasn't available."

"Certainly I will check into it. What are—" the guard said, resuming his inspection of the chambers.

"Demonstration chambers," my father chimed in with his calm, diplomat voice. I'd heard that voice growing up, when he was on the phone in his office with the door closed, Jonas and I listening over the ventilation grate in the floor.

"Professor Janoff teaches advanced pathophysiology classes at University of Bern and they're studying, I can never remember the term," Jonas said. "Professor, can you explain to the guard what your field trip today entails?"

"Of course," my father replied in English, using his knowledge of diplomacy to practice mirroring, speaking the same language the guard last spoke. It gave me time to get Lacy back here. Archie communicated with his eyes to the team of doctors in the room, tacitly letting them know that this invented story was their only way out of here safely.

Hey, I texted Lacy. *Bring the doctor back to the lab. The extraction team is here.*

"This semester," my father explained, "we're studying both cryogenics, which is used in medicine to freeze and store blood and tissue samples, as well as cryonics, which uses low-temperature freezing technology to preserve and store a human corpse upon death."

"Doctor Frankenstein?" the guard asked him and laughed aloud. Then he raised his hands into claw poses and growled, waving his hands in the air. No one moved except my father, the professional, who smirked and nodded his head to be polite.

"Oh no, nothing that extreme. These are all very common practices in medicine. I'm wanting my students to become comfortable with the components and technologies that are used."

"I think we're ready, Professor," Archie said.

I looked down at my phone. Nothing.

Where were Lacy and Dr. Falk?

CHAPTER 52

They performed a roll call. Jonas had a clipboard with the names of each doctor on it, which he showed to the guard for verification. How the fuck did he possibly get that? Lacy and Dr. Falk were, at least temporarily, missing. I had to let Jonas know before he roll-called him. He was looking down at the clipboard. There was no time.

"Okay," Jonas-the-tour-guide called out. "One at a time, please say here or present when I call your name, then we'll head out. Falk." He looked around the room.

"Here," I said without even thinking. The guard had no idea who I was and how long I'd been here.

Jonas stared. What else could be done? If the guard with Jonas knew that one of the doctors was missing from the supervised group, that could cause an alarm, delays, who knows what else. I did what I had to do to go along with the scenario he'd created.

"Thank you, Doctor," he said. "Step out into the hall, please. Mondragon?"

"Here."

"Thank you. Oberman?"

He went on like this through the rest of the list. I continued watching my father, observing this new George Janoff in the world of espionage, in the role of global diplomat. Crazy.

"Xavier, Nielssen, Winchester, Burke, Weiss, Nassar, Iskander, Collier, Young, Tabrizi, Durbin, and Vendi." They were all in the hallway outside the laboratory with Jonas and Archie, leaving my father and me to supervise the empty cryo chambers.

"Where are they?" he asked of Lacy and Dr. Falk.

"Missing. I texted. She's not answered yet."

"Have you checked the room I sent them to?" he asked.

I hadn't had time yet. "What were you—"

Two loud pops erupted in the same direction as the waiting room where Lacy had supposedly taken Dr. Falk to help him recover. I took off in the direction of the shots.

"BJ, no," my father hissed, concealing his voice from the guard outside. "They're not in there. Jonas, get the others out, now," he shouted down the corridor. "This floor will be locked down in two minutes."

"Right," Jonas said, still in character. "Doctors, with me please."

He motioned the huddle toward the elevators.

"Professor Janoff will be down shortly," he said, meaning my father.

It was hard to keep all our roles straight. And just then, Jonas had another flicker of genius; he spoke to the guard.

"I could use your help getting everyone downstairs," he announced. "Some of the doctors have had a strange reaction to the technology and I don't want anyone to faint and need medical attention that could require an ambulance coming on-site. That would be loud and distracting for everyone on the premises. Would you be able to assist?"

The guard paused then nodded. "I will go with you and send someone up to attend to them." He pointed to the others.

"Very good," Jonas replied and entered the elevators after the guard. Brilliant.

I assumed Jonas and Archie would wait somewhere outside with the group of fourteen doctors. I ran back down the hall to the waiting room where Lacy and Dr. Falk were supposed to have gone. The room was empty and appeared untouched.

"Where would they have gone?" I asked my father. "And could Dr. Falk have had a gun?"

"No," he said.

"Could someone have brought one in here somehow?"

"The guards have them, that's all I know."

"And Dr. Ek is still indisposed, right?"

"To say the least."

"Where's the other entrance to this floor?" I asked.

Lacy, my God. Would I be looking for her the rest of my life? I kept going past the waiting room and saw five similar rooms, one open conference area and two storage rooms. I checked the doors, both locked.

"What's in there?" I asked my father, pointing to one.

"I don't know," he said.

I tried to believe him.

"Stairs," my father said and ran toward the elevators, me trailing behind. "Up or down?"

"Down. This is the top floor," he said.

"No, it isn't."

He stopped in the staircase doorway and turned back.

"I found the blueprints to this building," I admitted, and hoped he didn't ask me where I got them. "This is the fourth floor. There's a fifth."

We ran into the elevators and checked. Above the 4 was a letter D.

"D, what's that?"

"French word, *débarras*, means storage," he said. "Just guessing."

We got in and pressed the button. The elevator ascended one floor, stopped, and nothing happened. I had about a thousand questions stacked up in my head. "Least we haven't heard any more shots."

He nodded and the doors opened slowly to a darkened floor.

"Dvali," I said before either of us moved. "Is he alive?"

"Yes."

"Would he have a gun?"

"I would think so. Did anyone search him when you entered?"

"No."

We stepped onto the floor and assessed the scene. I remembered how Lacy did it. "Lights," I said, and they magically came on, illuminating another similar interior structure of hallways, rooms, and tall ceilings.

"Nice."

"I have to know—is Dvali really here because he's chasing –"

"An antique sword?" he finished my question. "Interesting how he never tires of that story."

"Is it even missing?"

He shook his head. "It's completely intact in its original location as part of the Bilderberg Art Collection. It's never been stolen."

"Where is it? Here?"

He shrugged. "It changes. Sometimes certain pieces are stored here for a period of time, yes. Also St. Moritz, and many pieces, including the Boateng saber, are now on long-term loan to the Museo Barbier-Mueller. Here in Geneva." He gave me a long look, arms crossed, head down. "I'm sorry, BJ."

"I go by Brock now," I corrected him.

He shook his head slowly. He looked more than tired. Weary. "They knew you were my youngest, and so you were my weakness. I wasn't cooperating and this was how they applied pressure." He grabbed my shoulders. "I never, ever wanted you here, of all places. I hope you believe me."

"I'm trying."

I heard a voice call my name.

"BJ," a female voice.

"Lacy? Thank God. Where are you?" I followed the voice and turned left. She was leaning over Dr. Falk, sprawled on the blood-smeared floor, and another man on the floor behind him. Dvali.

"He shot Dr. Falk in the shoulder," she said looking at his assailant. "He had a radio with him and was communicating with someone outside, probably his driver."

My father quickly assessed the condition of both men. "Dvali's unconscious," he said kicking the gun a few feet away from him, "and Dr. Falk is gonna bleed to death if we don't get him to a hospital."

"We just came up the main elevator," I said to Lacy. "This floor's for storage. Where's the freight elevator?"

"There." He pointed and headed to the other side of the space. "Follow me."

"What about them?" Lacy gestured to the two victims.

"We'll call for an ambulance when we get downstairs," my father said.

"Do it now," I demanded and stood next to Andranik Dvali, slain villain—or was he a hero? I was still deciding.

My father pulled out his phone and pressed one button, then started speaking. I hoped it wasn't a fake call. I heard him report a shooting on the 5th floor, asking for emergency medical assistance.

"They're sending a team upstairs. Come with me, both of you," he said.

I followed him and Lacy.

"BJ..." Dvali moaned from the floor behind us. "I would have liked to play chess with you."

Me too.

CHAPTER 53

Two plain-clothed security guards met us at the elevators to escort us out into the back lot of the Geneva Freeport building from where we'd entered with Dvali and our driver a few hours ago. Three identical vans were waiting for us outside. Jonas, me, Lacy, my father, and Archie were able to stay together, along with three of the scientists. Were they really going to let us just drive away? Was an ambulance really called, and would they get to Dr. Falk in time?

I climbed into the second row of seats in the back of van #2 as I was instructed. I noticed the driver in a car behind the other vans. That bald, round head. *Oleg.* I leaned over to tell my father, when a loud siren from an ambulance headed toward the building as we pulled out, which meant my father had done what he said he would and tried to save Dvali and Dr. Falk. I still didn't know whether Ina had made it out or not. Maybe I never would.

The mumbling doctors in our van didn't like how Dr. Ek wasn't with us, and they weren't buying the 'he's detained' bit my father had been feeding them. He used more diplomatic phrases, big words, and promises that everything would be properly sorted as soon as we got back to "the premises", he called it. Archie was responsible for booking all of our flights back to LAX and he'd kept everyone's passports and ID intact while they'd been frozen in stasis. Again, I was struggling with the extreme level of trust that would be required here for any of these individual occurrences. It seemed too unbelievable to be true. But I'd just seen it with my own eyes. Hadn't I?

My father sat in front beside our driver. I heard them talking back and forth, looking in their rearview mirror. I didn't dare turn around, and I didn't need to. I'd already seen Oleg in the parking lot and told my father. So of course he'd be following up, taking every last step to prevent us from flying his cash cows back to California. We drove caravan-style on the highway headed to the airport, now in the right lane ready to get off at the next exit.

"Where are you going?" my father asked the driver.

"He is right behind me, on my tail!" The driver raised his voice, referring to Oleg.

Now it was worth the risk to turn my head around. I recognized all three of them, Oleg and his two soldiers in a dark minivan directly behind us, now pulling back at a slower pace and then speeding up to ram the bumper of the van directly behind us.

"Hold on." I tightened my seat belt.

The game went on for five minutes. Our driver sped up just past the first airport exit and it looked like we'd lost Oleg. When we approached the next exit, the ramp was elevated about fifty feet above the street below. I could see the two other vans right behind us. One was turning off. I told my father, who turned his body to face right.

"Oleg's following them. Slow down," he said to our driver.

A gun barrel pushed out of Oleg's driver's side window. It fired three quick shots. At almost the same instant, I saw the white van in front of them skid onto the shoulder, then the concrete step barrier. It flipped up to the right and cascaded down.

"Oh my God, it's going off the edge," I said.

"Keep moving," my father said to the driver, "not too fast, middle lane is fine. That's good."

"Dad, that van just flipped ov—"

"Before I got the words out, we heard the crash of the white van onto the ground below the overpass. The impact sound was followed by an explosion. Jonas was next to me. I put my hand on his arm to steady myself. Five, maybe six scientists were in that van. All likely dead.

There was no sign of Oleg's van. But I knew he'd be coming for us.

CHAPTER 54

By some miracle we got home from Geneva in one piece, all five of us, including me, Jonas, Lacy, Archie Dax, and my father. Miki Fine, according to Archie, was off limits (to us anyway) but was doing okay. I wouldn't be surprised to learn that they'd been secretly married all this time. My heart was still closed off from Archie Dax. I never really got over his loss and now, well, we had a lot to reconcile. So whether he was coming back to work for us was still under discussion.

After two days of recovering, we decided it was time to camp out in the backyard again, ignoring the fact that Oleg would be coming after us, if he wasn't already, searching for the missing doctors to re-ignite his underworld cash flow again. Our house growing up, where my father still lived, was too sloped in the backyard with not enough grass for a comfortable sleep. Lacy's parents' house was flat, lush, even, and perfect.

"You're quiet tonight." Lacy picked up the poles and helped me construct our ancient, smelly tent with a little more vigor than the last time we'd camped out here fifteen years ago. She was right, I was quiet tonight, but not because I didn't want to be here. I was deep in my head, processing everything that had happened, re-assessing conversations, relationships, loyalties and, more than anything, assumptions. I never had the chance to ask my father, at least not so far, about the pretty woman he'd been caught with late at night, the photographs that were taken of them, not caught in the act, nothing tawdry. Just in a hotel with a pretty woman in the middle of the night, sipping liquor in the dark, and talking. I was sure now the woman had been Anastasia Bergman, his ally and his enemy, his employer, nemesis, and scapegoat. Maybe he hadn't actually cheated on our mother. I liked the way that new thought felt in my head. It was unsubstantiated but it went down a lot smoother than the alternative. Of course he'd loved our mother. We watched him cry at the funeral, so much he had to walk away during the ceremony. Sometimes I loved it when assumptions were wrong. There was still time to decide.

"Just thinking," I said.

Jonas carried the tiny gas grill to a spot three feet from the tent, turned it on, complete with skewers and a bag of marshmallows.

"No Hershey bars?" Lacy asked.

"You're the only one who ever liked that. I personally would like to live to be forty. This," he held out a box of Graham Crackers, "is how you do it."

"Speak for yourself," I said. "I'd love to eat a marshmallow sandwiched between two Hershey bars."

"Fine. Next time."

The sky over southern California looked different tonight. Or was it me who was different? Clumps of stars blinked over us and I knew we were all thinking it, the idea of doing this again, of a next time. I jammed three marshmallows on each skewer and set them on the grill's roasting rack, which provided about four inches of clearance. Well-made tools were one of the things that made Jonas happy. He'd paid way too much for this grill when he bought it.

"We ready?" Lacy asked.

Jonas crept onto the grass beside her, and me to her right, aiming our faces up to the sky to see who might catch the first shooting star. Maybe we'd see none tonight, but on one camping trip we each saw one. That was something.

"Are we seriously all gonna sleep in that tent?" Jonas asked. "I could barely fit all three sleeping bags in there."

We didn't answer his rhetorical question. Instead we breathed in the cool night air, listened to crickets and night birds, and remembered.

"I'll be right back." Lacy vanished.

"You're gonna break the chain," I whined like a seven-year-old. I laughed out loud hearing it.

"Sorry, I have to pee. I'll be one minute."

I checked the skewers, which were almost getting black on one side. "Ooooh perfect," I said and rotated them. I looked at Jonas, staring up at the sky, and wondered if it was the right time.

"Hey, so are you going?" I asked casually, of the fishing trip Dad had invited us on next weekend. I wasn't sure I was ready for something so mundane. I think that's why I'd put his invitation out of my mind. I felt like I needed to spend an entire day with him in interrogation-mode, asking all the questions that needed answers. And then decide what our future might look like.

"No, I'm not going. This is your thing."

"Why is it my thing? He's your dad too, and neither one of us has seen him in three years."

He regarded the dark sky. "You and he fishing together is something special. You were the outdoorsy one, remember?"

"Yeah."

"I never went on those trips with you because it's not my thing. You guys enjoy it. I'll have him over for dinner or something so we can drink cognac and catch up in our own way."

"Okay, if you're sure." I knew he didn't want to go. I knew

he didn't want to sleep outside—tonight or with our father next weekend. I knew he didn't want to spend alone-time with him and remember the pain of our mother's death and relive the tension of not talking about it.

"Lacy's not going, is she?" he asked.

"What's the point of that question?"

Snickering. "Little defensive, aren't you? I just want you to have this time with him is all."

"Still not sure what you're implying here."

"Yeah right."

"Hey." Lacy handed me a piece of paper. I hadn't heard the door on her way back out.

"What is it?"

"I don't know. A note. It was on the kitchen table."

"Um...it's dark out. I can't see."

"Give it to me." Jonas grabbed it and turned on his iPhone flashlight. "Gone back to... Geneva for some cleanup, shouldn't be more than a week."

"From your dad? How did he get in the house?" Lacy asked.

"Courier, maybe, had your dad leave it on the table," I said.

Jonas went quiet for a few seconds, reading something else on the page. "Hey, listen to this:

The million dollars in the briefcase originally came from me, and Oleg stole it. I've gotten it back and it was intended to be used to invest in Janoff Investigations. I know you guys always liked a treasure hunt...let's see how honed your skills are. More to come.

I didn't know what that meant, and frankly, my brain was too exhausted for any more riddles. Tonight was about the beauty in simple things, like the way the moon lit up the right side of Lacy's face, the side she called her "bad side" in pictures. And the way Jonas took on the role of s'more-builder. We sat there munching on the gooey mess under that bed of stars, wiping our sticky hands on our pants like little kids. I loved falling asleep to the sound of Lacy breathing, and out of some primal territorialism, I loved how I was sleeping in the middle and had that precious sound all to myself. An old man once told me that unattainable things feel more like they're worth having before you actually attain them. I wasn't sure I'd ever find out, but right now our knees were touching through the sleeping bags.

CHAPTER 55

He chose Echo Lake Park as the fishing venue. I'd been there before once with Jonas, it was right off 101 southeast of the Silver Lake Reservoir, which had a 2.5-mile loop I used as a running track a few years ago. I'd tried to look forward to this trip, I really did. But his brand-new REI Old Town Saranac two-person canoe, shiny and never been used, just felt so contrived. And we'd had one argument already. He said LA doesn't require fishing licenses, but the State of California did. So that meant if Game and Fish approached us, we'd probably be fined. I wanted to ask him if he'd even been on the water in the past decade, but I held my tongue. This was his deal, he invited me, presumably to, I don't know, mend fences or get closer. So far it wasn't happening.

"Coffee?" He handed me the cap of his thermos.

Okay fine, I found one thing that didn't suck so far. He always made strong coffee and he took pride in brewing it perfectly. I sipped it twice and nodded. At least he looked the part. If he'd been a CIA operative or Bilderberg soldier all these years, he certainly knew how to assimilate correctly. He had on a pair of worn cargo pants, waterproof shoes, a faded t-shirt under a windbreaker, all worn and strategically threadbare. Fucking game theory.

"Thanks." I passed the plastic cup back over the space between our two seats, mindful of the emotional chasm still between us.

THE RIDDERS

There was no wind, no current. That meant an easy ride with a lot of silence to fill. I'd thought of a few conversation-starters, knowing how awkward it would be. I secretly hoped he'd invite Archie, since they'd worked so closely together, apparently, for the past few years. But in my mental simulations, all my innocuous questions veered down the twisty rabbit hole of a) Bilderberg, b) how he met Dr. Anders Ek, c) the fake-death of Archie Dax, d) the decoy sword, and e) his alleged extra-marital affairs, all things I knew he didn't want to talk about. So we sat idly on the still water in his new canoe pretending to enjoy the silence. Since we hadn't yet started paddling, I pulled the fated picture out of the pocket of my jean jacket. I held it out.

My father's features softened, his eyes slightly downturned. Was he sad seeing this?

"Where did you unearth that from?" He sounded surprised.

"Oh, you know Jonas, always stealing family pictures. I stole it from him."

"Well, don't ask me who the other men are because I never knew their names."

It was possible this was true. "Where was it taken?" I ventured, remembering Dvali had told me it was taken in the Netherlands.

"Italy. The Angelica Library, one of the oldest in the world, I think. We were part of a training class."

Of course I didn't ask him what the training was for, or who'd sponsored it.

"Can I ask you what's meaningful to you about this picture?" He leaned forward when he said it.

"The book," I said. "I always wondered what book you were carrying under your arm. Dvali told me it was a valuable first edition of a game theory book."

Now he raised his eyes and nodded. "He must've told you a lot of things about me." Long sigh.

"Let me guess – they're all lies?"

"Oh no. They're probably all true. I just wish I'd had the luxury of telling you myself, so I could explain the context and backstory. When you work for something as high profile as the State Department, your life isn't your own. That's probably the case with any federal agency, to greater or lesser degrees."

"So you had no choice about the things you were doing, the projects you worked on?"

"I didn't know at first. By the time I realized what I was really doing, I was in too deep to get out, or not without putting you, Jonas, and your mother at risk. They use that, you know, whatever's most dear to you. Your weakness becomes a sort of currency. It's a lever they push at times, to remind you of what you've given up."

Some wind came up and a few thick clouds collected over our heads. We both saw it at the same time and grinned.

"Remind you of anything?" he asked.

"I'm remembering we got stuck too far from shore in some really bad weather."

"What I remember," he said, and his smile faded, "is the sound of your mother's voice on that sandbar."

I watched my absentee father, the accountant, the agent, a purported spy, sob quietly, head down, shoulders rocking. Nothing was involuntary, for him, he was allowing this to happen, allowing me to see this display. But he was controlling the amount of emotion being released. Crocodile tears? I don't think so.

"She was fine, Dad. You paddled us in and you saved her. Right?"

Now android-Dad was back. "She was in no danger whatsoever. I really don't know what made her panic like that. She could have easily walked back; the water would have been barely up to her chest. But you can't ask a woman why she's afraid without sounding condescending. Or at least I don't know how to. Even still."

Well, he'd brought up women, not me. I hadn't planned to ask him anything of the sort. "I'll bet Anastasia Bergman was never afraid." There. I'd gone for it, thrown down my glove at his feet. "I'm sorry. I didn't intend to bring that up today."

"I never disrespected your mother or our marriage. No matter what you thought, what others might have told you, what your mother thought. Never."

"So why did you—" I let my voice trail off because I honestly had no idea what he'd done.

"It was my job, and it was determined to be in the best interest of US foreign relations for me to get close to her. And I did, but not in the way you think."

"So why did you let Mom go on thinking you were cheating on her? For God's sake, don't you know that's why she died?" My eyes were wet.

"She died of congestive heart failure," he said.

"Yeah, she did. Because you broke her heart."

* ❖ ⬦❖⬦ ✛ ⬦❖⬦ ❖ *

We rowed back to shore and took the boat in after that, never having fished. But we'd done something far more important.

CHAPTER 56

I woke up the next morning sunburned with three thoughts in my head: I really liked Lacy's father's crash pad, I'd always loved Santa Monica, and somewhere in the closet of my brain I remembered Lacy saying that her father rarely used the place anymore. Feeling empowered by the most romantic night of my life, just one week ago sleeping beside Lacy Diaz in our grungy little tent, I drove to Mr. Diaz's office and asked for an appointment.

"Of course, Mr. Janoff," his assistant said recognizing me.

And I asked him not for his daughter's hand in marriage but if he would sell me his condo to somehow make my entry into adulthood all the more real. Returning to my dreary apartment, with Ray's filth all over the house and the reality of his death making it even more sordid, I had to do something. Turns out he'd tried to give the condo to Lacy, but she said it was "bougie". Sounded like her. So he was thinking of unloading it. He'd made no improvements to it and offered it to me in a For Sale by Owner deal for exactly what he paid for it. I qualified for a conventional mortgage with private mortgage insurance. I about choked when I learned what the payments were going to be, but it was more impetus to solve my father's riddle and use his million dollars to pay off my loan. I had to grow up sometime.

Desperate for some semblance of routine, I started working

regular hours with Jonas, happy to be driving to Venice from Santa Monica, showing up at 9 a.m., making coffee, sitting with him to discuss open cases, and deciding who would do what. Even though I'd started as his IT and network guru, he'd finally started giving me small jobs. Getting my PI license hadn't changed much for me, except that now, after what we'd just lived through, I felt a sort of equality I hadn't felt before. Like I had more to offer him and the world now.

It was now two weeks after our backyard camp-out and I saw an envelope on the outside of my windshield held down by my wiper blades. My name was on the envelope in my father's handwriting. Inside was a folded piece of paper with what looked like a typed document.

Who is Karthik Panjali?

A renowned chip designer, who was testing a new chip that's gonna rock the world. Why? The internet runs on fiberoptic network that runs on visible light. Panjali has designed something different, an Extreme Ultraviolet Lithography Chip that would use ultraviolet light, so it could encode and transmit a lot more data. Besides his innovation, why is he important? He's an edgy qubit designer for quantum computing, and he's recently vanished. There's a story going around that he was abducted by the federal government to use his design for counterespionage. And there's another story that he was abducted by crypto gangsters who want to sell his idea to auction on the dark web.

Find Karthik Panjali, and you'll get your million dollars.
Here's your first clue: 21.9483° N, 120.7798° E

About the Author

Lisa Towles is an award-winning crime novelist and a passionate speaker on the topics of fiction writing, creativity, and Strategic Self Care. Lisa has nine crime novels in print with a new title, *Salt Island* (Book 2 of the E&A Series) forthcoming in the summer of 2023. Her novels *Hot House, Ninety-Five, The Unseen,* and *Choke* each won numerous literary awards. Lisa is an active member and frequent panelist of Mystery Writers of America, Sisters in Crime, and International Thriller Writers. Lisa has an MBA in IT Management and works full-time in the tech industry. She lives in Oakland, California with her husband and two cats. Learn more about Lisa at lisatowles.com and follow her on social media:

Facebook: @lisatowleswriterTwitter: @writertowles
Instagram: @authorlisatowles
Tiktok: @lisatowleswriter

And you can subscribe to her monthly newsletter here:
https://tinyurl.com/4a3bvdpn

Acknowledgments

Writing a book is an extraordinary experience and has many parts. Every book is not only different in storyline but also in its execution and process. Each one takes a team of kind souls who collectively keep you on track and sufficiently inspired to reach the last page. And then the real work begins.

I'd first like to thank my publisher, Lisa Orban, for her extraordinary vision in creating such a supportive community for the Indies United authors, for her amazing team, her patience and compassion, and her tireless marketing and social media energy.

And without my amazing editor, Cindy Davis, this book would not have been publishable in the first place. Thank you for your expertise, support, guidance, and encouragement, and for pushing me to the next level.

Warmest thanks to my kind and tireless beta readers – Gail, Lee, Missy, and Ana. Your helpful feedback was so important to improving this book.

To my graphic designer, Tatiana – you're a genius and incredibly skilled. Thank you for your talent and expertise, and for designing such a beautiful cover.

To Marsha, thank you for your social media and marketing consultation.

To my cherished MWA and SinC NorCal writing partners - thank you for your companionship, advice, wisdom, and inspiration. And to Michelle and Ana - kindred spirits, gifted writers - your friendship and support are a tremendous gift.

To Leo Bottary for your support, friendship, and consultation on the writing path.

To Jodie – my wellness touchstone - thank you for your wisdom and healing.

To my husband Lee, whose energy, passion, insight and verve are a constant inspiration. Your love and devotion bring me the greatest happiness of my life.

To my amazing parents who continue to inspire and surprise me with their wit, grit, talent, and wisdom. Whatever 'just do it' I have in me, I got from them.

To my sister, who was with me while I did the research for this book. You were my very first friend in this world and you're still a wonderful companion. Though I'm the older sister, you've always been my role model.

To my precious nieces, Olivia and Cassidy – watching you grow up is an amazing experience. I'm in awe of you.

To my cats, Coffee and Marmalade, sleeping beside me right now - such wonderful companions on the often-lonely writer's path.

And to the wonderfully supportive readers of this book and my other books – THANK YOU for your kind reviews, questions, comments, support, and feedback.

You are all a part of my village,
Thank You

Hot House

Indies United Publishing House
Released June 15, 2022
Book 1 of the E&A Investigations Series

When a former CIA operative and private investigator Mari Ellwyn starts digging into the blackmail case of a federal appellate judge, she becomes targeted by a van following her, threatening notes in her mailbox, and a breach of her home. Teaming up with seasoned investigator and former detective, Derek Abernathy, the crime-savvy pair begin looking into the wrongful death of a mentally-ill college student, Sophie Michaud, as well as two journalists – one dead, one missing, who were writing a story on the dead college student with allegations of her connection to the federal judge. The two investigators must uncover the truth about Sophie Michaud before her killer makes them their next target. But more importantly, Mari needs to find her missing father and reconcile her broken past and family.

"Towles has produced a knockout novel with Hot House. Towles's plot is as twisted and unpredictable as you would ever want a thriller to be. It's this kind of action that will keep readers engaged in this suspenseful crime novel. Nowhere will thriller fans find a more engaging keep-you-on-your-toes read." - *Literary Titan, 5 Star Review*

"A dark, edge-of-the-seat thriller. Highly recommended!" *Chanticleer Reviews*

"This meticulously constructed, remarkable mystery deftly explores people's darkest flaws while revealing hard truths about the hidden workings of the world. A fast-paced and psychologically astute thriller." - *Prairies Book Review*

Available now on Amazon and from other retail booksellers
https://amazon.com/author/lisatowles

Salt Island
Book 2 in the E&A Investigations Series
Indies United Publishing

Summer, 2023